MISSING PERSONS
A YOUNG INVESTIGATIONS NOVEL

DL WHITE

EDITED BY
ADOTK EDITS

AUTHOR'S NOTE

Dear Reader,

Welp, we are here again. I'm lookin' at you lookin' at me and asking you to open your eye holes and take in this work of art that I put together for you. And hoping you love it.

Y'all know I am weird, just go with it.

First things first: **I know that's not an El Camino on the cover.** I simply could not find an image that would do Yvette justice so I went with the next best option, a Chevelle. Unfortunately, I was married to the idea of Yvette driving an El Camino and didn't want to change the model of her car. *shrugs*

So, like many of my full length novels, I started writing this eons ago, hit a wall, put it away, then dragged it out every year to add seven words to the draft, then put it away. Then one day I was on the internet doing shenanigans and I saw a person talk about a missing person in their family and ALL OF A SUDDEN I knew where to go in this book.

Yvette Young is not a new character—we first met her in **Dinner at Sam's**. She is the Private Investigator that Gibson Kincaid hires to find Vanessa's ex-husband, who is in hiding and hoping to avoid being served with divorce papers and child support enforcement. I have always loved Yvette's story and my brain has been crafting the perfect hero for her for a long time. Wesley is a firm, gruff, bear of a man but there's something about Yvette that brings a certain softness to him.

And quietly, same for Yvette.

Now Sam's is a great story (you get to meet my FAVE of my heroes), but you don't have to read *that* one to read this one.

I'm calling this a spin-off of Ruby's even though there are no Ruby's characters in it. You'll see Minks (the restaurant the Ruby's ladies meet in at **Drinks at Minks)** and a couple of familiar locations but other than that, this should be considered a stand alone novel *in conversation* with **Brunch at Ruby's.**

As usual, there are lots of actual Atlanta businesses and neighborhoods. If you're local, I hope you recognize some spots.

Lastly, this is my first real, full length foray into a category that isn't what I call Capital R romance. I have been dabbling a bit in mystery, but **The Romance** just jumps out. In this story, we get a compelling missing persons case wrapped up in the love story I wanted to give Yvette. I really want this to be a light, romantic, slightly mystery tinged series, so my hope is that this hits right and gives me something fun and a little different to work on.

So there's nothing to it but to do it... read it that is.

Love it and spread the love via reviews at Goodreads, The StoryGraph, retail sites and social media. There is never ever a requirement to tag me or send me your reviews... I know where to find them! If you loved it, LET THE OTHERS KNOW!

I appreciate all of you more than you know.

OH WAIT! This book has a **Spotify Playlist: bit.ly/miss-ingpersonsplaylist!**

Enjoy!

Xoxo,

DL White
Author, Books by DL White

BooksbyDLWhite.com

authordl@booksbydlwhite.com

PO Box 310329 Atlanta GA 31131

MISSING PERSONS

CHAPTER
ONE

YVETTE

SNAP. Snap. Snapsnapsnap.

Through the telephoto lens of my Nikon, Sinclair Rowe's living room came into focus. Cream leather sofas arranged on either side of a glass table stacked with glossy coffee table books—Dior, Basquiat, some oversized thing about yachts. Abstract art on the walls, perfectly spaced. A gas fireplace flickering beneath a mounted flat screen.

New money, trying hard to look refined and impressive. But that wasn't what I was looking for.

Tonight, Marcel Simeon, my target, was at her home, doing more than snuggling on her couch.

"Finally."

Six weeks. Six weeks of following this cheating bastard through Atlanta traffic, sitting in parking lots outside his office building, trailing him to business lunches. Six weeks of watching him pick up dry cleaning, attend his son's soccer games, and have dinner with his wife at restaurants where appetizers cost more than most people's car payments.

Marcel Simeon had been the model husband. Until tonight.

I shifted against a tree, bark scraping my back through my hoodie and branches poking into unmentionable places. My feet had gone numb twenty minutes ago, but I couldn't move. Not when Simeon was about to hand his wife a life-changing divorce settlement.

Well, it would change *my* life.

Sinclair and Marcel moved to the bedroom, and so did I via the viewfinder. The sheer curtains might as well have been billboards. I switched to video mode and let the camera roll while they put on their little show.

I pulled out my phone and opened the messages app, typing to the attorney who'd hired me to follow Simeon.

VetteY: Finally caught them. Pics, video coming.

The reply came back fast.

WPayne: They doin' the do right now? Send me a preview.

VetteY: Affirmative, pervert. Will send pics when I get to a computer. It's pitch black out here & I'm cold.

VetteY: & there is a bush in my ass. A courier will drop the file and my invoice tomorrow.

WPayne: Bring it yourself. I haven't seen you in a while. Take you to breakfast? Lunch? The Bahamas?

I snorted and shoved the phone back in my bag.

Ten minutes later, I had enough evidence to sink the Titanic twice.

The crawl back to my car took forever. Twigs caught in my hair and something that felt suspiciously like spiderwebs stuck to my hands.

My El Camino sat where I'd left it, tucked between two pine trees like a sleeping panther. Jet black glossy paint, white leather interior, chrome hardware, and an engine that purred like she was happy to be alive. The wide white racing stripe down the center of the hood was a signature touch—a little much for my taste, but the car had been Jason's dream.

She turned over on the first try. I backed out of the trees and onto the main road, gravel pinging off the undercarriage.

Atlanta's late-night crowd was in full swing. Cars packed the streets bumper to bumper as everyone tried to beat last call or find a Waffle House to soak up the alcohol. Bass lines thumped from open windows. Groups of women in too-high heels and too-short dresses picked their way down uneven sidewalks.

I flipped through radio stations, looking for something that wouldn't make me want to put a fist through the dashboard. Love songs, breakup songs, makeup songs—the whole cycle of romantic bullshit that kept people like me in business. I settled on a satellite station playing R&B hits. Ludacris and Ciara's "Oh" came on, and I cranked the volume.

The photo I kept in the visor caught my eye when I flipped it down to reduce the glare from the streetlights. Jason smiled back at me from a family cookout years ago.

We spent the afternoon on my parents' deck. His parents had come down from DC and within an hour, he had my father talking cars and my mother showing Mrs. Porter her tomato plants.

After dinner, he dropped to one knee and asked me to be his wife.

I couldn't wear the ring on my finger anymore, but I kept it close to my heart on a chain around my neck. Quarter-carat diamond, white gold, nothing fancy.

"We'll get you something bigger later," he'd promised, but I'd told him I didn't need bigger. I needed him to come home from Afghanistan so we could separate from the Army together, get married, and start our lives.

I pulled at the chain, pulling the ring out from under my clothing. The thin metal was cold against my skin. It had been three years since Mrs. Porter called to tell me Jason's convoy hit an IED on the way back from a supply run. Three years of knowing he should have been safe in the motor pool, not riding shotgun.

He was a mechanic, for fuck's sake.

My parents' house appeared through the trees, porch light glowing yellow against the dark brick. Dad's Escalade and Mom's Mercedes were tucked away in the garage. I shared the carport with whatever my brother Yancey was working on this month. Lately, it was a cherry-red Acura NSX that he'd bought for next to nothing and spent six months making roadworthy again.

I parked next to it and killed the engine. I let myself in through the back door and climbed the stairs, moving by memory in the dark.

The apartment had been Dad's surprise for me when I separated from the Army and opened my P.I. firm. A separate entrance, a galley kitchen, a small living space—enough to pretend I lived alone while still being close enough for my mother to force-feed me leftovers. The rent he charged barely covered utilities, but it gave us both the illusion that I was an independent adult.

Yancey pitched a fit when he found out about the apartment. Twenty-eight years old and still sleeping in his childhood bedroom, complaining that I got special treatment.

Maybe I did.

I'd also spent years in places most people couldn't find on a map and I'd buried the man I was supposed to marry. Yancey's biggest hardship was running out of cable channels to surf.

I dumped my gear by the door and headed for the bathroom. Dad had gone all out on the shower and tub: upgraded tile, rain showerhead, multiple jets, water pressure that could knock you over. I cranked the hot water until steam fogged the mirror, pulled on my shower bonnet, and stood under the spray until my muscles loosened and the pine sap washed off my skin.

After smoothing coconut oil over my damp body, I went through my evening skincare routine, then pulled on Jason's Army t-shirt, threadbare and faded to gray after years of nightly wear, and a pair of boy shorts.

My laptop was plugged into the alcove near the kitchen. I ran my finger over the trackpad to bring it to life, then popped the memory card from the camera and plugged it into the adapter.

Moments later, I was watching Marcel Simeon's marriage implode in high definition.

Muttering to myself, I copied a sampling of the images to a folder, then zipped them up and attached them to an email.

To: payne.wesley@courtneypaynegroupllp.com

From: Yvette@younginvestigations.com

Re: Simeon Surveillance results

Wesley—

See attached images. I'll save photos and video to a thumb drive as usual but these will whet your appetite and should be enough to show the client. Hope that mousy dishwater blonde with no discernible ass was worth losing $$$ to his future ex.

Per your request, I'll come to your office. See you soon.

–Vette

CHAPTER
TWO

WESLEY

"WELL."

Julia Simeon's voice cut through the silence of my office, cold as ice. "I suppose that's that."

Her perfectly manicured fingers clenched a stylish scarf as she studied the surveillance photos spread across my desk. The muscle in her jaw twitched once. Twice.

She looked up at me, steel in her spine, all business now. "How can we end this quickly and quietly?"

I began gathering the photos into a neat stack. "We file, citing the evidence of infringement of the prenuptial agreement. Marcel and his attorney will try to negotiate—"

"I don't want to negotiate." One corner of her mouth lifted, not quite a smile. "I want this over with."

Perfect. They were always easier to represent when anger replaced hurt. "I'll have video and the full report from my investigator this afternoon. The video evidence leaves no doubt. He won't have a leg to stand on."

Julia nodded, then stood. Her cream suit hadn't wrinkled

despite time in my guest chair. "Set up the next steps." She strode to my door, then turned. "And Mr. Payne? Money is no object. I want this done right."

"Yes, ma'am."

I waited until the door closed behind her before allowing myself a smile. The Simeon divorce would bring exactly the kind of high-profile case our firm needed—expensive and potentially precedent-setting.

I reached for my coffee, sighing when I found the cup empty.

"Payne!" my partner's voice boomed through the desk phone intercom. "You free?"

"Come on in."

I glanced out of the tall windows at the Beltline Trail foot traffic below. The converted warehouse space we'd chosen for Courtney & Payne gave us the best of both worlds: modern amenities with Old Fourth Ward character, close enough to downtown courts but removed from the stuffiness of traditional legal districts.

Nick Courtney looked like someone carved him from granite—square jaw, broad shoulders, permanent lines etched between his brows. His suits probably cost more than my first car. He'd always dressed the part of the successful attorney, even when we first met and he tried to convince me to join his practice when I retired from JAG.

"I saw Mrs. Simeon. How'd it go?" He dropped a file on my desk before heading to the coffee machine.

"I'd say it went well. She doesn't want fanfare. Just wants it over. Don't break my machine, man."

"I just want a damn cup of coffee." He jabbed at the machine with more force than necessary. "You think he'll fight the prenup?"

"For about five minutes. Yvette's photos will shut that down fast." I didn't reach for the file he'd brought but pointed at it. "What's that?"

"Missing person. A friend's sister needs some assistance finding her husband, who is due to come into some money."

My brows rose in curiosity. "This is a law firm, Nick."

"Guy's been missing three years," he continued, as if I hadn't lodged a protest. "His father's dying and there's an inheritance hanging in the balance."

Nick finally got his coffee made, though he'd probably broken something in the process. He cradled the mug in his bear paws and settled into one of my guest chairs. "Interested?"

"Not particularly." I had enough on my plate with the Simeon divorce about to explode. "We are not an investigative agency. If she really thinks there's something funny with his disappearance, I can bring in Young Investigations."

Nick's face cracked into a scowl. "Wesley..."

"Those are my terms," I said, my tone dropping to the register I used for hostile witnesses. "You're bringing this to me because you think I can handle it. The only way I take this is if I bring in Yvette."

"You have a thing for her, Payne."

"Yvette plays by the book and gets the job done. Yeah, I like that a lot."

"Her methods can be...questionable."

"Always within the law. She doesn't investigate in any different manner than any other P.I. you've used." I let that hang in the air between us. Nick had the grace to look uncomfortable. "Is it because I insist on hiring a Black woman-owned agency? Even if she's ex-Army CID? Even if I worked with her over the course of my JAG career?"

"Wesley, that's not what I—"

"You want me to look at this case? I'm bringing in Yvette." I turned to face him fully. "And we both know I'm not asking."

Nick took a long sip of his coffee, probably burning his tongue in the process. Eventually, he lowered the cup to a saucer on the desk. "This is why I nabbed you, you know that? No political sense whatsoever. Stubborn as fuck."

"You recruited me because I'm a damn good lawyer." I picked up the file. It felt thin to me. "And because you needed someone who could handle themselves in court instead of settling everything in mediation."

"What I got was someone who insists on hiring his favorite investigator for every damn case."

"Nick..." I sighed. I was getting tired of this merry-go-round of an argument every time we had a case that needed a private investigator. "When's the last time we lost a case Yvette investigated?"

"That's not the point—"

"That's *exactly* the point. Tell me about this missing person."

Nick sighed, a familiar sound of surrender. "Edward Foster walked out on his wife and twin boys three years ago. Just...vanished."

"Okay. I assume she called the police?"

He nodded. "They gave her the usual line...he probably ran off with someone, it's not illegal to leave your marriage."

"If you leave your marriage and don't provide support for your children, it becomes a state priority. Is that how this becomes my problem?"

"Ed's father bought a small chain of bagel shops a few years ago. Got featured on some cooking show, business exploded. He sold the whole deal to some venture capital group. He's doing pretty well, several million in the bank. But Daddy's dying and his son still being missing isn't sitting right with him."

I flipped through the file, locating the police report and the wife's statement when her husband packed a bag and walked away.

"If Ed's dead, the entire inheritance goes to..."

"His sister. Who hates the wife, so she and the kids get

nothing. Anjelica could use Edward's portion of the inheritance, considering he's been gone this whole time and she's raising their children alone."

Nick's smile turned grim. "January marks four years. With no evidence that he's used his social security number, hasn't been seen or heard of, he can be declared dead."

The legal implications clicked into place—presumption of death statutes, inheritance law, the burden of proof shifting to anyone claiming he was still alive.

"Dad has made it clear that if Edward isn't found, Eileen —sister—gains control of the estate and determines who gets a disbursement."

"So wife needs him found alive to ensure he inherits. So she can divorce his ass and take it?"

"She'll get at least half, thanks to Georgia's equitable distribution laws."

I studied the single photo in the file. Edward Foster was an average man with a receding hairline and the beginning of a beer gut. "What's the story with the father? How sick is he?"

"Pancreatic cancer. Terminal."

"And he won't change the will?"

"He says if his son's alive—and he thinks he is, just hiding —he deserves his share. If he's dead…" Nick shrugged. "Sister gets it all."

"And what's your connection?"

"Sister of an Army buddy. I said I'd take a look." Nick set his cup down. "It's a long shot, I know. But the wife's raised those boys alone, struggling. If Foster's alive, she deserves that money. And if he's dead, she wants to fight for her portion of that inheritance."

I closed the file. "You're getting soft in your old age."

"Says the man who insists on bringing in his favorite investigator, who he also served with." Nick stood, adjusting his tie. "Speaking of which, when are you gonna make something shake with that situation?"

"What situation would that be?"

"The one where you're in love with her and she's still wearing a dead man's ring around her neck."

I kept my face as neutral as possible while my chest tightened as if it was being squeezed by a vice grip. "This not a conversation topic."

"Never is." Nick headed for the door. "Don't let this case get personal. I know how you feel about Yvette, but—"

"Get out of my office, Nick." The words came out sharper than intended, but I didn't correct my tone.

I tapped the intercom line and buzzed my assistant. "Samera, I need you to clear my afternoon. And get me everything you can find on an Edward Foster. I'm forwarding the details to you. We need to set this up and get Yvette on it."

"Yes, sir. Would you like me to call her?"

I glanced at my watch, the tightness in my chest lessening at the thought of hearing her voice. "Nah. I owe her a phone call, but I want to set some things in motion first."

"Okay. Your ten o'clock just walked in, by the way."

"Great. Send him back."

I had just enough time to glance through the file again before my door would swing open and I'd have to pivot to saving someone else's life. I kept the Foster file on my desk, though.

Something told me this case would be anything but simple. Good thing I had the best investigator in Atlanta on speed dial.

CHAPTER
THREE

YVETTE

HEAVY, decadent smells wafted through the air vents, pulling me from a fitful slumber.

I lay on my stomach, one pillow bunched beneath my head, the other pushed onto the floor, likely during one of my sessions of thrashing about in my sleep. My eyes felt gritty like I'd been crying.

I dragged myself from the bed and rifled through my closet for something to wear. Since closing the Simeon job, I hoped it could be a paperwork day. I'd love it if my cousin and fellow investigator, Nia, and my office manager, Estelle, could just sit around catching up on busy work, watching TV and shooting the shit.

I mumbled to myself, praying that my jeans would zip as I jumped to pull them on. I slipped on a white button-up blouse and slid my feet into a pair of ballet flats. Grabbing my camera and my bag, I left the apartment, locked it behind me, and skipped down the steps to the house below.

"Smells good down here, Mama."

I dipped to drop a kiss on my mother's lightly rouged cheek as I passed her in the kitchen. My mother stood not more than five feet tall on a good day, pleasantly plump, with a kind face. Her graying hair swept into a gracious bun and she wore her usual powder blue nursing scrubs. She worked in the NICU at Piedmont Hospital and loved it. She said she'd love on those babies until Yancey or I gave her some grand-children to spoil.

"Thank you, baby. Go on ahead and sit down, get it while it's hot and before the menfolk get to it," Mama ordered, her soft voice carrying over the din of ESPN in the living room.

My father sat at the head of the table in his usual uniform of worn jeans and a collared shirt, one of many with the Hamilton Construction logo embroidered on the right breast. A battered yellow hard hat hung off of the chair behind him.

Yancey was a younger version of Daddy. Both had deep chocolate skin tones and light brown, expressive eyes, but Yancey was thin where Daddy had gained a few around the midsection. Yancey moved with lithe, active energy, while Daddy had succumbed to middle age. Both flashed a bright smile of straight white teeth and a single dimple on the left cheek. That dimple caught my mother. The same dimple got Yancey into a lot of trouble with the ladies.

"Turn that TV down, Michael," ordered Mama, bringing a basket of biscuits to the table.

I eyed the expanse of food across the table—fluffy, cheesy scrambled eggs, crisp bacon, a basket of biscuits with jam and honey, and buttery grits. It wasn't always like this. Sometimes there was more food.

I loaded up my plate. "This table is why my jeans just barely zipped this morning."

Mama twisted her lips into a frown while she spread strawberry jam across half of a biscuit so fresh it still steamed. "If you ask me, a few pounds looks good on you. Between the Army and…"

She paused before continuing, glancing at her plate. Mama found it hard to talk about Jason. "I'm happy to see you put on a little weight. You were so thin when you came home."

That had been after. After the call from Mrs. Porter. After the funeral. After sleepwalking through the last few months of my enlistment and leaving Virginia without Jason. Grief snatches away any semblance of a normal life. Steals your joy. Makes you feel guilty about enjoying life after losing someone. I'd been numb and hadn't particularly cared about how my clothes hung off of my too-thin frame. It made my mother happy to see me eat. So I did.

And now my jeans didn't zip. "A *little* weight? I've gained upwards of a *little* weight."

"Nobody told you to load up your plate like that," said Yancey with a mouth full of food, his eyes full of mirth. "Not Mama's fault she's a good cook. Not ours either, so don't go giving her any ideas about low-fat meals."

"Hush up, Yancey," Mama ordered from across the table.

"Yeah, hush up Yancey," I goaded and, as if I hadn't just been complaining about my weight, chomped down on a forkful of bacon and eggs.

"Both of y'all hush up!" Daddy grumbled, his body twisted around to see the TV in the living room. "Trying to hear the scores from last night."

Mama rolled her eyes. "I just do not understand this obsession with sports scores. What does it even matter? Can't you look that up on your phone later?"

"I don't know about you women, but it's what men talk about while we work. Can I hear this, please?"

I cleaned my plate despite my protests. Years of living in barracks and eating mess hall food made me long for my mother's cooking. Now that I had it daily, I'd never turn it down. I'd just have to buy new jeans.

Mama finished her breakfast and stood, piling a used

napkin on her plate. She walked around the table and plopped a kiss on her husband's cheek. "Your lunch box is on the counter. Don't forget it."

Daddy nodded, half-listening to his wife, half-listening to the TV. He'd never, in thirty years, forgotten his lunch box.

"Yance, I packed some of last night's dinner for you. You don't need to be wasting money going through somebody's drive-thru every day when you have plenty of good food you can just warm up."

"Thanks, Mama." Yancey glowed as she brushed past him, running a hand over his low-cut hair. "Don't mess up the fade!"

"Oh, hush. Nothing there to mess up, you keep it cut so short."

"What about me?" I feigned hurt feelings. "I don't get a lunch?"

"You don't *need* a lunch," said Yancey. "Weren't you just complaining about your fat ass?"

"Yancey." He snorted, dipping his head toward his plate. Mama waved a hand in my direction. "I never even know if you're in town, coming or going, here and there at all hours. Did I hear you come in after one o'clock this morning? I can't even imagine what you're seeing at that hour."

I chuckled, thinking about the images I'd emailed Wesley. "Trust me, Mama. You don't want to know."

Mama rinsed her plate at the sink and added it to the collection of dishes in the dishwasher. "Don't let me come home to breakfast still sitting on the table. Thank you!"

She grabbed her day bag, a sturdy leather number that I bought her many Christmases ago, tossed it over her shoulder, and headed toward the garage. A few moments later, her Mercedes backed down the driveway and headed down the street.

Satisfied by ESPN, Daddy finished his breakfast, then grabbed an extra biscuit before dropping his plate into the dishwasher. "Vette, you and Yance get breakfast cleaned up. I got to make the rounds at all my projects today."

At the sound of Daddy's truck clearing the driveway, Yancey stood, picking up his plate, which was practically licked clean. "I gotta get to the shop—"

"You're helping me clear this table and get the dishes taken care of before you go."

"Can't," he protested, rinsing his plate and setting it in a neat row in the dishwasher. "I got a schedule I gotta keep."

"Like I don't?"

"You don't have a real job, Vette. You can show up any time you want."

"Excuse me?" I turned to face him fully, hand on my hip. "My job is as real as yours. You run your own schedule at Hot Wheels anyway."

The custom body shop did everything from repairs to rebuilds, specializing in classic cars. My El Camino was a flagship project for Hot Wheels. Yancey still bragged about how he'd transformed it from a rusting, barely running clunker into a sleek, sexy machine.

"So what? I still got responsibilities."

"You have time to satisfy your *responsibilities* at home." I stood, carrying my plate to the kitchen. I handed it to Yancey, who frowned but took it. "Mama does everything for you, so I'm not hearing anything about how you don't have five minutes to help around here."

"She likes doing that stuff—"

"She shouldn't *have* to do that stuff. You're twenty-eight years old, living at home, getting your meals cooked, your laundry done, your lunch packed like you're still in high school."

I started clearing the remaining dishes from the table while he leaned against the counter, scrolling his phone. "I am not in the mood for a lecture about my life choices."

"Somebody should lecture you. You got it made here and

you know it." I stacked plates with more force than necessary, the ceramic clinking together.

"So? That's my business."

"Your *business*?" I turned from the sink, crossing my arms. "Like last Sunday, when you told Mama and Daddy that you had to work, and the minute they left for church, you let a woman in here? She stayed for *well* over two hours despite there being a rule against that. That business?"

Yancey stopped mid-step, his hand frozen on the door frame. His gaze shifted left to right, back and forth.

"How you know about that? You weren't even home, Yvette."

I tilted my head and crossed my arms, leveling a stare at him.

In surrender, he sucked his teeth and dropped his shoulders in a shrug. "Right. You're nosy for a living."

———

I PULLED into my parking space in front of a two-story brick mill off of Moreland Avenue that had been converted into office suites. Daddy had transformed the space while keeping the original facade and tall windows. Inside, the office felt open and bright with high ceilings and polished concrete floors. Having family do the renovation meant we got a good deal on a renovated space in the heart of Atlanta's Little Five Points neighborhood.

"Mornin', Vette," came a gritty voice, aged by years of smoking and not living right, as Estelle put it.

"Good morning, Estelle," I chirped, passing the neat desk perched near the front window. Estelle was like Mrs. Jenkins from 227, always hanging halfway out of her space, talking to everyone that walked by and keeping an eye on things. "How you doing?"

"Too blessed to be stressed," she said, issuing her standard response while using the end of a pen to scratch an itch. Her chestnut brown hair was streaked with lovely gray strands in a short style tapered near the ears, the rest in delicate finger waves. Her big brown eyes didn't miss a thing, not with the bifocals hanging on a chain around her neck.

Estelle was a machine, clocking in at 7 a.m., buzzing around the suite, making coffee, filling the printer drawer with paper, checking the messages. She ran our case management system like she'd been born to it. I started getting emails about cases and updates by around 8 a.m. and if I hadn't checked in or shown up by 9 a.m., Estelle got cranky.

"How I'm supposed to assign cases to you and you ain't even around?" she'd often grumble, sounding like she'd just smoked a pack of cigarettes.

She settled into her chair, watching me move around the office. "How's ya mama and them?"

"I'm okay. My parents are fine. Yancey is a punk." I flipped through a stack of mail piled neatly in an IN box on the front counter. Bills. Paperwork. Junk. "Anything new pop up?"

"A slip and fall case that I gave to Nia since it's close to the other one she's doing. Same attorney." Estelle's nails click-clacked against the keyboard as she spoke. "Nothin' going on but the rent, but the day ain't over yet." She reached across her desk to swipe nonexistent dust from the picture frames holding snapshots of her three grandchildren, always in her line of sight.

"I'm going to finish my time sheet for the Simeon case and then I need the invoice to add to the package going to Mr. Payne."

Estelle nodded, pulling up the time tracking software and retrieving the saved file with the glut of hours I'd already accumulated. "You gave up on Simeon? Or did you catch him?"

"Oh, I caught him. Red-handed. Well…"

"Red somethin'!" Estelle snickered, bringing her glasses to rest on her nose. "These dirty bastards. Thinkin' they can't get caught. They don't know Yvette Young, do they?"

"They sure don't, Estelle."

"Well, they're about to find out. Alright, send me the rest of your hours and I'll have an invoice ready in a jiffy."

I tucked a stack of mail into the crook of my arm and grabbed my bag. I handed the camera to Estelle before heading to my office. "I need a new battery in this one. She put in some hours last night."

I'd already begun walking away when I stopped and took a few steps back. "Oh, and I don't need a courier for the Payne file. I'll drop it over there myself."

"Mmmhmmm," hummed Estelle, taking a sidelong glance at me—my tight jeans, a feminine blouse, and flat slippers instead of sweats, an Army t-shirt, and boots.

I felt my face flush. I knew what that sound meant. "Don't *mmmhmmm* me, Estelle. I have an appointment near there. No sense in wasting the fee for a courier—"

"Girl, I'm just playing with you. Gon' and get me those hours so you can get over to Mr. Payne."

When it came to my office, I needed a blank slate. I got enough stimulation in my line of work, so the muted tones, white walls, plain carpet, and no decoration worked for me. My dad gave the walls a fresh coat of eggshell white, replaced the carpets, and added wood blinds to the single window in the room.

I bought myself a functional work desk from the local office supply store and aside from two tall metal filing cabinets, a desk lamp, and a guest chair, the room had no particular mood or feel. It was plain. Uninspired. No mementos. No memories.

Just how I liked it.

Jason had been the complete opposite. He spent his days underneath vehicles, elbow-deep in motor oil, so when he was out from under a car hood, he liked his space to be warm and inviting. His desk at work was a mess, littered with photos of his parents, siblings, friends, and himself at various stages during his career. And of course, more than a few pictures of him with me.

We met through mutual friends after boot camp. We had been introduced and then left alone, seated side by side on a bench outside of the Exchange, an on-post department store. After a few awkward moments, Jason had leaned over and said, in a loud stage whisper, "I'm onto them, you know."

I giggled but refused to give the handsome, rugged, light-skinned brother with the dark grey eyes any attention. He was a stranger, after all.

"I mean," Jason continued, leaning closer to me, letting the light scent of cologne waft past my nostrils. "I think they might be trying to set us up."

"You're just now realizing that?" I laughed again. "I'm way ahead of you."

"Oooh. We got a smart one over here."

"More than smart," I replied. "I want to join the Criminal Investigations Division."

He shook his head. "CID? You was a tattletale as a child, wasn't you?"

I shrugged, letting a sly grin answer for me. "My brother, Yancey, got into enough trouble all by himself."

"Yancey!" Jason's laugh turned into a cough as soon as he saw the stiff set to my jaw and the narrowing of my eyes. "Uhm. That's an interesting name…Yancey."

"He was named after our great grandfather, who fought in World War I."

"Okay. So you come from a line of servicemen?"

"You could say that."

"Me too. Everybody in my family is Army. Is that why you joined up?"

I shrugged, pulling at the shreds of my homemade jean

shorts. I wished I'd wore something different. "I guess. My great grandpa Yancey was at Fort Belvoir, Virginia. My grandfather didn't enlist, but my Dad joined up for a short time. He was injured and discharged before they could send him overseas."

"And your brother? Is he Army too?"

I laughed so hard and so suddenly that I snorted. The thought of my rebellious, headstrong troublemaker of a little brother volunteering for the Armed Forces was comedy. The only way Yancey would join the military was by force.

"Yancey is in high school but he's not soldier material. I have a feeling nothing would be honorable about his discharge."

"So what does he want to do instead?"

"He wants to go to a trade school for something like tricking out cars or whatever."

"A man after my heart," he said with a big, wide, toothy... *sexy* grin. "I think me and Yancey ought to hook up. I'll be training to keep those military vehicles on the road."

I nodded, my eyelids slipping closed. *Great. I'm attracted to a mechanic.*

"I see you judging me. I didn't say nothin' about your nosy military police ambitions. Not cool, Yvette."

Jason stood and began to walk away. I was sure I'd just ruined things for myself.

So what if he would eventually be a mechanic? They performed a valuable service to the Army. And he was cute. Manly. Thick biceps, wide chest, strong thighs—not that I noticed.

He had the kind of body that wasn't built at boot camp. I especially liked how the bass in his voice skipped down my spine and how the way he looked at me made my belly flutter.

So he'd be an Army mechanic. *So what?*

He spun to face me with half a grin on his full lips. "I

don't think our friends are coming back and I'm hungry. Want to go to the mess hall?"

I swiveled back and forth in my faux leather office chair, caught in a web of memories. Sometimes they tortured me, like around his birthday. Sometimes they comforted me, like when I remembered something funny he'd said.

Today, the memories were just…memories.

The phone on the desk chimed its melodic three-tone ring. I picked up the line, always chuckling that I could hear Estelle better through the wall than through the phone.

"What, woman?"

"I'm ready for your hours. Do I need to come and get them?"

"I just got to my office, Estelle."

"You've been sitting there staring at the wall. Are you alright?"

I checked my watch, then the time on the desk phone, finally emptying my lungs with a deep sigh. "Yeah. I'm okay. I'll send those to you right now."

CHAPTER
FOUR

YVETTE

"YVETTE YOUNG FOR WESLEY PAYNE."

"Do you have an appointment with Mr. Payne?"

I paused, willing myself not to stare down the perky young lady at the reception desk of Courtney & Payne LLP wearing a telephone headset, her finger poised to just press the damn button and let Wesley know I had arrived. I didn't recognize her, though I hadn't been to the office in a while.

"He knows me," I muttered, scratching my name on the guest sign-in sheet.

"Mr. Payne insists that he's not to be disturbed unless—"

"Do you know what this is?" I waved the padded envelope in front of her face. Her eyes, wide and glossy, followed my movements right to left, up and down. "This is the complete evidence package that Mr. Payne's client is waiting for. Tell him Yvette is here."

She paused, swallowing hard, then asked, "Would...you like to leave it for—"

"Forget it. I know where his office is."

I tucked the envelope under my arm and stomped past the front desk toward a set of double doors, pulling them open and marching down the hall until I reached the two corner offices at the end of the suite.

Wesley's office was on the right; his partner, Nick Courtney, occupied the office on the left.

I rapped my knuckles twice on the thick wooden door. From the other side, I heard, "Come in."

Wesley's offices had always been as tastefully appointed as the Army allowed, even violating a few minor guidelines for office decor. At Courtney & Payne, he took advantage of the freedom to decorate as he pleased.

He just skirted the line between ostentatious and gaudy with enormous dark furniture, brass antique lamps, valuable art, and rugs so expensive, I was surprised he allowed me to walk on them.

Wesley stood at his desk, bent over the telephone, handset to ear. He waved me in.

"Yes, it's fine, Samera. Yes, I'm sure. No...no security, and from now on, she can see me without an appointment, alright?"

He sighed, replacing the handset in its cradle and leveling a glare at me. "Just once, could you come up here without upsetting my front office staff? You don't want a jumpy former cop to roll up here, do you?"

I shrugged. "You should train her better. All she had to do was call you."

He stepped around the desk, pointing toward one of his guest chairs. "Good to see you, Vette. It's been a while."

Wesley Payne in a suit was a *problem*. Today's was deep plum, tailored close at his broad shoulders and trim at the waist, paired with a deep eggplant tie that brought out his rich sable skin. He propped one ankle on a knee, showing off his socks that matched his tie like he had all the time in the world.

Strong jaw. Full lips. Neatly trimmed beard. He kept his haircut low and tight back in the day to fit into grooming standards, but now it was a little longer on top, just enough wave to run your fingers through.

If you thought about that sort of thing on occasion.

It didn't matter that he looked like somebody's fantasy—tall, broad, cut in all the right places. I was at his office on business. Nothing else.

Private practice didn't bring him the same level of satisfaction that military law provided. Helping a client prove a complainant had falsified evidence of an injurious fall on their premises or standing between a bickering husband and wife didn't compare to investigating charges of treason, processing a court martial, or defending a soldier accused of murder, but it was work. It was the law, and when he won, he won big and he made sure to make a splash.

"Is that my evidence?" Wesley nodded toward the envelope I held. I handed it to him and he ripped it open, pulling out my invoice and the supporting documents. A flash drive dropped into his palm.

"I want to review everything before we file. You said you had video too?"

"About thirty seconds on the flash drive. No sound, but you can play some Luther Vandross in the background if you'd like."

Wesley went back to his desk and plugged the drive into his laptop, humming a few bars of "Here and Now" while flipping through video screenshots. "I know I don't have to ask, but this stuff is going to stand up in court, right?"

"You're right, you don't have to ask. What's the deal with this case anyway?"

"According to Julia Simeon, the marriage was more like a

merger between businesses than a love affair. Julia came to the marriage with a lot of money and even more clout. Her father built the Savings Hut empire."

"That chain of discount stores full of cheap shit?" I scowled, squinting. "My mother loves that place. It's like an indoor garage sale."

Wesley shook his head, brows lifted. "They do *billions* in business."

"Get outta here!"

"I kid you not," said Wesley. "The prenup was more of a formality. Protecting each other's images, et cetera. It's the world's worst kept secret that they married for money. But now…"

Wesley sat next to me again, laptop in his hands. "Mrs. Simeon has met someone. And she'd like to divorce Marcel, but he won't have it. She doesn't need the public watching her get her ass handed to her while her husband is offering himself to everything on two legs."

"Why? What does he care? He can freely date whoever now. Besides, Simeon Industries does a good book of business on its own."

"Her old man has been out of the business for a minute. She's running things in his absence, anyway. When he dies…"

"She inherits the company."

Wesley nodded, rubbing his dry palms together. "More importantly, Marcel has been trying to buy Savings Hut, or at least a portion of it, for years. The old man has always refused. With him out of the way, Julia, and Marcel by marriage, come into controlling shares."

"So Julia needs to be good and divorced before she inherits Savings Hut to avoid Marcel controlling any of her company."

Wesley rested his chin on his palm while thumbing through the photo images. "Unbelievable," he mumbled.

"They must have thought they were safe since there were nothing but trees behind the house."

"He was such a Boy Scout, playing the doting husband, the loving father. He wasn't counting on me following her. I knew he'd show up."

He hummed his agreement. "That's why you're good at what you do."

"Welp…" I slapped my jean-clad thighs as I stood. "He's lost a good chunk of money thanks to her not being careful enough to close her blinds. I'd be mad as hell if I were him."

Wesley laughed. "He probably will be. This divorce is going to be messy. Quiet, but messy."

"He'll probably roll right over, agree to whatever she wants. Never hit a courtroom."

"Don't say that," he groaned. "I need to see a courtroom." Wesley rose to his feet. "You, uh…you taking off already?"

"Got places to go, creeps to investigate." I took a step toward the door but stopped when he spoke my name.

"We can't talk? Catch up?" He gestured me back toward the chair. "Have a seat. Tell me how you're doing. I mean, really."

"I'm fine. I have an appointment—"

"Vette." His expression softened as the V between his deep brown eyes deepened. "I know the anniversary just rolled by. He was my friend too. I loved him too."

He paused, then added quietly, "I miss him too. Jason was—"

"Do not even start with that, Wesley. Jason was barely even cold before you were hitting on me."

I watched him roll his eyes. "Vette. It's been—"

"Three years. You gave me three years to get over the love of my life before…"

I couldn't even get my words out, I was suddenly so unreasonably angry.

"It's not like I proposed, Yvette. We were spending a ton

of time together. I asked if you wanted to make things official. You made it clear you weren't ready for that and I accepted that."

"I know exactly what you did, Wesley. What you didn't do was show any kind of loyalty to your friend. Or his girl." I spun, headed for the door. "Have my check cut and don't give me any shit about payment terms."

"Yvette. Wait!"

I gripped the handle and yanked the door open, nearly bowling over the receptionist.

"Oh!" she yelped, jumping back, teetering on her high heels.

"You suck at eavesdropping," I muttered, passing her as I left the suite and stepped into an open elevator.

My heart thumped—fast, then faster. My hands trembled so hard I could barely press the button to go to the lobby. I was going to pass out or scream or both.

Not here. Not here. *Not here!*

The walls of the elevator pressed in, the polished brass panel reflecting a twisted version of my face. I couldn't breathe. Couldn't think. Wesley's voice echoed in my head:

He was my friend too. I loved him too. I miss him too.

The elevator doors opened and I stalked out, my legs stiff. Across the marble floors, through the revolving doors, out onto the sidewalk. The mid-morning air hit my face, cooling my skin and drying the beads of sweat that had popped up, but it wasn't enough.

My chest squeezed in a vise. I braced a hand on the stone facade, trying to reset myself.

That happened more often lately. Not being able to handle talking about Jason.

Talking about moving on, moving past him. Letting go. And fighting this…*whatever* with Wesley.

Finally able to breathe and heartbeat still at a rapid but slowing rhythm, I climbed into the El Camino and drove the short distance to a converted sunroom turned home office at the back of a 1920s bungalow off Ponce Avenue.

Veterans' benefits paid for services post separation. Training. A degree at an accredited college or university. Medical care. Disability care.

Therapy for Post Traumatic Stress Disorder.

"YOU'RE LOOKING BETTER. Are you sleeping?"

Paula Chapman slipped a pod into the Keurig and waited for it to brew a dark, aromatic blend.

"Kind of. I had a case that kept me out late and when I got to sleep..."

When the cup was full, she added a splash of cream and handed it to me. I sighed, cradling the mug in my hands.

"Go ahead. You got to sleep, and..."

I shrugged. "I still wake up crying some mornings. Not all the time, though, so...it's getting better."

"Same dreams?"

At my nod, Paula sat and crossed one leg over the other. Her black pencil skirt rode up, revealing muscled thighs and smooth golden-brown skin. Her bob was honey-blonde, parted low and swept across one eye. Smooth, blunt at the ends, not a strand out of place.

Also ex-Army, Paula still kept up her exercise regimen: five miles at dawn, strength training and kickboxing on alternate evenings. Bike rides on the weekends. She could jump into uniform and return to duty tomorrow if needed.

"Tell me about the dream."

"We were working together. Clearing a building that seemed empty. I heard footsteps, turned to say something to him, and he was gone. No sound, no flash, no warning. Just... his gear on the floor. Like he'd never been there at all."

My eyelids dropped as I pinched the bridge of my nose. "I

made myself wake up but I still heard the footsteps. Turned out to be Yancey stomping down the stairs. I swear, for someone so skinny, he walks like he's carrying a twenty-pound rucksack with ten-pound boots on."

Paula laughed. "Your brother needs to work on his stealth."

"He moves like a damn elephant."

"You said you and Jason were clearing a building. That wasn't either of your jobs, right?"

"No," I said, shaking my head. "He fixed whatever needed patching together. I was CID. I followed paper trails and talked to people. Neither of us were trained for what we were doing in my dream."

She nodded, letting that settle. "But you were doing it. Together."

"Yeah." I dragged a finger along the seam of my jeans. "Moving like a team. Like we'd done it a hundred times before."

Paula was quiet for a moment. "You think there's a reason your brain put you and Jason in that kind of scenario?"

I exhaled slowly, tipping my head back against the couch. "Maybe because I keep thinking that if I'd been there, maybe I could've done something. Told him to take a different route. Spot the danger before it hit. I know it's not rational, but—"

"But that doesn't stop the loop."

She gave me a moment before adding, "It wasn't your job, but your mind keeps rewriting it like it could've been. Like if you'd just been on that scene, in that building…you could've changed something."

"They changed his assignment at the last minute that day," I said, recalling the only bit of detail I'd been able to get from Jason's parents. "A parts delivery turned into a convoy escort. They hadn't investigated the road…sent him out there anyway."

I didn't realize how tight my chest had gotten until I tried to inhale.

Paula's voice was gentler this time. "So maybe the dream isn't about combat at all. Maybe it's about rewriting how this happened. And how you still couldn't stop it."

I stared at the floor. "He disappears in the dream. That's what it felt like. One day he's emailing me corny jokes and we're counting down to when we get out of the Army and arguing...kinda...about where we're going to settle down—by my parents or his. We were making plans to get a house. The next day, he didn't email me back. And then days later, I'm getting a phone call I do not want to take."

She let that hang there for a moment before saying, "So your brain puts you back in the moment. Lets you be there with him. Doing something. Watching his back."

"And I *still* lose him."

Paula didn't flinch. "Or maybe you're not losing him. Maybe your grief is giving you a different ending. One where you were by his side, like you wanted."

I sat there, twisting the ring around my neck until the chain pulled tight.

"You disagree with my interpretation," she said, reading my body language. "What are your thoughts, Yvette? Verbalize them."

I pushed up from the couch and walked to the window. Her garden stretched just beyond the back deck. Low beds were tucked along the fence line, full of color and movement even in the heat. Black-eyed Susans, something pink and leafy, a few tall stalks that might've been lavender. In containers on the porch, she was growing her own herbs. She'd once mentioned that getting into the dirt, pulling weeds, cultivating life helped to clear her head after hard sessions.

"I feel like it's my brain saying that I'm on my own now. I have to figure out how to do this life thing without backup."

"And… how does that feel?"

"Terrifying. Lonely. It pisses me off."

I whipped around to face her. "I'm fucking *pissed* that he's gone. That's how it makes me feel."

The words burst out louder than I expected. I didn't even realize I'd raised my voice until I heard it bounce back at me. Paula didn't flinch. I hated that I was still rattled.

"What's got you wound up today? Besides the dream."

I dropped back onto the couch with an irritated huff. "Your friend Wesley Payne."

"Oh." She clicked her tongue. "Now he's *my* friend? What did he do now?"

"He's just been…Wesley. Making me feel guilty, like I've been avoiding him."

"Have you been avoiding him?"

Of course, I had. Knowing how he felt about me—had felt about me for years—made me keep my distance. Not because he made me uncomfortable. The opposite, actually. Being around him made me feel too much. He looked at me like he still wanted me, like he never stopped. And if I wasn't careful, that tall, broad, aggravating man was gonna have me laid up with my legs in the air, getting thoroughly handled and forgetting all about my good sense.

Wesley Payne wasn't just fine. He was familiar. Safe. Devastating. And I missed Jason. I missed him so bad I could barely breathe some days.

But not all the time.

Some nights, it was Wesley I dreamed about. His hands, his mouth, the way he said my name, only it was in my ear with a seductive growl.

That was its own kind of betrayal.

"Only after he pushed up on me." I shifted, unable to get comfortable, but it had nothing to do with Paula's couch.

"Pushed up on you?"

"You know what I mean. We're friends. We work together

a lot. We've spent a lot of time together, worked a lot of cases together. He's always...kinda flirting. He recently asked me if I wanted to be with him. Like *date*."

Paula worked hard to look surprised, like she and Wesley didn't discuss me behind my back. "And you said..."

I bit my lip, then confessed, "I didn't handle it well. I feel so weird when he looks at me. Like...*looks* at me."

"You don't want him looking at you?" Paula seemed amused. "Don't you kind of...care for him? Didn't we work through that some time ago?"

She was right, we had. Whether I was ready to accept those feelings was a different story. I stood again, restless. I had to pace, exert some energy.

"That is not the point, Paula."

"What is the point, Yvette?"

"He was my superior officer. And my friend. And eventually, he was *Jason's* friend. So...it's wrong." Defiant, I folded my arms across my chest.

"Who says it's wrong, Yvette?" Paula tilted her head.

"Jason's been dead three years and Wesley's already trying to move in."

"*Already?* Three years is a considerable amount of time."

"Not long enough."

"How long would be enough?" she lobbed softly.

It landed with a thud. "I hate when you do the therapist thing."

She chuckled, setting down her notebook. "What therapist thing?"

"When you ask me questions I can't answer."

"If you can't answer the questions, we have work to do. Have you told Wesley to stop *pushing up* on you? That you're uncomfortable with his attention, that you understand he's attracted and he'd like to date you, but—"

"No. I just...ignore him."

"You know you're going to have to say the words, Yvette.

He can't read your mind. Now...you may want to investigate if you really *want* him to stop flirting with you, asking you out, acting like you're together."

I glared at her.

She threw up her hands in a helpless gesture, then glanced at the clock on the side table. "How about a safe topic? How's the family?"

"That's *not* a safe topic. Yancey's spoiled ass is still on my last damn nerve. How my parents ended up with a kid like him..." I huffed a breath of frustration. "And it's like they love it. They don't even see how they're not helping him be a responsible adult."

"What do you think is behind that? Their babying of him?"

"They're trying not to make another me. Someone who felt like she needed to go out in the world and risk her life for Uncle Sam. Every time I had to travel to some war-torn country, Mama needed a phone call every day to reassure her I hadn't died."

"That's a tough load to carry. But you managed."

"Yeah. But they're not trying to repeat that with Yancey. Maybe he'll marry someone and they'll both live in his bedroom."

Or maybe they would kick me out and let their golden boy have the apartment. The thought made me seethe.

"And...work?"

"Work is okay. I'm not hurting for cases. I'm not a millionaire either. Between Nia and me, we stay busy but..." I leaned forward, resting my arms on my knees, and pushed out a puff of air, expanding my cheeks. "I'm bored, Paula. I'm just... bored."

"Bored? How could investigating cheating spouses ever be boring?"

"It's really not that exciting. It's just sitting. Listening to audiobooks. Eating sugar and sucking down coffee, trying to stay awake, waiting for some man to come out of some place he isn't supposed to be. I feel like if you have to go to the lengths of spending the kind of money that I charge to prove your spouse is cheating, save the time and money and file a quickie divorce."

"Worked for me," Paula quipped. She brushed a lock of hair from her eyes. "But people want to be proven wrong. They'll do whatever they need to do, pay whatever they need to pay to tell themselves their hunches were incorrect. That it wasn't lipstick on his collar. That the perfume you smell is a brand you wear. That he seems sexually satisfied, and you know that feeling didn't come from you."

"I guess that's why I'm in business. Maybe I'll expand to some different kinds of cases."

"We're not going the bail bondsman route again. Your mother won't hear of it."

That made me laugh. Paula glanced at her watch. "A few minutes left. Anything you want to chat about?"

I cringed, unable to meet her gaze. I clasped my hands and squeezed them together until my knuckles protested.

"You're going to hear about this anyway. I had an argument with Wesley today."

Paula chuckled. "I know you don't believe me, but Wesley and I do not talk about you, Yvette. What was the argument about?"

"I don't even know. I don't know what to do with...*this* between me and him. I know you hate that phrase, but I don't know."

"If the situation were different—say your relationship with Jason ended in a typical way and not with his death, might you accept Wesley's advances?"

"You mean date his friend after we broke up? Isn't there some kind of bro code against that?"

"Let's pretend there isn't. Wesley is available, free and clear. Would you feel differently? Act differently?"

"I don't know. Maybe. And…I feel like that's a problem."

"It isn't, Yvette. The problem is that it isn't a problem and you're fighting yourself on it. Time's up."

Paula pushed herself up from the chair and guided me to the office door with an arm over my shoulder. Before I walked out, she gripped me by the forearm.

"See you sooner than later, I hope?"

I nodded once, then left before she could say anything else.

———

WHEN I RETURNED to the office, Nia was leaning a hip against Estelle's desk while they watched a dramatic scene unfold on the TV mounted on the opposite wall. It was mid-afternoon, time for Estelle's stories.

The life of a private investigator was often more boring than people imagined. Much of the job was computer research, drafting reports, and tallying hours. If I left the office, it was to spend time in the car in the shadows, camera prepped and ready to catch some action.

I wanted the office to be a place where we could comfortably spend a long span of time, thus the built-in kitchen, the large high-definition flat screen with cable, and even one of those streaming boxes so we could pull up a Netflix movie while filing.

A commercial blared through the surround sound speakers. Nia grabbed the remote and muted the TV.

"She knows good and well that man is lying through his teeth."

"Mmhmm," Estelle hummed. "But she's gonna hang on until she gets that money."

Nia followed me to the kitchen. "You smell like Wesley. Did you see him today?"

"I what?" I opened the refrigerator and reached for a can of diet soda, then sniffed my blouse.

"You smell like his cologne. That Jean Paul Gaultier he wears all the time. Y'all gettin' down and I don't know about it?"

I popped the top on the can of soda. "Don't piss me off, Nia. How did your case end up?"

"Fine. I got what I needed, turned it over. Wesley called here for you, by the way. He said you weren't answering your phone."

I hadn't checked my phone after leaving Paula's office. I always turned it off during my sessions. I reached for my bag and unzipped it, retrieving the phone and pressing the power button to bring it back to life.

The screen flashed for a moment, then several notifications rolled in—missed texts from Estelle and Wesley, two missed calls, and two voicemails from Wesley.

"I'll call him." I needed to apologize anyway.

"Tell him I do good work too. He only ever wants his *Vette* to work his cases," she remarked.

"I'll pass it on."

In my office, I set the can of soda down and dropped into my chair. Before I could lift the handset to dial Wesley, the *beep boop beep* sounded.

"Stelle, you don't need to call me from your desk," I yelled.

"Pick up the phone, girl!"

With a huff, I picked up the line. "What?"

"I'm transferring Wesley to you. Talk to the man, please, so he can stop bothering me during my stories. He knows the rules!"

"You know you can't call here in the afternoon," I said when Wesley's call patched through. "Got Stelle mad."

"Oh…" I heard him snap his fingers near the receiver.

"Forgot about Estelle's stories. Tell her I said sorry. So... listen—"

"I know." I was suddenly hot, feeling my body flush. "I'm sorry, you're sorry, we're both sorry."

"I am, actually. I didn't mean to hurt you. I know it's hard. But you don't talk, so I don't know where you are in the process, you know?"

"Well, you're pretty clear now, right?"

A moment of silence passed before he answered. "Yeah. I just...I'm here. I understand."

"Oh, yeah? I remember when your fiancée who wasn't ever supposed to see combat went to Afghanistan and died. You totally get it."

He heaved an audible sigh that seemed to come from deep in his chest. I should really leave this man alone.

"Okay," he conceded. "I don't understand. I do care. And I know this sparring is probably fun for you, but I don't want to fight."

"I don't want to fight either. So let's not fight. How about that?"

Wesley paused like he had more to say, but in the end left things where they lay.

"I had another reason for calling. You left before I could tell you I might have a good missing persons case. I'm meeting with the client first thing tomorrow. You want in?"

"Is Nick okay with it? You know he whines whenever I work for y'all. I can transfer my work to Kincaid—"

"Don't even think about it. Gibson can't keep you busy like I can."

I laughed, then sat up and reached for a pen and a pad of paper. *Finally, something exciting.* "What's the deal?"

"It's a long story, but you know how if a person disappears and stays gone for four years, they can be declared legally dead?"

"Uh-huh..."

"Now let's say that almost legally dead, total deadbeat runaway husband and father has some money coming to him. Wouldn't his near-widow want some of that?"

"Of course. Especially if he's been gone long enough to be declared dead. So is he?"

"Don't know. I need you to find out what's up and we're up against the clock. Dad is terminally ill. If this guy is dead, all the money in question goes to the sister. Sister hates my client, so it's likely she'll get nothing. But if he's alive..."

"It's community property. Or whatever y'all call that in legalese."

"Equitable distribution," Wesley said. "He can't keep his wife from getting half when she divorces him."

"If the money was that big of a deal, why isn't there a prenup?"

"They're 'new money,' as we say. Either way, if he's alive, he inherits, and if he inherits, she's entitled to half."

"And sister? How's she feeling about a potential reunion with her deadbeat little brother?"

"She hopes he's dead. Then she doesn't have to share."

"Hmmm..." I chewed on the end of my pen. "Dad must be sure his son is alive."

"I think so too. The PD didn't look real hard, but no traces of him were ever found. No car, no...backpack, nothing. We need to bring him out of the dark, dead or alive. Preferably alive, if it's up to my client."

"Or dead, if it's up to his sister."

"You're so morbid," Wesley said, his laughter carrying over the line. It lightened my mood a little to hear it.

"I thought you liked that about me."

"One reason of many," he answered, then quickly added, "Uh, come to the office tomorrow morning around ten. We'll do some background, start a file. And put you to work."

"I like the sound of that. Does your client really think her husband is still alive?"

"She can't afford to think anything else." The line went silent for a full beat. Then… "Vette?"

"Yes, Wesley."

"I'm just trying to be here. You know?"

"I know, Wesley. I appreciate that. I don't know if I'm ready for more than that. Part of me wants…"

I sighed, expelling a long, loud breath. The weight of that breath carried the struggle of the last three years.

"Yeah," came the gruff, emotional response. "I know, Vette. See you tomorrow."

CHAPTER
FIVE

WESLEY

I SAT on one side of a round meeting table in my office, trying not to watch Anjelica Foster tug at her too-tight suit jacket. Deep lines creased alongside her tense smile as she halfway stood to shake Yvette's hand.

Yvette had breezed past my new receptionist as usual, wearing her standard PI uniform—baggy jeans, an oversized t-shirt with a zip-up hoodie, and boots. She dropped that ever-present crossbody bag on the nearest chair and offered her hand to Anjelica as I made introductions.

"Before we begin," I said, pulling out a legal pad and clicking my pen, "our conversation today is confidential. Yvette Young is a licensed private investigator who works under contract with this firm. She's quick, and she knows how to stay hidden."

"Not to mention cheap. Right, Wesley?"

My eyes shifted to hers, narrowing slightly. Yvette never could behave in a meeting. "And she can work with a budget."

"I hope so," Anjelica muttered. "I mean, I don't have much now, but if Edward is alive, I'll have more than enough."

"For the moment, we're working on contingency. You won't owe attorney fees unless we locate Edward and you receive the inheritance. Ms. Young's investigative fees will be covered under the same arrangement." I made a note on my pad. "Let's focus on finding him."

Anjelica nodded. "What do you need from me?"

"Why don't you walk us through the timeline?" I said, pen ready. "Start with when Edward disappeared and take us through to today." I pushed back from the table and adjusted to a more comfortable position, arms folded across my chest, legs stretched out under the table.

She sighed, gearing up for what I knew would be a long story. Her middle Georgia drawl thickened as she settled in. "Me and Edward have been married goin' on twelve years now. He's been gone a bit over three years. When we first got married, we struggled, like couples do. Edward worked on a construction crew for a long time, but the work was hard on him, you know? He never made enough and he was always stressed out. He drank a lot. He showed up to work still drunk a lot."

Anjelica inhaled, her chest heaving, then paused. "Could I get a glass of water? I'm already parched."

I stood to retrieve a bottle from the mini fridge next to my desk, unscrewed the cap, and handed it to her. She gulped down half the bottle in seconds, then let out a loud belch.

"Whoa, excuse me. Sorry."

I caught Yvette's glance and shrugged. Our client wasn't exactly refined, but I'd worked with worse.

"Anyway. Me and Edward have twins. We shouldn't have had them 'cause we could barely afford to feed the two of us, but...they're here. They're the spittin' image of their daddy and I admit, they are a handful. And why wouldn't they be?

It's just me taking care of them while their daddy is out God knows where, doin' God knows what. I swear if we find him on a beach somewhere, I'm gonna kill—"

"Never say things like that in front of an attorney," I interrupted, my voice sharp. "I don't care if you're joking. Never say that again."

Anjelica rolled her eyes but continued her story. "So Edward lost his job, and I had to go to work. Ed ain't no Mr. Mom, I'll tell you that." She chuckled. More like gurgled. "He had a tough time handling the boys. They were four. I tell you, men really don't understand what it's like to be a housewife until they have to be one. Then there's so much complaining about how much work it is and how he never gets to talk to anybody and—"

"So, when exactly did Edward disappear?" Yvette interrupted, and I silently thanked her. The story needed direction or we'd be here all day. Not that it mattered to Yvette—she was billing for her time.

"Oh. Well. Anyway, the twins were wild and he couldn't find a job except under-the-table work, but that wasn't doing much more than buying bread and peanut butter. When I was home with the boys, he expected a clean house and laundry done and dinner on the table and his kids to be all…not evil. When I was the one working, the house stayed a mess and the boys stayed dirty and nothing ever got done but a lot of TV watching. I was on him a lot, I guess, and…well, he just snapped. He says, *'You know what? You can just keep all this shit!'* And he packs a suitcase and walks out the door."

I watched Yvette's fingers moving quickly across her notepad, her head nodding along to Anjelica's meandering story. So far, I could understand wanting to get away from this woman and her deep country accent, bless her heart.

"I didn't think he'd stay gone," Anjelica continued. "I thought he'd just blow off steam or whatever. But he never came home."

"You called the police, I assume?" Yvette asked.

Anjelica nodded, her head bobbing. "Yep, sure did. At first, they thought I killed him. But when they couldn't find any evidence of that, they said it wasn't against the law to leave your family. That he was probably laid up with some young thing. I mean, I don't know what gal would choose an unemployed, middle-aged, short, balding guy with a beer belly, but it takes all kinds, I guess."

"It...certainly does," Yvette quipped, and I had to hide a smile. "The police never looked for him, then?"

"After he'd been gone a couple weeks with no word, they let me file a missing persons report. They half-assed looked for him, like turned over one rock, said, 'Well, ma'am, looks like he's done left ya,' and closed the case."

"Typical," I muttered under my breath.

She paused, swiping at a tear. "I guess I thought...hoped like a dummy is more like it, that he might come back. He dumped a whole entire life and left it behind."

"And now you need him found? Tell us about that," Yvette prompted.

Anjelica sat up straighter, crossing and uncrossing her legs. "Right. So George, Edward's daddy, has owned a few bagel shops for years now. Always did good business, you know? But in recent years, they really took off. Got featured on one of them Cooking Channel shows that goes to towns and profiles small businesses. Well, everything exploded after that. When George got sick, he sold the whole franchise for a huge chunk of money. Several million dollars, plus he kept shares in the company."

I noticed Yvette's pen moving faster now that we were getting to the heart of the matter.

"George and I... Well, we don't get along. Edward and Eileen's mama died when they were kids. Them two is all he ever had since he never remarried and Edward was...is the baby of the family. George always thought I drove him away, so it was my fault that his son wasn't around to share in the avalanche of money he was throwing around town. Plus, Edward chose construction work over joining the family business, chose me and starting our family over making bagels for a living. George never got over that."

She took another sip of water before continuing. "But then George got sick. It came on real fast and he don't have much time left. That's when he decided to sell the whole business while he could still manage everything himself. In his will, he's supposed to be leaving money to split between Edward and Eileen, but only if Edward is alive. If he's dead, his entire estate goes to Eileen to distribute as she sees fit and… Well, me and Eileen don't get along too well neither."

I watched Yvette's expression carefully as Anjelica laid out the stakes.

"Eileen is pissed because Ed has been gone and it's like… it's like leaving money to a dog. She's been after me for weeks to have Edward declared dead, but I couldn't do that if I wanted to. And I don't. A person has to have been missing for four years past the last date of contact—"

"Which would be?" Yvette cut in.

"January. He can be declared dead in January."

I saw Yvette suck in a sharp breath and made a note about the timeline. Not enough time to find a man that vanished into thin air.

"Then Eileen gets the money that Edward's father set aside for him. Millions of dollars. And I get nothing, and the boys, his children get nothing because she's a petty, spiteful, evil—"

I leaned forward, resting my arms on the table. "Let me clarify something important. If Edward is alive, anything he inherits while still legally married becomes marital property. Georgia follows equitable distribution laws. We need to focus on that angle."

She huffed, sticking her chin in the air. "Which is also why

I'm not filing for divorce until we find that sumbitch. He owes me. I been payin' all the bills, takin' care of his brats. He was so excited when he found out we was havin' twins, then he up and left them with me."

Her hands trembled as she pushed a lock of platinum blonde hair behind her ear. "Listen, can we take a break? I need a cigarette real bad."

I nodded and showed her to the door. After closing it behind her, I leaned against it and looked at Yvette. "What are you thinking?"

She studied her notes, her shoulder lifting and lowering in a shrug. "They don't sound like the sharpest tools in the drawer."

I had to laugh at that. "Neither of them are particularly sharp, except he's managed to disappear and stay gone for four years."

"Honestly, Payne, this case is a dog. This man doesn't want to be found. Is it even worth it for you? How much is your fee? What if I don't find Edward?"

I took a moment before answering, drawing my lips inward and inhaling deeply. "I'm taking this case as a personal favor. She was getting the runaround with the cops, and now this situation. There's no record of a will for Edward. He didn't have life insurance. This is her last chance to establish some kind of future for her boys. Once he's declared dead, everything goes to the sister and Edward's children get nothing. Her brother asked us to step in and see what I could do."

"You're taking this on contingency. You don't normally do that either."

"I'd do anything for a friend." I tried to catch her eye, to convey my deeper meaning, but she ignored it as usual. "So I really need this to close, Vette. Can you do it?"

"You know I don't like to promise results."

"Yes, I know that. But…"

A light tap sounded at the door and I turned to open it. Anjelica came back in, looking less manic but reeking of nicotine. She eased into her chair with a deep sigh.

"Do you have any idea where your husband could be?" I asked, diving back into the conversation. "Do you own a cabin somewhere, does he have a reclusive cousin living in the North Georgia mountains? Any hits on his social security number? He has to be working somewhere."

Anjelica shook her head through the litany of questions. "If I knew, I'd have found him and dragged him back here by his ass. His family led this huge search, called everyone they could think of, looking for him. They don't have any private, secluded land. He doesn't have any hiding spots that I know of. And Edward is handy. He's most likely working under the table, construction or something like that."

Yvette scribbled a few more notes, then closed her notebook and stood. I watched her shift into professional mode, all business now.

"I'll need a comprehensive information package about Edward. Photos, Social Security number, employment history, known associates, habits, preferences. The more detailed the profile, the better our chances." She glanced at me. "Standard missing persons documentation."

After offering a limp handshake, Anjelica's blue eyes followed Yvette out of the room. "That's it? She's...she'll start looking now?"

"Miss Young is thorough," I assured her. "We'll schedule a follow-up meeting once she's had time to review the initial information. You should have those documents to us within forty-eight hours."

"Oh. She won't...shoot him, will she?"

I had to chuckle at that. "She's an investigator, not a bounty hunter. Her job is to find him. That's it."

"Good. If he's gonna get shot, I'd rather do it myself."

I groaned. Anjelica laughed, pushing her chair back to stand. "I know, I know. Don't say that in front of my lawyer."

After Anjelica left, Nick filled my doorway, his Brooks Brothers suit perfectly pressed, a permanent frown already in place. "So?"

I gestured to the chair across from my desk. "She's rough around the edges, but her story checks out. The father's will, the sister's hostility, the timing of it all…"

"And Young's taking the case?"

"She is."

He settled into my chair with a sigh. "Any chance of finding this guy before January?"

"If anyone can do it, Yvette can."

I didn't mention the nagging feeling I had about Edward's disappearance. Something about it felt too clean, too planned for a guy who could barely hold down a construction job.

"Patrick will appreciate the help. Man's been worried sick about his sister, those boys." Nick leaned back, studying me. "But Wesley…"

"Nick. Don't." My tone was a warning.

"Someone has to say it, Payne. You're distracted when she's around. You showed up late to the Hoffman deposition because you were at lunch with her."

"We were discussing a case," I shot back, my lip curling. "A case that made us a lot of money."

He leaned forward. "Look, excuse my language, but you're wasting the best years of your life sniffing pussy that doesn't want you. If she was going to move on at all, let alone with you, you would have already had her—"

"We're done here." I stood, stalked toward the door and pulled it open. "I have work to do."

I watched his expression morph into his usual stoic, stony visage. "I need you focused, Payne."

After Nick left, I pulled up Yvette's initial report on my laptop. The photos from the Simeon surveillance were perfect as always, impossible to dispute. I thought about how she must have looked taking them, crouched in those woods for hours.

She'd bring that same dedication to finding Edward Foster and I'd be there every step of the way, staying close but not too close, walking the line between professional and personal that had become our routine.

Nick wasn't wrong, though. I *was* distracted.

Aching for someone who was off-limits, supporting her while she learned to breathe again would break any man's focus.

CHAPTER
SIX

YVETTE

I LEANED against the wall just outside the office door, watching Estelle with an ever-present cigarette dangling between two fingers. She wore jeggings that looked painted on and did little to accentuate her wide hips, paired with a tunic that was supposed to cover and minimize. I'd tried telling her countless times that the combination did nothing of the sort, but she wouldn't listen.

"First one today," she said, lifting the cigarette to her lips.

"Not counting the one you have to have as soon as you wake up? And the one you usually have right after breakfast? And the couple of puffs you take on the way to work?"

The tip glowed red. She blew a column of smoke into the air. "I meant the first one since I got here, smart ass. Where you been?"

"I told you I had a meeting at Courtney & Payne. Give me one."

Without a word, Estelle handed over a cigarette and her

lighter. I lit it and sucked in a long drag. With a cough, I let the smoke evacuate my lungs, waving it away from my face.

"Your mama know you smoke, girl?"

"I'm grown. And I don't smoke. I just take a puff here and there."

"That's how I got started." Estelle finished her cigarette and crushed the butt against the wall. I did the same, then followed her to the office door. "A puff here, a cigarette there from my sister's pack. Forty years later..."

She let out a sigh that quickly morphed into a wet, rasping cough.

"How many are you down to now?"

"Pack, maybe two a day. It's still a lot, but I was going through a carton every other day. I see the difference in my pocketbook."

I laughed as I walked past Estelle's desk toward the kitchen. "Where's Nia?"

"She finished both of those injury cases she was working on. She was dropping the paperwork to the attorney and then coming in."

"Good. We've got a new case from Wesley and it's going to have to be a group effort."

"Oh, yeah?"

"Mmhmm. Missing person. There's some money wrapped up in finding him alive. I'll explain everything when Nia gets in."

"Sounds like a good one. I better fire up my programs."

Estelle had been a teenage mother back when that would get you sent away to live with an out-of-town aunt or grandmother. Instead of running away, she'd raised her daughter with her mother's help. While her daughter was in school, so was Estelle, taking typing and computer courses. She took a comfortable secretarial job, ended up marrying her boss and having two more kids. Once they were grown and having babies of their own, Estelle was ready to re-enter the work-force, but the world had changed.

Undeterred by words and terminology, she dove in, making quick friends with her much younger classmates. Her grandchildren helped her at home, showing her shortcuts and websites. Her open nature made her a natural ally; Estelle had connections everywhere with everyone. What she couldn't do herself, she had a contact in her cell phone that could.

"Text Nia and see if she's already on the way. We're going to need all the help we can get." I settled into a seat at the table pushed into a corner of the kitchen and opened my notebook to a blank page.

Minutes later, Nia's Prius zipped past Estelle's window, sliding into a spot beside mine. She marched into the office carrying a box from Krispy Kreme and set it on the kitchen counter. "I was in line when I got your text. The hot sign was on."

Nia's sweet tooth was legendary—she never came in without a box of donuts, a chocolate bar, or a bag of candy. Unlike me, however, her svelte figure didn't betray her obsession. She was tall and long-legged, with a body that was designed to show off clothing.

"Why is the box all the way over there, though?" I asked, holding out a hand, which was soon filled with a hot glazed donut on a napkin. "Do not tell my mother about this. I was complaining about the size of my ass yesterday."

"I ain't seen nothin'," said Nia around a mouthful, before sliding into the chair across from me. Estelle joined us with a mug of coffee and a notepad. "So what's the deal?"

I spent the next half hour filling Estelle and Nia in on my meeting at Wesley's office and the pending case, including the challenge set before us to find Edward before Anjelica lost everything.

"It's a shame that man cut his grandsons out," Estelle said, shaking her head. "I understand if you don't like their mama.

My husband is not fond of our son Stevie's wife, but he'd do anything for his grandbabies."

"Well, you know how money changes folks."

"And now he's basically saying, find my son so your sons can have a future and if you don't?" Estelle dusted her hands together. "Through with you. This is him getting back at her, seems like."

"Maybe," I said, steering the conversation back toward the investigation. "More than anything, he's pushing Anjelica to find him. And from what we're seeing, I'm convinced he had help disappearing."

"He's got to be out there somewhere," offered Estelle.

"Right," mumbled Nia. "But where? I mean, where do we even start?"

"With what the police didn't do," I said, closing my notebook. "We'll dig deeper than they ever bothered to."

I AWOKE the next morning with a headache, which wasn't helped by the bright beam of sunlight streaming into my bedroom, nor the pounding of Yancey's feet on the steps below. The thought of food made my stomach turn, so though I smelled Mama's famous pancakes—the ones she served with maple syrup and toasted pecans alongside a gorgeous batch of fluffy eggs, thick cut bacon, and jalapeño grits—I rolled over onto my stomach and slammed my eyes shut against the onslaught of light.

My phone chimed. Without looking, I stuck an arm out from under the sheet and reached for the device on my nightstand, bringing it close to my face. I slid my finger across the screen and read the message from Wesley.

WPayne: Package coming to you today. Police report, information you asked for from Anjelica.

I thumbed out a short message: Thx.

WPayne: That's it? No snappy comeback? Too early?

VetteY: Late night researching with the team. I'll catch up with you after we've gone through the package.

WPayne: OK. Call u later.

I groaned and set the device aside.

I'd met Wesley in Heidelberg, Germany. He was the JAG Attorney assigned to defend a soldier arrested in a drug bust. On my first case as a Special Agent, I was assigned to investigate, follow the clues, and present the evidence regarding the soldier's misconduct. We butted heads frequently since every piece of evidence that I turned up proved the soldier was lying, that he was the drug connection, that there was no frame or conspiracy.

Wesley was a bulldog, sending me on ridiculous missions and interviews. "Captain Payne," I fumed, "you seem hell bent on finding something, anything to prove Sgt. Parsons' innocence when everything I've found says he's guilty."

"Because, Special Agent Young, it's my job to prove he's innocent," Wesley had snapped. "I don't want any surprises from trial counsel. Parsons says it was his drug connect that framed him. Keep looking."

I eventually uncovered a ring of military drug smugglers and got an underling to admit to framing Parsons for the drug buy gone bad. The day before I was to leave the base, Wesley called me from the lobby of the Heidelberg Marriott where we were both staying for our temporary duty assignment.

"I feel bad about how hard I pushed you on the Parsons investigation."

I chuckled. "You should, Captain Payne. But you were right. I shouldn't give up just because the evidence says to stop looking."

"I hear you're on the first flight out of here tomorrow. Could I talk you into a celebratory drink?" The pause on the line before I answered prompted his next statement. "I did some investigating of my own, you know."

"Did you now?"

"I did. And word via the underground is that Special Agent Yvette Young has been romantically involved with an E-5 Mechanic, Sgt. Jason Porter, for the past few years."

I clicked my tongue but couldn't hide a smile. "So you're telling me you know I'm involved and you're not a threat?"

"Correct. Come on down. I'm at The Grill."

The Grill wasn't fancy, but it offered small pockets of privacy between groups of German businessmen winding down after work and clusters of American soldiers seeking a taste of home. Two hours, two drinks, and half a salad later, I was seated at a cozy table across from Wesley.

"You have some pretty good investigators," I told him. "Jason and I aren't exactly hiding our relationship, but I didn't take out any billboard ads."

"The gossip flows pretty well, if you didn't know."

"Oh, I know. I hear a lot of things through the grapevine."

"Like?"

Feeling pleasantly untethered from months of investigation and paperwork, I had switched to merlot. I swirled the bold red before sipping a mouthful, then answering.

"Like…Captain Payne is a hot commodity. And that he doesn't disappoint the ladies. *Any* of them. And there are… *lots* of ladies."

Wesley's head dipped with his laughter. "My reputation precedes me, I guess."

"That it does. And it's juicy."

He sat up straighter, folding his hands in front of him, as if preparing to cross-examine me. "So much of the grapevine is noise. Out of curiosity, what do your sources say about me?"

"Do you want the classified report, or the rumor mill version?"

"Both," he said, after some thought.

I pretended to thumb through imaginary files on the table. "Captain Payne will take shit from superiors so his staff don't have to. He's dogged. He's clever. Possibly a little self-destructive when it comes to taking on lost causes."

"Fair," he said, raising his glass.

"You're generous with your charm and—" I paused long enough for him to arch his eyebrows. "There's a whole section about your drunken rendition of 'Purple Rain' at Commander Millhope's retirement party."

He groaned in mock embarrassment. "One time. The Prince thing was *one time*. I was ordered to sing and I was drunk off my ass."

"It only takes one time, Captain," I said, not bothering to hide my grin. "The gossip train rides both ways. Though I appreciate that you respect my relationship. It's hard enough, you know?"

I sipped more wine and took another bite of perfectly prepared schnitzel with spätzle, a delicacy I would miss when I left Germany.

"I do. I once attempted the rigors of a long-distance relationship. I can do a lot of difficult things but..." He shook his head. "It was hard to stay connected. And the minute a person tells me what I can't do..."

"That's the first thing you want to go out and do. I know the feeling."

"So how do you keep it going?"

"I guess..." I shrugged my shoulder, pondered my answer further. "I hate to be all love at first sight about it, but...Jason and I have been inseparable since we met. He's the first person I think about every day, no matter where I am. The last person I think about at night. No matter where I am. Speaking of—"

I glanced at my watch, frowning. "I'm due to call him in a half-hour."

Wesley stood as I did, watching me gather the unfashionable bag I always wore. "Thanks for joining me. I hope we'll work together again. Soon."

"Looking forward to it, Captain." I stepped back from the table and saluted.

"Go on with that, Agent Young. Fly safely."

Since that assignment, Wesley had stayed in touch through voicemail and email. And when I was again assigned to his investigative team, I felt guilty about feeling giddy. He was attracted to me. I knew it. But he respected my relationship with Jason. And I knew that too.

I had never banked on the obstacle between me and Wesley not being a factor anymore. And although I still wore Jason's ring and still cried in my sleep and still went into a panic attack at the thought of letting go of my memories, the underlying attraction to Wesley Payne that had begun so long ago on that Army base in Germany, that attraction that I'd ignored because I was so much in love with Jason...was blooming.

The phone chimed again:

Stelle: You coming in?

VetteY: Headache. Payne is sending a package. Scan it when you get it, send it to me.

VetteY: You and Nia work the paper trail. Trace everything as far back as you can. The last time he used his credit cards, bank cards, IDs.

VetteY: Let me know if anything interesting pops. I'll be online later on.

I dropped the phone and rolled to my side, wrapped in a cocoon of sheets and a goose-down comforter. I was comfortable, but the bathroom was calling my name.

Sitting up, I tossed the covers back and headed to the bathroom. A noise in the hallway made me detour. I pulled the door open to my mother holding a plate and a mug of coffee, her leather purse on her shoulder.

"You look terrible," she muttered, walking in uninvited.

Technically, the place belonged to my parents, so I didn't protest. I pushed the door closed and followed her into the small kitchen.

"Thanks. Two late nights in a row. I have a headache."

"You need to take better care of yourself, Vette. All this running around—"

"It's my job, Ma. I know we've gone over this before."

Mama set the plate covered in foil on the counter and plucked a fork from a drawer. "Don't interrupt me when I'm complaining. It's dangerous. Do you still carry your gun?"

My pistol stayed in the glove box of the El Camino, right in reach if I needed it. I'd never needed it. It had only been fired at target practice.

I reached for the plate and slid it across the counter. I still wasn't feeling well, but the mixture of smells filling my apartment was tempting. I'd been so caught up in my research the night before that I'd skipped dinner. Maybe I just needed to eat.

"I don't even feel comfortable with you owning one but I'd rather you carry it than not. Have you thought any more about—"

"Mama." I rolled my eyes as much as I could get away with. "I don't know what makes you think a job with the FBI would be less dangerous. I'd still carry a gun, I'd still work late. I'd still be doing all of this running around, but I'd be running after real criminals, not cheaters and fakers."

"Not if you took the research job. You could have just sat at the computer, all nice and safe, and stayed in Virginia. Or you could have taken that investigator job with the Georgia Bureau."

Daddy had done renovations for several agents and the Deputy Director of the Georgia Bureau of Investigation. I had a good word and plenty of references if I ever wanted to apply.

"That was a desk job. Pushing buttons in a Cyber Crime Division."

"So?"

I dipped the tines of the fork into a puddle of grits and scooped some into my mouth. The spice of the jalapeño spread across my tongue. My stomach didn't lurch at the introduction of food, so I kept eating.

"*So?*" Mama repeated, tilting her head and lifting an eyebrow, a gesture that had always meant *answer me if you know what's good for you.*

"So...it would have been boring. I like being busy. I like being in the field. Even in the Army, I was glad to get off post and do something interesting."

Mama sucked her teeth as she leaned against the counter. "Flying off to all kinds of places. How much wrong can someone even do in Whatever-stan?"

I almost spit coffee across the counter. "I told you...you don't want to know."

"Well..." Her lips pursed. "All I know is, you'd best be careful out there. You just never know what might happen."

"I am careful."

"How's Stelle doin'? Still smoking like a chimney?"

"She's down to a couple packs a day, actually."

Mama made the same humph sound she'd made earlier. "And Nia?"

"Still about as big around as my wrist. Bought us Krispy Kreme donuts yesterday. Ate half of them herself."

"See, that's your Aunt Erin's genes right there. She got all the skinny from our daddy. I got all the plump."

"I love your plump, Mama."

"And...how's Wesley?"

I felt my face flush. "Saw him yesterday. He's fine."

"Just *fine*? He was so good to us after Jason died. Always checking on us, making sure we had what we needed." She tilted her head, studying me. "When am I going to meet his people? I know they raised him right."

"Mama…"

"I'm just asking questions. He's single, successful, fine as aged whiskey. A good man with a lot going for him." She leaned against the counter, getting comfortable like she was settling in for an extended conversation. "How many men like that you think are just walking around Atlanta?"

"Mother…don't start."

"Don't start what? Pointing out that a good man with his own law practice is interested in my daughter?" She crossed her arms. "Baby, men like Wesley don't come around every day. Educated, well-mannered, treats his mama right—"

"You do not know that, Mama!"

"I can tell, Yvette!"

I went back to my plate, mumbling, "I'm not having this conversation."

"Somebody needs to be having it. What good is going to see Paula if she's not telling you that Jason wouldn't want you shutting yourself off from life? And Wesley's not going to wait forever."

"I didn't ask him to wait as long as he has."

"And I bet you haven't asked him not to." Mama's eyebrows rose. "Seems to me like you're setting up to do something about that situation. You need to get a move on about it."

She pushed off the counter, pulling her purse further up onto her shoulder. "Speaking of getting a move on, I'm heading out. I know you love my pancakes, and you didn't come down for breakfast." She paused, trying to look stern. "Make sure my plate gets back downstairs."

Then she was gone, the sweet scent of vanilla gone with her. I stood at the counter and finished the plate of lukewarm breakfast, feeling better. I heated up the coffee in the microwave, then sat at the desk and turned on the laptop.

I was still waiting on Estelle to email the contents of the file on Edward Foster. Once I figured out where the police investigation left off, I could pick up the trail. In the meantime, I'd conduct my investigation the way I always did.

First, find out everything there is to know about the subject.

The night before, I'd done an in-depth search on Edward Foster, George Foster, Eileen Foster, Anjelica Foster—anyone the Fosters might have thought about knowing or being connected with, looking for information or a hint of a clue where Edward might have disappeared to. Men didn't vanish. Not without a plan.

Second, follow the paper trail.

Estelle and Nia were both skilled at skip tracing. If a scrap of information about a client existed, one of them would find it. Old utility bills, former addresses, telephone data. The trick was to get your information through legitimate channels when possible or get someone to collect it for you. Both Nia and Estelle had contacts at various agencies but didn't like to call on them too often since doing so could put someone's job at risk. I preferred they exhaust public records before reaching out for help.

Third? Get tricky if necessary.

If skip trace and background investigations came up empty, I had to dance along the edge of what was legal to get the answers I sought. That part was the most fun. It often involved travel, some disguises, and sneaking into places where I wouldn't be welcome.

I sipped my coffee and looked through the links I'd curated the night before. From the information I'd received from Anjelica, I would dig through the list of Edward's friends and coworkers, people he liked and spent time with. And, more importantly, people who didn't like him and would betray his secrets.

An hour later, a notification popped up on screen. Estelle

had emailed the contents of the file from Wesley. I downloaded it to my desktop and started sorting through the information. There was a copy of the very thin missing persons file from the DeKalb County Police Department, photocopies of Edward's identification from official sources, a brief list of people that had been interviewed and theories that hadn't been investigated. Last, there was a lengthy list of Edward's friends and family. We'd start there.

My phone rang. The caller ID said it was Estelle. I picked it up on speaker. "Hey. I just got your email."

"Not much to it. Nia and I found about the same stuff online. Looks like Anjelica was right. They didn't look hard."

"And that could either be a blessing or a curse," piped in Nia. Estelle had put me on speaker. "Maybe he hasn't really vanished without a trace. Maybe they just didn't look for him."

"His wife would have, I imagine."

"Not necessarily. From what you told us about her, she didn't have money to send people out to find this guy and if the police didn't find him, he would not be found."

"That's a good point. But wouldn't his father have spent money to find him if he thought he was alive?"

"Maybe," said Estelle. "But you said he got real sick real fast. There may not have been time. This stipulation in his will is his way of making sure his son gets found."

"And if he's alive," added Nia, "Anjelica gets her money, and it's like he paid for the search in the first place. But if he's dead, he hasn't wasted a penny on a futile search."

I gulped a swallow of coffee. "That sounds very new money to me. Flossing like the money is endless but counting every dime that gets spent. I've never met someone so cheap as a person who just became wealthy."

Both ladies on the other end laughed.

"So what did you guys come up with, skiptrace-wise?"

"Not much," said Nia. "I know you suspect he didn't

disappear alone and I'm starting to agree with you. The only utilities in this guy's name are the utilities at the current Foster residence—"

"So Anjelica still has Edward's name on the accounts at the house?"

"Yep. His name is on the power, the gas, the phone. The mortgage is still in his name. She was never on the deed and can't transfer it without Edward's consent. He's not been declared dead, so it wouldn't transfer to her yet."

"I guess I see that. Just...after four years, I would have transferred some things to my name."

"She reminds me of when a child disappears and the parent leaves everything just like it was when they left," said Nia. "I wouldn't be surprised if Edward's pants were still on the floor and his boots were still in a corner and his toothbrush was still in a cup in the bathroom. She was really holding out for her man to come home."

"Well, let's hope," said Estelle, "for Edward's sake, that he's not been holed up with some other woman for four years while she's been struggling."

"Keep going on the skiptrace results."

Estelle picked up where Nia left off. "I don't see any other accounts he's opened. No credit cards, no utilities, no apartment leases, no cell phones, *nothing*. Of course, these days it's easy to get a prepaid that's not tied to your name. And there's been no activity on the cards Edward had in his name since he disappeared. The trail on Edward literally goes cold."

"But there's no indication that he's dead, right? Did the police check neighboring counties, maybe even neighboring states, for unclaimed bodies? What about fingerprints? Edward was a bit of a drunk...what are the chances he got in a bar fight somewhere and got arrested? That would put his prints in the system."

"I might be able to check that through my contacts," said Estelle. Running Edward's prints would require reopening his case, which wasn't likely to happen. After their brief investigation, the DeKalb County Police had closed it, stating that he'd simply 'left the area.' Without a crime, there was no legal reason to pursue him further.

"And that would only help if his prints are in the system," said Nia. "I'm looking through this pitiful file and I don't see any mention of his prints. Maybe they're stored somewhere else."

"If I need to, I'll go to the house and collect them. I'm almost positive Anjelica has something with Edward's prints on it."

"She's probably got a candlelit shrine to the man on her mantle," said Estelle with a cackle.

"Stelle!" I scolded but couldn't help laughing along. The second line on my phone beeped. Wesley.

"I'm getting another call. You ladies keep at it. I'll be in touch with you later."

I ended the call with Estelle and picked up the second line.

"Hello, Wesley."

"What up, Vette?"

There was something in the way he always called me Vette. My family called me Vette too, but my skin tingled—annoyingly so—at the timbre of his voice when he said it.

"You feeling any better?"

"Yes," I answered with a smile, eyeing the decimated, sticky breakfast plate. "My mama knew just what I needed."

"She make you some chicken noodle soup?"

"Pancakes."

Wesley laughed.

"With syrup and pecans. And jalapeño grits with bacon."

"You always bragging on your mama's cooking. One of these days, I'd like to experience it myself."

"I'll bring you a plate the next time she throws down."

"Sounds like she throws down every day."

"She does," I said, laughing.

"You seem like you enjoy it."

I narrowed my eyes, even though he couldn't see me. "You saying I've gained some weight, Payne?"

"No," he said quickly. "I'm saying you look like you've been enjoying her cooking. Tell her I said hello the next time you see her."

"I will."

And then she would pressure me to see him as more than a friend, a fellow veteran, a business partner.

"Did you check through the package I sent over?"

"Estelle scanned it and sent it to me. DeKalb PD didn't do Anjelica any favors."

Wesley snickered. "Not a single one. You saw how thin that file was."

"I'd like to look around the house. Maybe I'll see something she didn't. Also, I don't see any prints on file for Edward, and I'm going to need them."

There was a pause.

"How—you know what, Vette? I don't need to know how you're going to get prints identified."

"If I was going to do something illegal, I wouldn't tell you."

"I appreciate that."

"So, about getting into the house…"

"I would prefer if I were there. Anjelica is a little jumpy."

"Understood. That's why I'm asking you to get me into the house."

"I could arrange a meeting tomorrow. She'll have to get time off work. Is that soon enough?"

"It'll work."

"We could go to lunch after, if you'd like."

I shifted on the couch, adjusting the throw over my lap. "Wesley…"

"As friends. Partners, even. We could talk about the case."

"I know where you like to eat, and you don't pay me enough to treat you to lunch."

Wesley laughed loud and hearty. "Fair enough. I'll treat you to lunch. Let me give Anjelica a call, set up the meeting, and then I'll text you details."

"Sounds fine. We'll keep working on this end."

"I'm looking forward to seeing you, Vette."

The way he said it made my stomach flip.

"Wesley…don't do that."

"Don't do what? Don't be real with you?"

"You and I both know you're being more real than you need to be. I just want to work this case."

"We are working the case." I could practically hear the smile in his voice.

"You're also working on my nerves. Let me know about tomorrow."

I hit the end button and dropped the phone beside me.

CHAPTER
SEVEN

WESLEY

THE FOSTER HOUSE was a two-story colonial nestled in a quiet Doraville community of aging homes and larger than it appeared from the outside—but not by much. For a family of four with rambunctious twins, the two-bedroom, two-and-a-half-bath home must have felt like a pressure cooker. No wonder Edward had left.

Anjelica met us at the door in a ponytail and casual clothes, her face bare of the heavy makeup she'd worn to my office. "I have to be to work at noon," she said, leading us inside.

"Where do you work?" Yvette asked. I watched her slip into investigator mode, cataloging details most people would miss.

"I'm a coordinator at Candler Park Residential Living Facility. I basically make sure they're not fallin' all over the place. Feed 'em their meds, make sure they eat. Do activities. Stuff like that."

"Is that the job you picked up when Edward lost his job?"

Anjelica's cheeks flushed pink. "I been through a few jobs since then. I worked as a hotel maid, a cashier at the Food Lion for a long time. Worked my way up to Assistant Manager, but then after Edward disappeared I kinda...fell apart. I lost that job and I was on the welfare for a while. And then I got off that 'cause I got tired of folks feelin' sorry for us. Then I got this job. I been there about two years now."

I hung back, watching Yvette work. She moved through the living room, taking in the shrine of photos on the entertainment center, the threadbare but clean furniture, the thin carpet. Through the window, a dilapidated swing set sat beside what looked like a hand-built deck.

"Did Edward build that?" she asked, gesturing outside.

Anjelica nodded, pride lighting her face. "It was the first thing he did when he bought the house—tore out the old deck and built this new one. I told you, he's handy. He can do this stuff in his sleep."

"Does he have a workshop or something?"

Smart. If Edward was as handy as Anjelica claimed, his workspace might tell us more than the rest of the house combined.

"In the garage."

Anjelica led us through a door off the kitchen. The space was frozen in time—thick dust coating tools arranged neatly on the walls. "I haven't touched anything out here. Everything is just as he left it."

"Good. That's exactly what I needed to hear." Yvette set down her kit—an old tackle box that seemed to contain everything she needed for evidence collection. I watched her snap on gloves and pull out lifting tape.

"Is that just like...Scotch tape? I could have got some prints for you."

"It's special tape," Yvette explained, moving toward the woodworking equipment. "Specifically designed for lifting fingerprints. Regular tape is too sticky."

I stepped around Anjelica, drawn to Yvette's methodical process. "You're looking for something he would have held, something that would give you a good print, right?"

"Yeah. Maybe…" She studied the stacks of wood by the table saw. "He would have brought these in. Stacked them. Handled them."

"He wore gloves when he was going to work with the saw," Anjelica offered. I caught Yvette's glance and shrugged. Even a dead end could tell us something.

"I'll take a look anyway." Yvette moved to the next tool, already focused on her work. "Did he leave anything behind like a toothbrush? A hairbrush?"

"I might have an old hairbrush. But why? How will his brush help you find him?"

"If I can get the GBI to look into it, they'll ask for it. I just want to have it ready."

My eyebrow lifted. "You think you can get them interested?"

She shrugged. "Don't know until you ask, right?" Then, without looking up from her work: "Do you mind? You're in my light."

I stepped back, suddenly aware of how out of place my Italian suit looked in this dusty garage. The smell of mildewed wood clung to everything. While Yvette examined tools on the wall, I studied the space through an attorney's eyes. Tools hung in their proper places, projects appeared completed rather than abandoned mid-task, workbench cleared and organized. This wasn't the workspace of a man who'd lost control and walked out. Edward had finished what he was doing, put everything away, and then left. Planned, not impulsive.

Yvette's small sound of triumph drew my attention. She'd lifted a handsaw from its peg, examining the handle with her flashlight.

"Got something?" I asked.

"Clear prints on the protected side." She grinned. "Okay. I need the hairbrush, toothbrush, whatever you've got with something from him on it."

We followed Anjelica upstairs to the bedrooms. The boys' room looked like a war zone—two twin beds barely visible under mountains of toys and clothes.

"They won't clean their room," Anjelica said, noticing Yvette's raised eyebrow. "So I told them if they want to live in filth, go right ahead." She swung the door closed quickly. "I mean... I don't leave it like that. Every once in a while, I make them clean it out."

"We're not with DFACS, Anjelica."

Anjelica led us to the main bedroom. The room was surprisingly neat, nothing like what I'd expected based on Anjelica's description of preserving everything exactly as Edward had left it.

"Tell me about the day he left," Yvette prompted. "Did he take everything, or did he just toss some things in a bag?"

"He threw some things in a bag, but..." Anjelica paused. "It was like he had been thinking about it for a while. Like he knew exactly what he wanted to take and what he wanted to leave."

Everything about this screamed premeditation to me. Edward hadn't snapped—he'd executed a plan.

I watched Yvette methodically search the closet and dresser drawers while Anjelica retrieved the hairbrush from the bathroom. The lack of personal effects struck me as deliberate. No receipts, no notes, no business cards. Edward had sanitized his trail.

"I've got some follicles," Yvette announced, examining the brush. "Looks like the bulb is attached."

"Is that good?"

"It's great. That's where the DNA is." She worked quickly, collecting samples. "No toothbrush?"

"No. He took the one he used and he always threw away his old one when he switched toothbrushes."

Of course, he did. Another sign this was no impulsive exit.

"Did he leave any boxes?" Yvette asked. "Old pictures, documents, eighth grade English papers?"

Anjelica bit her lip. "Not in here, we didn't have much room. But he might have left some boxes in the attic. I tried to get the police to look through stuff up there, but they didn't seem interested. On all those TV shows, the cops tear your house apart when they're lookin' for somethin'."

Yvette chuckled, catching my eye. "Well, those cops on TV are pretty much a fantasy. We all wish it worked like it works on TV."

"You've done more in the time you've been here than they did the couple of times they came out here. They hardly touched a thing... They didn't look for prints or collect hair or anything."

"That's why I hire Yvette," I said. "If there's something to find, she'll dig it up."

"I appreciate the vote of confidence, Payne. Let's hope I live up to it." She turned to Anjelica. "Attic?"

By the time we loaded the last of five boxes into my SUV, my suit was covered in dust and cobwebs. Yvette tried not to laugh at my disheveled state but failed.

"I'll let you know if we dig up anything in these boxes," she said, checking her watch. "They could be junk, but you never know what kind of clues people unintentionally leave behind. We'll let you get to work."

She slipped into the passenger seat of my Range Rover. I started the engine and D'Angelo's "Untitled (How Does It Feel)" poured through the sound system, his voice shifting between rich baritone and soaring falsetto. Yvette settled back in her seat, then slowly turned her head toward me.

"What's up with this music?"

"What do you mean?"

She chuckled. "It just seems like you're trying to seduce me with this romantic neo soul."

I rolled my eyes and switched to sports radio. "Better?"

At her nod, I asked, "So, do you think there's anything in those boxes that'll help you find Edward?"

"Don't know. But a wise man once berated my investigative technique, telling me to keep searching until I find the answer I'm looking for. I'm just following procedure. Turning over stones, seeing what's there to be found."

I tried not to smile. Failed. "I hadn't lost a case yet and I was really feeling myself. I could have been—"

"You were fine. The pressure was what I needed. Besides, if you hadn't pushed, that soldier would be serving time on drug charges."

"And he would have been court-martialed. You saved his career."

"I didn't do it alone," she said.

I nodded, remembering how well we'd worked together even then. "We've always made a good team. Please tell me I wasn't the biggest ass you ever worked with."

"Not quite," she said, almost laughing. "But close."

I steered us into the valet line at Chops Lobster Bar. After handing over my keys, I led Yvette into the restaurant. We were seated immediately at my usual table near the window.

She ordered sweet tea. I opted for red wine.

"Do you always drink at lunch, counselor? Especially during a business lunch?"

"Does it bother you?" I asked.

She shook her head, her eyes on the menu. "Just busting your chops."

"Just tea for you?"

"I'm not much of a drinker. Anymore."

I knew why. I'd been at Jason's funeral and the celebration of life afterward. I watched her try to drink away the pain until she had to be carried out. The Porters hadn't spoken to her for weeks after.

The waiter appeared and I ordered a cowboy cut ribeye with all the trimmings. Yvette went with a modest skirt steak and baked potato. Once he left, she leaned forward, resting her forearm on the table.

"What do you think are the chances that Edward ran off with someone else?"

I paused mid-sip. This was what I'd been thinking all morning but hadn't voiced. "You're saying he didn't just get fed up with his wife and kids but actually left town with someone?"

"That's exactly what I think."

"Alright." I matched her posture, forearms on the table. "I'll bite. What tells you that?"

She bit into a roll, considering, then smiled. "Woman's intuition."

"I need more than that, Vette."

"Think about it. You hate your life and you want out. So do you throw some things in a bag and bolt? All by yourself? And once the money runs out, you don't slink back home, poor and hungry, tail between your legs?"

"If a man wants to stay gone, he can find a way."

"You said it yourself, Edward and Anjelica are not smart people. The guy just barely graduated high school." She sipped her tea. "There's no way he did this himself."

"So, we're really looking for an accomplice."

She nodded. "Someone that left town around the same time Edward did. Someone he knew."

I snapped my fingers, pointing at her as the pieces fell into place. "That's why you took those boxes."

She grinned, pointing back. "I'm hoping old Ed is the sentimental type. Could be a dead end, but maybe he saved something that would give us a clue."

"Good thinking." I found myself grinning. "I like this theory. You think Anjelica knows his partner in crime?"

"I doubt it. If she does, it would be someone she hadn't seen, heard of, or talked to in forever. Otherwise it would be too much coincidence that someone else left town around the same time."

"We're looking for an old relationship, then. A former flame."

"When and where did Anjelica and Edward meet?"

I recalled the details from her file. "They met at a bar, on her birthday. Her twenty-first, to be exact. She said he sort of had his stuff together back then. Had just bought the house they live in now. Was real handy around her apartment. Things got serious fast. She moved in with him to help pay the bills. They got married. She got pregnant. Ed lost his job. Things seemed to roll downhill from there."

"So, Ed meets this hot young thing in a bar. They have a whirlwind relationship. Before he knows it, he's husband and father. The pressure is getting to him. He's drinking a lot. The economy tanks, or whatever happened in the world around the time Edward lost his job."

"He's looking for a way out. A way to take the pressure off."

"Maybe go back to a life he used to know, before he met the blonde at the bar."

Our theorizing paused as the waiter set down our plates.

Yvette eyed my steak. "You're seriously going to eat that entire thing. And then go back to work."

I cut into the perfectly cooked meat, savoring the first bite with closed eyes. "Almost fork tender. Just hot enough. Just cool enough. Practically melts in your mouth." I opened my eyes to find her watching me. "Oh yes, I'm going to enjoy this."

"My girly steak and I are going to have a similar love affair," she said, starting on her own meal.

"You were saying," I prompted, "Edward might have been looking to restore his youth or something of the sort."

"Right. I think people go back to what's comfortable. If something's not working, we go back to what did work. Maybe what worked for Edward was a simple life. Fewer responsibilities, less dealing with real life."

"Less demanding wife and monster children and possibly meddling family."

"Perhaps."

"So when you're digging through those boxes, what are you going to be looking for?"

"Evidence."

"Obviously." I rolled my eyes. "What kind of evidence?"

"Evidence of that simpler life that he would have been yearning to go back to. And someone that would have helped him get back there."

CHAPTER
EIGHT

WESLEY

THAT MASSIVE STEAK was sitting heavy in my stomach as I lugged the fifth and final box from my SUV into Young Investigations. The wine probably hadn't helped either.

"I told you about all that beef, plus all those potatoes, plus two glasses of wine, and then trying to do some work," Yvette said, watching me struggle with poorly concealed amusement.

"You could..." I puffed out my cheeks, sliding the last box onto the kitchen table. "You could have grabbed a box, Miss 'I Ate a Lot at Lunch Too.'"

"I could have. But nah, Captain Payne. You don't keep up on your PT?"

"Major," I corrected her, groaning as I straightened. "I separated as a Major, thank you very much. And as much as you complain about the size of your ass, it's not like you do, either."

"I thought I smelled a handsome man."

Nia's voice had taken on that sultry tone she always used

around me. She stood in the doorway in a short skirt and tight blouse, batting her eyelashes. I'd dealt with this kind of attention my whole career, but it felt awkward here, in Yvette's space.

"Nia." I turned to greet her, offering a professional hand, but she stepped in close and wrapped her arms around my torso. I returned the hug reluctantly, keeping it brief.

"It's good to see you again," she purred. "You never come see us anymore."

I pulled back, gently disentangling myself. "It's just... Yvette is so efficient—"

"Wesley is too busy to be hanging around this office," Yvette cut in, squeezing past us in the small kitchen to examine the boxes. "If you can put the Slut Kitty away for a second, I have a project."

Nia sucked her teeth but joined her at the table. Estelle leaned against the counter, and I noticed how cramped the kitchen felt with all of us in it.

"What we got?" Estelle asked.

"These are from the attic at the Foster house," I explained, pulling the lid off one box. "Edward's wife said this was mostly his stuff that's been sitting up there for years. They could be junk, but maybe there's something useful. This is a good place to start if we're looking for someone from Edward's past. Maybe someone he knew a long time ago. A high school sweetheart or something like that."

I watched her examining the contents.

"Let's try to make a list," Yvette said. "Then start cross-checking people. Find out where they are, if they're still in the area, and if not, if they left town around the same time Edward left—even if it was a year before or after."

I watched Nia paw through the box I'd opened. "This looks like junk. Credit card statements... receipts... a Christmas card from twenty-five years ago..."

"Anything else come up on the skiptrace?" Yvette asked.

"What about those hair samples? Any chance your contact could help with DNA testing if we had a match to compare against?"

Estelle pushed off from the counter and retrieved a thin file from her desk. "We can't run DNA without law enforcement involvement or a specific match to compare against. As for the skip trace, there are still no hits on anything in his name in the last four years. He had a driver's license, but no hits on it. No tickets or anything." She shook her head, closing the file. "Only way his license would show in the system would be if he used it when he was arrested."

Yvette nodded, processing this. Private investigators had limited access compared to law enforcement, and they couldn't request official DNA testing without an open case. They had to work within tighter constraints and higher costs.

"What about running his name through NCIC or state databases?"

"Worth a try," Estelle said. "I don't know if she can run random searches without an active case, but I'll ask. Might cost us, though."

"Nia, we need to keep an eye out for anything in those boxes that points to anything he did or was before he met Anjelica. Those Christmas cards you saw might be a good start."

Nia nodded. "Mmhmm, I gotcha. Old life."

As much as I wanted to stay and help them dig through Edward's past, I had my own work waiting. I retrieved my key fob from my pocket. "I need to head back to the office. Keep me posted on anything of value."

I made my way to the door, aware of Yvette following me.

"Need a nap?" she teased.

I laughed, then lowered my voice, leaning in slightly. "Among other things. Thanks for the company. I really enjoyed spending time with you today."

"Business lunch, Payne. Don't get caught up."

"I'm not, especially since I know you're going to bill me for all of this time today." I headed for my SUV, forcing myself not to look back. "Talk later, Vette."

"For sure," she called after me.

Back in my car, I could see Moreland Avenue already backing up. The door thudded shut as I started the engine and pulled out of the parking space. "Call Nick Courtney," I told the Bluetooth system.

"How'd it go at the house?" he asked when he picked up.

"Mixed results. Yvette collected hair samples for potential DNA testing, but we can't process them without law enforcement involvement. The skip trace is still coming up empty—no activity under Edward's name in four years."

I merged into the slow-moving traffic. "But she's convinced he didn't just snap and leave. Too clean, too planned. She thinks someone helped him disappear—probably someone from before he met Anjelica."

"What kind of help? She thinking he had a woman on the side he ran off with?"

"That's what we're trying to figure out. We pulled boxes and boxes of old stuff from the attic: high school yearbooks, Christmas cards, work records. Looking for connections that predate the marriage."

"Not to throw fuel on the fire," Nick said, "but George Foster's not doing well. Doctor says maybe six weeks, eight at the outside."

The traffic light ahead turned red. I stopped, gripping the steering wheel tighter. "Six weeks to find a man who's been gone four years."

"Yeah. Clock's ticking."

CHAPTER
NINE

YVETTE

WHEN I PULLED into my spot in the carport, the Acura was gone. In its place sat a classic Chevy pickup, fading paint and rusted spots, but otherwise in good condition from the outside at least. The kicker was always the engine and interior.

I'd developed my love for classic cars through osmosis. Yancey's dream had been to run a restoration shop, and when MTV's *Pimp My Ride* was on the air, he never missed an episode. Jason and Yancey bonded over retro car magazines and debated about throwback auto paint colors. I couldn't help but pick up lingo and knowledge here and there. Before long, I was as much of an admirer of classic cars as they were.

I admired the old machine for a few moments before heading inside. No simmering pots, no sizzling pans, nothing baking in the oven gave away that Mama wasn't home. But laid out across the counter were a loaf of bread, packages of lunch meat and deli cheese, condiments, and sandwich fixings.

"Yance!"

"Huh?"

Following the drone of the TV through the kitchen and into the living room, I found Yancey stretched from end to end across the couch. He was still in his uniform and a plate bearing the mutant sandwich he'd built—whole wheat bread, lunch meat, cheese, pickles, banana peppers, and at least four condiments—was balanced on his belly.

"Nice rig out there. That your new project?"

"Yeah," he answered. "Came in today."

"What's the year?"

"'68. Needs a rebuild, so we're going to give it a little update while we're at it. Probably leave the interior mostly intact. Just do a cosmetic update, recover the seats, stuff like that."

"That'll turn out nice."

"Yeah." He glanced at his watch, then at the muted TV. On-screen, vintage muscle cars glided across the stage at an auction show. I imagined deep-voiced commentators exchanging meaningless banter about the condition of the vehicle and the journey toward restoration.

"Where are mom and dad?"

"Church meeting."

Our parents were members of the Bethel Baptist leadership team. They met monthly for dinner and discussed upcoming programs and special events at the church.

Yancey picked up the overstuffed sandwich and took a bite. Bits of bread and filling fell from his mouth as he chewed; he brushed them from his cheeks and shirt, sending them flying to the carpet.

I frowned, watching him eat. "I'm headed upstairs. Don't leave that stuff out on the counter, okay? And make sure you take a dustbuster to those crumbs you're leaving on Mama's nice couch that you're not supposed to even be eating on."

"Ma'am, yes, ma'am!" Yancey barked, snapping an exaggerated salute from his sprawled position on the couch. "Right away, ma'am! Anything else, ma'am? Should I stand at attention, ma'am?"

I slowly turned around. "The fuck is your problem, Yancey Young?"

"Nobody need you to come in here and start dictating shit," he whined. "Take your bossy ass up to your apartment and do whatever the fuck it is you do up there."

I crossed my arms. "I'm trying to make sure you respect this house and the work Mama puts into cleaning it, and especially the work she puts into cleaning up after you."

I gestured at the crumbs scattered across the couch.

Yancey rolled his eyes. "I don't see you down here helping her."

"I don't live down here. You do."

"You know what, Vette?" Yancey sat up, tossing the plate onto the glass coffee table. Another no-no—he'd already gotten fingerprints all over it and it would be just his luck that he'd crack the glass. "You need to get out my face and mind your business instead of mine."

"You don't *have* any business. You're so ridiculously spoiled, Yancey."

"So what?" he bellowed, no longer a lazy drawl but a full-throated outburst. "I know whose business it ain't. *Yours.* This ain't your house. I'm not your child. Mom and Dad wouldn't let me leave even if I wanted to. So like I said, butt out."

I scoffed, letting him see my eyes roll. Hard. "You? Leave this pleasure palace where you get to spend all your money on cars and not have to lift a finger and let everyone baby you like you're some kind of special snowflake?"

Yancey stood, rising to his full height. "I don't need this shit. I was having a good time before you got home and now I got to hear your mouth."

He dug into his pocket and pulled out a set of keys, then walked past me, lightly pushing me aside.

"So you're really leaving this mess?" I followed him to the kitchen, where he bypassed the counter and headed for the carport door. "All this shit on the counter—you're leaving this too?"

He sucked his teeth, giving a nonchalant shrug. "Clean it up if you're so concerned about it."

"I'm not cleaning up shit. This is ridiculous—"

"I'm outta here—"

"Nuh-uh! Get back here!" I grabbed him by the back of the neck and pulled him away from the door, then stepped between him and his escape. "You are not leaving this house without cleaning this mess up."

His nostrils flared as he stared down at me, his petulance just barely contained. "You need to get out my way, Yvette."

We hadn't been this close to blows since we were teenagers. The tension between us crackled.

"Or what, Yancey?"

A muscle in his jaw jumped beneath his skin. For a second, I thought he might actually try to move me physically. "Move, Vette."

Unfortunately, I wasn't built to back down. I stared up at him, defiant. "Or. *What*. Yance?" I planted my feet firmly, arms crossed. "I'm not asking you to scrub the whole kitchen. Just put away what you took out and clean up your mess."

I saw his weight shift, then the surprise in his eyes as he realized I wasn't going to flinch. I dropped my hips, grabbed and hooked his wrist, then torqued his elbow back just like I'd learned in security training. His arm rolled in my grip and the look on his face snapped to panic.

I spun him, forced him toward the floor, and anchored a knee in the middle of his back, pressing the palm of my hand against the side of his head.

Yancey crumpled, howling. "*Ooowwww!* Let go, you psycho bitch!"

"You're a spoiled brat! You think everyone should

worship the ground you walk on but you're not special, Yance. You're lazy and I'm sick of it."

"Ow! That hurts, Vette! I'm serious! *Ooowwww!*" His eyes watered, face streaked with snot.

"Are you going to clean up your mess and stop acting like you're so goddamned privileged?"

He bared his teeth, snarling at me. "Let go of me, bitch!"

"Yvette!"

Daddy stood in the doorway to the garage, keys in hand. Yancey yanked himself out of my hold and rolled away, rising to his knees.

Mama stood directly behind Daddy, peering quizzically at her children on the floor. "Vette, what are you doing to that boy?"

I pulled myself up, dusting my pant legs. "He is a grown man. And I was just playing with him."

"Didn't sound like playing to me," Daddy said, offering a hand to Yancey, bringing him to his feet.

"If you're going to kill each other, don't do it on my floors!" Mama brushed past Daddy, her eyes landing on the sandwich fixings spread across the counter. The sight of a mess, no matter how trivial, activated a sequence in her brain. "Y'all are in here rolling around and screaming at each other like you're toddlers."

"Mama, don't touch that. Yance is gonna clean up his mess."

I glared at him. He glared back, refusing to move. "Don't think I won't knock your ass back in front of our parents, punk."

Yancey's eyes darted to Daddy, but he merely shook his head and walked to the fridge to retrieve a beer.

"That's enough, you two." Mama had already begun putting items away and wiping down the counters. "It's just a little mess, not worth getting so upset."

"It's not just *this* mess. It's *every* mess. You baby him like he can't do anything for himself. I'm tired of watching him take advantage of you!"

"Then maybe you should go to your *apartment*," Yancey snapped. "Or better yet, get your own place, then I can live in the apartment and you don't have to worry about anyone doing anything for me."

"Like you would cook and clean and do your own laundry, with your mother downstairs making sure you don't have to do shit."

"Alright!" Daddy stomped through the kitchen and pointed toward the back stairwell. "Vette, it's time you went on up upstairs."

My jaw dropped. "I'm being kicked out because I don't like to see him get away with being lazy?"

"You're being kicked out because you're getting loose at the mouth." He pointed, again, toward the stairwell. "Take five, Vette."

"You know what?" I retrieved my bag and pulled my keys out, headed instead to the carport. "How about I just leave and let you kiss his boo-boos and make him feel better in peace?"

"I don't much like your tone, young lady," Mama said.

"Mama, I don't like—"

Instead of finishing my sentence, I stormed out of the house and threw myself into my car. I fired it up and slammed it into reverse, speeding out of the carport and the yard like Yancey would.

Once I hit the end of the street, I hung a left, then a right and shot out of the subdivision.

I had no particular destination in mind, but of course, ended up at Young Investigations. It was like a second home anyway and if I needed to, I could sack out on the futon for the night. The suite was empty, lit only by the glow of the screensaver on Estelle's monitor. Piles of paper and half-emptied boxes from Edward Foster's attic littered the kitchen. I ignored them, opened the refrigerator and retrieved a soda, then grabbed two granola bars from the cabinet.

I'd had my mouth set on a hot meal. Nature Valley granola wasn't even close to cutting it.

Carting my light dinner to my office, I settled into my desk chair and turned on the computer. It booted quickly, logging me into email and Communicator.

A message bubble appeared on my desktop.

WPayne: Working late?

I unwrapped one of the granola bars and took a bite, crumbs falling onto my desk.

VetteY: Not exactly.

VetteY: You?

WPayne: Always working, wherever I am. Late, early, in between.

VetteY: At the office?

WPayne: Nah. I'm working, though.

I brushed the crumbs away and opened my soda, then typed with one hand while I gulped down half the can.

VetteY: See, that's why you're going places. Work ethic.

WPayne: *LOL.* I'm worried about where I'm going. I can't take too many more of these cheating spouses and missing people cases.

VetteY: So don't.

WPayne: So easy.

VetteY: Yeah. So easy.

WPayne: Maybe for you.

I stared at the screen for a moment.

VetteY: You know more than anyone how easy this hasn't been for me.

WPayne: Yeah, I do. Hoping the Simeon divorce will be the last. It sucks to be doing this penny ante shit when I want to do criminal defense.

VetteY: why didn't you just start there…

WPayne: I needed to build a name for myself. I'm ready to switch focus though.

VetteY: I hear you. I'm a little bored myself.

WPayne: So what are you doing if you're not working?

I glanced around the empty office before typing.

VetteY: Bad night at the house. Yancey was on one. Had to get out of there.

WPayne: So you went to work? Laughing @ you.

VetteY: Asshole. Work is who I am.

WPayne: Would you care to do something besides work?

I couldn't help but smile. Wesley was so predictable.

VetteY: Such as?

WPayne: Join me for a drink

VetteY: Haven't you had enough to drink today?

WPayne: It wore off. I'll let you bitch about Yancey.

VetteY: *And* my parents?

WPayne: Don't push it. You know I love Valerie Young.

VetteY: You don't know Valerie Young.

WPayne: And I won't be talking shit about her until I get to taste some of her food

VetteY: You're paying

WPayne: Always. You coming?

My stomach growled, reminding me of the hours it had been since lunch and that granola bars weren't really dinner.

VetteY: If you'll spring for dinner too. Left the house before Mama even got started cooking.

WPayne: Dinner too?

I pushed back from the desk and grabbed my bag, slinging it across my body.

VetteY: And I'm not cheap. What do you say? Going once...

VetteY: Going twice...

WPayne is typing a message

WPayne: SOLD to the pretty young lady. Since I'm paying, let's go someplace nice.

VetteY: Always.

Minks was only a few miles away but with evening traffic, it took me over half an hour to drop my car at the valet station and push through the glass carousel doors. The restaurant boasted a bar scene that felt more like a nightclub than a posh midtown eatery. The lights were low, the music was loud, and blue neon stars danced across the ceiling. The bar was packed, standing room only. I could see the elevator to the rooftop where Atlanta's elite preferred to dine.

A man of Wesley's build and stature was hard to miss. He sat on one of the pristine white leather couches just past the hostess stand, face illuminated by the screen of his mobile phone. His thumbs moved across the screen at a rapid pace. He'd changed into jeans, loafers, and a thin cashmere sweater.

"Time to clock out," I said, plopping down next to him. "Vette is here and she is hungry. What are you doing?"

"Talking to Anjelica's brother," he answered without looking up. "He's asking questions about the investigation."

"You're typing a lot for not having much to say. We haven't gotten anywhere yet."

Wesley grimaced and closed the texting app. "He knows that. Just reassuring him that we're not giving up and we'll get some answers."

"You shouldn't make promises you can't keep. Well, promises I can't keep."

He stretched an arm across the top of the couch behind me. "You said you could close this, Vette."

"I said I would *try*. You know I don't promise outcomes. Just that I'll give the work my best effort."

"I'm going to need a little more than your best effort on this one."

"Do you not see me sitting here, tired from working your case? Hungry because I haven't eaten since lunch? Feed me and get off my nerves."

He stood, pulling me up with him. When we were both

standing, he pulled me into his molded chest. I stiffened…
then gave in and wrapped my arms around him.

See. That wasn't so hard, I told myself.

Then he dipped to drop a kiss on the top of my head.
"Good to see you, Vette," he said, smiling when he released
me.

"You just saw me," I said, rolling my eyes but smiling
back.

"Still good to see you."

The hostess interrupted to let Wesley know our table was
ready. We followed her through the packed restaurant up a
flight of stairs to a booth at the rear of the room. Each table
around the perimeter had its own chandelier, the flickering
flame of a tea light candle bouncing off the crystal. From up
here, I could see the entire downstairs bar area.

"These are nice digs," I said after we were seated and had
placed drink orders. "Like…the best seat in the house."

Wesley nodded. "I once got the owner out of a…serious
bind. Let's call it that. Now if I want to come in for dinner, I
give him the heads-up, I get this table."

"Even on short notice? So you just have connections
everywhere. You're a household name among certain
households."

"That's not what I'm trying to be…"

"But the size…fifteen? Sixteen? Fits."

"Sixteen," he answered, reaching for the menus that the
waitress had left to begin perusing the options.

I followed suit, almost swallowing my tongue at the
prices.

"Stop looking at them dollar signs. Order what you want,"
he said from behind the menu.

"How'd you know what I was thinking?"

His menu lowered enough so that I could see his eyes. "I
have known Yvette Young for a long time."

My eyes skipped down the options. Something heavy

after our decadent lunch out and when I'd already been complaining about how my jeans fit would bring serious regret the next day.

"What looks good?" Wesley asked, setting his menu aside.

"My waistline is asking for baked white meat and a kale salad."

He nodded. "I agree with going lighter. I think I'll have the duck."

I leaned my elbows on the table as I grinned at Wesley. "You can eat duck after having to eat it at the Ft. Belvoir Officers' Club?"

Wesley had started laughing before I'd even finished my sentence. "The most traumatic meal of my life. It was supposed to be duck à l'orange. It tasted like chicken à la tang."

I shuddered at the memory of dry, tasteless bird simmering in a congealed goo. "I also remember command banned that menu item until further notice. You can't even say *duck* at Belvoir."

Wesley shuddered too, frowning. "I bet Valerie Young knows how to make a delicious duck à l'orange."

"I don't think she's brave enough to try it."

Wesley sipped from his drink. I gave mine a taste too and sighed, licking my lips. A vodka lemonade always hit the spot.

He watched me for a moment, the remnants of a smile still playing on his face. I recognized the gentle tilt of his head, the way he set his drink aside and squared his shoulders, ready to absorb any unfiltered nonsense that might spill from my lips.

"So…what happened, today?"

"Gonna have to be more specific," I said, aiming for flippant.

He gave me a look. The kind that said *I know you know what I mean, Vette.* "At the house. Had to be something big if you missed dinner. And I promised you could talk shit about Yance. Proceed."

I'd already nearly forgotten about the fight with my brother, then my parents, and then storming out of the house. Wesley had that effect on me...made my troubles slip away, if only for a moment.

The problem, though, was that I was comfortable in my misery.

"In my defense, Yancey was being a shit. My parents were out for the night, he decides to make this big ugly sandwich and eat it in the living room. On the couch. I don't know if you know this about the Young household, but we do not eat in the living room and *definitely* not on the couch."

"Similar rules at the Payne household."

"So I'm on my way upstairs and I said, 'Hey, make sure you clean up your shit.' I know and he knows Mama is going to have a screaming fit about it. He went *left*. Talkin' bout 'Ma'am, yes, ma'am! Should I stand and salute, ma'am?' I wasn't even..."

I shook my head, ignoring Wesley trying not to laugh.

"Anyway, we bicker. He gets pissed, decides he's leaving, I said 'the fuck you are' and proceed to physically restrain him. I was getting him good when my dad walked in and made me stop. I hate his relationship with my parents. They're content to not let him grow up and that..."

I gripped the arms of my chair and sucked in a long breath through my nose.

"Really gets to you," said Wesley. "You've probably been an adult since before you were even an adult. Taking on a lot of responsibility, even joining up right out of high school. Didn't you say you enlisted because of your dad?"

I swallowed the lump that always formed in my throat when I talked about Daddy. He joined the Army right out of high school but had injured his knee during the early years of his service. The injury kept him from serving in overseas skirmishes. He stayed behind on post and managed projects in the absence of his fellow soldiers. Once he had fulfilled his minimum service commitment, he was honorably discharged.

Daddy told a lot of stories about his friends and fellow servicemen who were wounded in battle. He felt like he couldn't complain about a little knee pain, not when so many came home with Purple Hearts and missing limbs. Or worse, had died in service.

I thought maybe I could, somehow, experience the Army like he always wanted to.

"And he souped up the car for you," Wesley argued, pointing with one finger while the rest of his hand clutched his glass. "Because it would have meant a lot to Jason. And to you."

"You're not gonna hop on this train with Paula, are you? Talking about how Yancey loves me, he's just jealous?"

"I wasn't aware that train was taking passengers."

"Well, he doesn't love me much after I almost broke his arm and shoved his face into the kitchen tile tonight." I took a sip of lemonade, deadpan.

Wesley laughed aloud this time, his mouth dropping open. "He's never gonna learn that you can kick his skinny ass, is he?" He nodded to the waitress across the room, indicating that we were ready to order. I slid my menu to the edge of the table. "So y'all got into it?"

"The boy was screaming like a toddler in Walmart. I'm not sorry about pinning his face to the kitchen floor. Is that wrong?"

Wesley grinned. "You ever think you were maybe a little *too* good at the security trainings? Like you took something home you weren't supposed to?"

I shrugged, innocent. I knew better, though. Yancey was a civilian and was never a fighter. I had weight, muscle, and skill on him. He was a shit, though—who knew what would happen when he challenged me?

"He can handle himself. Or he should be able to. My parents were not happy to walk in and see their baby boy with his face mashed sideways against the floor. He actually scares me sometimes with how much he doesn't know about the world. I guess taking it out on him was not the best reaction."

Wesley considered me, head tilted, hands folded politely around his glass. He did not look away, which meant I had to, so I found the chandelier above the next table and focused on the light.

"I know you fought with your brothers," I said, unwilling to stay in the spotlight any longer. "And some of your sisters. How are they, by the way? And Mom and Dad Payne?"

His face softened at the mention of his family, the edges of his features rearranging themselves into an expression of fondness. "Everybody's real good," he said. "We're all working, which makes Mom and Dad Payne happy."

"Is Gloria still teaching?"

He nodded. "Mom's at Auburn University in Montgomery. Tenured, so they'll have to force her out someday, I guess. Dad's still with the Guard's legal office. I don't think he's ever going to retire. Again."

"On top of thirty years as JAG? He should be tired."

"Leonidas Payne doesn't know the meaning of the word." Wesley's drink must've been good and strong because he stretched his legs under the table. His foot brushed mine. I didn't move. "Passed that on to all of us. Makai's here in Atlanta, I just saw him the other day. Tariq's in Orlando, working for Lockheed. Anissa's working at LG in Huntsville. Jazhara…"

He sighed, tracing the rim of his glass with one finger, then took a long sip. "…skipped graduation and flew to Brazil."

I leaned back and pressed my fingers to my temple, feigning exasperation. "Oh, honey, no."

He nodded. "The folks were hot about it too. But I guess it was for some internship and it led to her landing a job in her field—junior editor at some tech magazine. Every time I talk to her, she's at some convention in Vegas or LA or…Antwerp, writing about the latest gadgets and whatever's about to hit the market. She's thriving, I guess."

"Good for her. Hope she sowed some wild oats."

"I'm not thinking about my baby sister's wild oats."

I snorted. "I never got a chance to sow any."

He went quiet for a second, like he was weighing whether to say anything at all. When he spoke, his tone was careful.

"I'm not trying to be…you know. Just saying, you've still got time. That's why I left the service when I did. Figured I had more to do, and I wanted to do it while I still had youth on my side."

"Yeah. I get that."

I had a whole different reason for leaving the Army. I couldn't stay enlisted one second longer than I had to, and I hadn't set foot on a post since the day I left.

The waitress finally came to take our dinner order and I could've kissed her for the interruption. I wasn't in the mood to talk about Jason.

"So," I began after placing my order, attempting to steer the conversation away from my dead fiancé. "Any bets on where Edward will turn up?"

"Somebody's bed. That's all I've got on that. I definitely get the feeling he's alive, though."

"You really think so?"

"You all but convinced me of it today. But he's not smart enough to do this alone. Anyone can leave. But to stay gone? With not a speck of activity in over four years? He's with someone. I'm interested in who."

"Me too," I mused. "You think he knows his dad is dying?"

"Probably. So why hasn't he appeared with his hand out?"

"There must be some reason he can't," I mused. "At least we know we're after some wily sumbitches."

Wesley chuckled. "Been hanging out with Anjelica too long."

After dinner, we milled outside the restaurant waiting for the valet attendant to bring our cars around.

"Thanks for dinner," I said quietly, meeting his eyes for just a moment before looking away. "I needed this. Tonight."

He nodded, almost shyly. "Can't have you starving to death. Those granola bars wouldn't last you long."

My eyes narrowed. "How'd you know I was eating granola bars?"

My El Camino rumbled at the curb and Wesley walked around to the driver's side with me. "I have known Yvette Young for a very long time."

He brushed his lips against my cheek before urging me into the car. "Drive safe. Let me know you got home. And stop being so mean to that boy. It's not a fair fight."

I laughed, ducking into the car and pulling the seatbelt across my torso. With a honk, I pulled away from the restaurant, noting how long it had been since I'd opened my mouth to laugh aloud.

It felt good.

Too good.

The problem with Wesley was he made everything feel too good.

He made it too easy to forget how heavy grief was.

He made me feel like myself again. Like the woman I was when I was happy.

CHAPTER
TEN

WESLEY

TEN FLOORS above the Beltline trail, the law offices of Courtney & Payne were dark. Save my office, which was lit for the long night ahead, the silence broken only by the sounds of my fingers pounding the keyboard and the low hum of the beverage cooler under the credenza.

Photos of Edward Foster's workshop were spread across my desk. I'd been studying them, reading Yvette's notes scrawled in the margins:

> *Wear patterns on the workbench suggest regular use*
> *Tool drawer partially emptied. Selective removal, no signs of theft or a rush exit.*
> *Scuff marks near workbench*
> *Cabinet handles dusty, uninterrupted*
> *No trash or scraps. Space seems to be cleared methodically*

Next to Foster's file sat the Simeon divorce folder. Julia Simeon's statement stared up at me, mostly legal jargon dressed up to mask disappointment, anger, betrayal and a demand for consequences. Marcel might argue a little, might waste his attorney's time pretending he could win, but in the end, he would settle.

Some cases were just that simple.

The door swung open without a knock. I didn't look up, but I recognized the sound of familiar footsteps crossing my office.

"Don't even think about it," I said without raising my head.

"I'm not gonna break it. If it worked like a normal coffeemaker—"

"There's nothing wrong with that machine except your inability to use it." I glanced up as Nick ignored me and prepared to do battle with my espresso machine. Rolling my wrist, I glanced at my watch, then at Nick. "What are you still doing here?"

He poked at the touchscreen, waited, then tapped again when nothing lit up. Muttering to himself, he pulled open the reservoir lid and peered inside.

"My wife set up some dinner," he said. "The restaurant over at Ponce—Nine Mile Station? I'm killing time." He turned just enough for me to see his suit jacket slung over one arm, his tie still knotted as if it were 9 a.m. "I heard the Simeons are going to settle."

"That's the hope. Can't beat the cheating allegations. Surveillance must've hit harder than we thought."

Nick grabbed a mug from the shelf, pushed it under the spout with too much force, then twisted the brew dial the wrong way. The machine beeped in protest. Undeterred, he crouched to open the beverage cooler, grabbed a carton of milk, and sloshed some into the frothing pitcher.

"I mean..." He shrugged, leaning in to read the button labels while steam hissed faintly from the frother. "We can put it in 4K if he needs to see it more clearly."

I stared at Nick's back. "Did you just compliment Yvette's work? You have a fever or something?"

"I'm feeling generous. Don't get used to it." Nick glanced toward the desk while the machine went through its machinations. "How's that albatross around your neck coming? Yvette find anything in those boxes?"

"Still sorting through them," I said. "Photos, letters, junk from his high school days. Could be nothing. Could be the thread we need."

A tinny clang cut me off. Nick had knocked over the milk frother.

"Fuck, man. What are you doing over there?"

"This is why normal offices have break rooms with normal coffeemakers," he muttered, pulling out a handkerchief to clean up the spill.

"We have a break room with a normal coffeemaker."

"That one sucks. I like yours."

I picked up a pen and clicked it repeatedly. "The workshop tells a story. Everything's organized. Tools arranged by size, no half-finished projects. This is not the space of a guy who snapped and walked out."

"So he planned it," Nick said.

"Yvette thinks so. And she's usually right."

Nick dropped into one of my guest chairs, the demitasse cup looking ridiculous in his large hands. "Patrick says his sister called Edward lazy. Impulsive. Not the planning type."

I opened Yvette's preliminary report. "The way he did this says something different. He wants it to look like he just up and disappeared, but he was actually pretty calculated about it. He seemed to know what he was doing."

"I don't know," said Nick before taking a sip of his brew. "No prints. No credit activity. No traffic cams. Nobody's that good at disappearing, Payne. That man is dead."

"Or someone is helping him appear to be dead. It's not

like the CIA is the only agency that knows a thing or two about disappearing a person."

Nick's brow hiked. "You think he's a witness?"

"Don't know. Vette might be onto something, though, looking for someone he's connected to."

My phone sent a buzz-buzz-buzz into the air. I picked it up from the charging pad and frowned at the screen. "Speaking of connections," I said, tapping the speaker icon. "Patrick. Nick's here with me. We were just talking about your brother-in-law. What's going on?"

"Hey. Uh... I might have something?" Patrick's voice had an edge I hadn't heard before. He hesitated before speaking again. "I ran into Eddie's old supervisor from the Miller Creek development. It was the last real job he had."

"The condos that never got built," I said. "What'd he say?"

"There was a woman in the office—Carmela Verona. She worked in finance. Bernie said she mysteriously quit, packed up, moved away. Left no forwarding address...right around the time Ed vanished. Thought it was weird but never put the two together."

I sat up, grabbing a pen. "How close to Ed's disappearance?"

"A few weeks, maybe a month before. They weren't in the same department. He didn't think they knew each other, but they both worked there."

"Nobody quits a steady job for no reason," Nick said.

"Yeah," said Patrick. "Especially when you work for the developer or the investor. That's not the only job they've got going on."

"Had to be something with the Miller Creek project in particular," I said.

Patrick sighed. "It's probably nothing. Bernie mentioned it and the more I think about it, the less it seems like a coincidence. Just...sounds funny to me."

"Funny's enough to check out," I said. "Thanks, Patrick. We'll dig into it and keep you posted."

I pressed the button to end the call. Nick had shifted his posture: elbows on his knees, his fingertips steepled under his chin. "Interesting," he mused, his eyes narrowed.

"Very," I muttered, already pulling up Yvette's number. If Patrick was right, if there really was a second disappearance wrapped inside the first one, then either Edward Foster wasn't alone in running, or someone else had vanished and we had more than one missing persons case.

She picked up on the third ring. "You better have a damn good reason for pulling me from the dinner table," she said, voice rising above the clatter of plates and background hum of familial chaos.

"I would apologize, but frankly, Yvette, I wasn't invited to dinner, so you'll have to deal."

"Talk fast, Payne. Mama's pasta bake and garlic toast wait for no one."

"I need Stelle to look into a woman from Edward's past. Patrick ran into Edward's old supervisor at the Miller Creek job, the development that flamed out. Supervisor says a woman named Carmela Verona worked in finance there. She quit, packed up, disappeared maybe a month before Edward did."

"Two people connected to the same failed development project disappearing within weeks of each other? That's not coincidence."

"Yeah, that's what we're thinking."

"I'll let you know what we dig up. Anything else?"

I checked the time, squinting at the hour. "You working tonight?"

"Nope," she popped back right away. "I will be in a food coma, planted between my mama and my daddy. It's *NCIS* night."

I cringed, as did Nick. "How do you even watch that

show? They invent procedure, fuck up chain of custody, get jurisdiction wrong, and don't even get me started on the courtroom scenes—"

"It's comfort TV, Payne."

Nick and I rolled our eyes at each other, mostly because Yvette couldn't see us.

"Fine. Enjoy your unrealistic military entertainment television."

"I will. Stelle's with her grandkids. I'll have her dig into Carmela in the morning."

"Appreciate it, Vette. Enjoy your pasta bake and say hey to the family."

Yvette hung up without saying goodbye.

The old-school romantic in me spun a scenario on demand where instead of sitting in the blue glow of my office with Nick, I was next to Yvette at a raucous, overlong dinner with her meaty thigh in my grasp.

"You good?" Nick asked, eyebrow raised. "You zoned out."

I cleared my throat and shuffled the Foster photos back into their folder. "Yeah, I'm fine. Just thinking through the timeline."

"Uh-huh." Nick's smirk said he wasn't buying it. "You get distracted every time Yvette calls."

"Drop it, Nick."

He placed his empty cup on my desk and grabbed his jacket. "Despite that, you were right to bring Young in on this."

"Good night, Nick."

He paused at the door before stepping out. "You've got it bad, Payne."

After he left, I sat in the quiet and listened to the after-hours shuffle—janitors emptying trash, wiping down glass, chatting over the echo of a Bluetooth speaker playing music.

The Foster file sat open in front of me, but I didn't see it.

I saw Yvette with me at my place. Her in my kitchen, a glass of wine in one hand, her hair up and off her neck. I stood behind her, arms on either side of her, breathing in the scent of her perfume. She turned, mouth ready with a smart ass comment that went unsaid because I kissed her instead.

The baggy clothing she wore as armor slipped from her body. I imagined picking her up and tossing her onto my bed, laying her out spread eagle and open for me as I coaxed a curling moan of orgasm. In this fantasy, she didn't push me away. I felt her hands gripping my ass cheeks as I plunged deep into her. I pictured her hips rocking up to meet mine, our bodies battering against one another, her cries echoing off the walls, all the unspoken things between us burned away by the friction of our bodies.

In my mind, the years of wanting her, of imagining what it would feel like to have all that intensity focused on me instead of using work to distract herself from grief, were over.

I blinked and came back to myself. My dick was hard as concrete and the only woman I wanted to help me deal with that ran at the first hint of anything serious between us.

I scrubbed my hands over my face and forced myself to focus on the Foster file.

Two disappearances connected to a failed development project meant money was involved.

Money complicated things.

CHAPTER
ELEVEN

YVETTE

THE RED NUMBERS on the wall clock flickered a digital 8:02 as I shouldered into our office suite juggling my laptop bag, a carrier of coffee cups, and a box of fresh donuts from a shop down Moreland Avenue. I hadn't slept much, but the sugar and caffeine would buy me a few hours of focus.

I made a show of placing the donuts on Estelle's desk, then the coffee tray. "Breakfast of champions."

Estelle's eyes stayed glued to her monitor, though her hand reached for coffee. "You brought donuts? This must be good."

"Wesley called last night with a name. Carmela Verona worked in finance on the Miller Creek project when Edward was there. She disappeared a few weeks before he did."

"Miller Creek?" Nia appeared, still in her jacket and one of her typical form-fitting outfits, wafting a citrus-based perfume in her wake. She must have just beat me to the office. She plucked one of the coffee cups from the carrier and asked,

"That development that went belly up? That had Edward taking under-the-table work?"

Then she saw the pink box. "Revolution? Tell me you got me some maple bacon."

My top lip curled. "Against my better judgment, I know I don't dare come in here without your nasty bacon donuts. Hand me a fritter."

I settled onto my usual perch on the edge of Estelle's desk with my fritter on a napkin, close enough to see her already pulling up her programs. "So, according to Wesley's source, Carmela disappeared a few weeks before Edward left. No forwarding address, no one has seen her since."

"Hmm…" Estelle's fingers flew across her keyboard, the click-clack echoing through the office. "Was she ever declared missing? Or is she just…gone?"

"Good question. I never found evidence of that."

"Lemme take a crack at it. Carmela Verona, you said? V-E-R-O-N-A?"

"That's what Wesley gave me." I pulled out my phone and scrolled through last night's notes.

Estelle's screen filled with search results, her eyes scanning rapidly. "Carmela Verona, if this is the same woman. I don't see a missing persons report filed with Atlanta PD. Could be another county…"

"That's convenient timing if she dipped right before Ed," Nia said around a bite of her maple bacon monstrosity. "Too convenient."

I nodded, washing down my fritter with black coffee. "Wesley thinks she could have been Edward's inside contact. Someone who could have shared with him where the bodies were buried, so to speak. We really need confirmation that they knew each other."

"I'll start on news archives," Nia said. "See what pops up about when Miller Creek collapsed. Might give us some context for why they both ran."

I headed to my office before I could grab another donut from that box. Edward's boxes still covered most of the available floor space. We'd been through them before, but now I was looking for something specific.

An hour into sorting through every piece of paper I'd come across, I'd yielded only dead ends. I was starting to think we were chasing wild geese when Estelle's voice carried through the open door.

"Well, ain't this some shit."

I set down a stack of useless receipts and went to her desk. "Found something?"

"Born in Miami, 1985. Parents moved them to Atlanta after a job transfer. She graduated from Riverside, class of '03."

"Hmm. That's where Edward graduated from."

She nodded, satisfied. "Same exact year." Estelle had pulled up a digital yearbook archive and centered on the screen was a formal portrait of Carmela Verona. Her hair was an inky mane that spilled past her shoulders, parted in the middle and feathered.

I leaned closer to the monitor. "What's that caption under her senior photo?"

Estelle zoomed in: "President of the Drama Club, member of the Debate Team, and the National Honor Society."

"Check Edward's activities," I said.

More clicking. "Drama Club all four years. Looks like he worked in production and set construction."

"Fitting."

The image showed students in elaborate costumes, a Shakespeare play judging by the ruffles and doublets. Edward stood just offstage, one arm raised dramatically. And just behind him, Carmela in an elaborate gown.

"*Midsummer Night's Dream*, spring production." Estelle scrolled through more photos. "Here they are in *Oklahoma*...

Guys and Dolls. Looks like she was in all the shows and he was in the background."

"What happened after graduation?" I asked. "Where did she go?"

"University of Georgia." Estelle was already searching. "Business degree, then MBA. Worked for some big accounting firms before landing at Miller Creek. Edward stayed local, tried community college, dropped out..."

"Until Miller Creek brought them back together," Nia mused. "They knew each other. And they worked together. And probably disappeared together."

My phone pinged. I pulled it out of my pocket. Wesley's name flashed across the screen in a notification banner.

WPayne: Nothing like a long day at Superior Court. How you doing?

I typed back: *Ed and Carmela went to high school together. They knew each other well before Miller Creek.*

His response came quickly.

WPayne: Good find. I was asking about you though.

I stared at the screen, heat creeping up my neck. Trust Wesley to turn an average conversation personal. And trust me to like it more than I should.

I watched the cursor blink. Deleted two replies before landing on *I'm fine. Working.*

Another ping.

WPayne: Evading the question, Agent Young.

It wasn't that I didn't have words. I had too many words. Too many feelings.

There was too much I was still sorting through, too much I was *almost* brave enough to say aloud.

He cared. I knew that. I was grateful for that. But Wesley saw more than I was prepared for him to see. And he kept showing up for me despite that.

Which...was unnerving, because why?

I was still carrying too much. Still holding pieces of

someone I hadn't let go of, but I knew I had to in order to have any semblance of happiness.

VetteY: I'm good, Payne. Promise. Focusing on finding this man and closing this case.

VetteY: Let me know when you're out of court so I can update you.

"Nia." I locked the phone and shoved it into my pocket. "What did you find about Miller Creek's collapse?"

"Business section, *Atlanta Journal-Constitution*, September 2018." Nia pulled up an article on her tablet. "The headline is *Miller Creek Development Faces Mounting Delays, Cost Overruns*."

I leaned over to read. "Representatives cite unforeseen structural issues requiring significant additional funding…"

"That's where it gets interesting." Nia pulled up another article on her tablet. "Three months later, they announce urgent foundation repairs would push the completion date back a year. But the site manager was quoted as saying initial testing showed no signs of instability. So which is it? Faulty foundation, or is it fine? Then…"

She flipped through more saved articles. "Four months later, two months before Edward disappeared, they scaled back the whole project."

"Did they say why?"

"I found a link to a blog that intimated that they were trying to use substandard materials on site, basically unusable stuff. The post got taken down pretty quick and I could only read what had been cached."

I pulled my bottom lip between my teeth, deep in thought. Then I shook my head, glancing at Estelle, then Nia. "No way Edward didn't know about cutting corners on materials. And Carmela—"

"Would have seen all this happening in the books." Nia tapped the screen. "I bet she was being forced to cover it up."

"And Edward was being forced to sign off on materials he knew were substandard…"

I stood, pacing. "They were running from what they discovered. But who else was involved? The developer? The contractors?"

"At the very least. Maybe the building inspectors too," Estelle suggested.

———

HOURS LATER, I laid out our findings across the kitchen table for Wesley.

"I need to make sure we aren't just seeing things and making them fit because we want them to fit."

Wesley leaned in to study the documents. "I want them to fit too. But I'm picking up what you're putting down," he said. "These inspection reports are suspicious as hell. The report on my kitchen renovation was more thorough."

"Exactly. Edward would have overseen all of it. If they were using substandard materials…"

"He'd know." Wesley picked up one of the permits, studying it closely.

"Someone was skimming money," Estelle added from her desk. "And somebody is working hard to hide it."

Wesley straightened. "So…Edward and Carmela discover they're being used to cover up fraud. Maybe worse, if those materials were as bad as the blog suggested. You know those condos that collapsed in Miami? Champlain Towers? Same kind of situation."

His expression clouded over. "A friend of mine is representing the families of the dead."

"So, they ran?" I stood and began to pace. It helped me think. "From…who?"

"Whoever it was had enough power to bury that blog post about the materials," Nia pointed out.

"And enough reach to make two people disappear without a trace." I stopped pacing.

Wesley was already reaching for his phone. "I'll have Samera dig into board members, major investors of the developers. Gotta be something there."

Estelle spun her monitor around. "Might have something. The original permit applications for Miller Creek were filed by a company called Apex Development Group."

"Never heard of them," Wesley said, phone in his hand.

"Because they didn't exist six months before the project started."

"Can you trace the ownership?"

I leaned forward, bracing on the edge of Estelle's desk as she navigated the web of shadow companies. I watched her screen as each layer of shell corporation peeled away to reveal another, each with a nonsense address or a registered agent that was just a mail drop somewhere in Delaware.

"Every one of these is only about one project old," she narrated, eyes flicking across years of digital filings, "and then they dissolve or get rolled over into the next one down the line. But..." She pointed to a line. "The bank accounts all tie to First Southeast Partners. It's not a bank you walk into. It's private investment, mostly offshore, so they just have a P. O. Box."

I whistled. "Are we in mob territory?"

"Not exactly," Wesley said from the kitchen, where he'd grabbed a Coke and popped the top. "Old Atlanta money. They're connected to half the major construction projects in the southeast. More names than you'd expect have their fingers in that pie, including that casino development that was all over the news last year and was never finished."

"Same pattern—cost overruns, delayed inspections, structural issues," said Nia.

"Nick handled some work for First Southeast Partners

years ago," said Wesley. "One of their higher-ups. Richard Barrett."

I grabbed a pen and a sheet of paper to write the name down. We'd research him forward and backward. "What kind of work?"

"Standard real estate stuff. Zoning, liens, boring stuff. But Nick said Barrett made it out like he had all kinds of friends in all kinds of places."

"The kind of friends that can make people disappear?"

Wesley paused. "Vette…these seem like the kind of people that play hardball. If Ed and Carmela were scared enough to run, we need to—"

"Don't even say it, Payne." I knew that tone. "If I'm running toward danger, it means we're on the verge of finding something that needs to be found. I've gone up against worse than white-collar thugs. We don't have anything concrete to turn over. You can't cut me off."

He ran his tongue along the inside of his cheek, considering. "Then tag me in," he said. "I've got contacts in the DA's office, the GBI— hell, the FBI if we need them."

I shook my head. "The more people who know we're looking, the more dangerous it gets. I need a few more days of flying under the radar. If we find something solid, we'll bring in the cavalry."

Wesley was quiet. Pondering. Pontificating. For way too long. "Promise me you will be careful, Yvette."

"I always am," I said, affecting an innocent tone.

"No. No, you're not." I could hear the smile in his voice even if it wasn't on his face. He pulled his key fob from his pocket. "I have a meeting, but I'll dig around for anything current on Barrett. Maybe Nick remembers something that didn't make it into a file. You call me if you so much as smell trouble. Got it?"

I wanted to say I could take care of myself. I wanted to say that I wasn't afraid of people like Richard Barrett, that old

Atlanta money didn't have the same bite it once did. But the truth was I'd already caught the whiff of something dangerous in this case, and bravado wasn't going to change that.

And I knew Wesley would never forgive himself if something happened to me while working his case.

"I will. Promise." I held up a hand as if I was taking an oath. "Scout's honor."

"Does that work if you were never a Girl Scout?"

"You don't know I was never a Girl Scout."

Wesley's hand hovered over mine for a second, as if he might squeeze it, or maybe just anchor me to the moment. Instead he picked up the Coke, drank the last inch straight from the can, and nodded to Nia and Estelle as he left. The door shut behind him with a hush, not the thud I was expecting.

After Wesley left, I rejoined Nia and Estelle, who were huddled around Estelle's computer.

"I got more gossip," said Nia. "Miller Creek's safety inspector was replaced right before Edward disappeared. The rumor is that the old guy just stopped showing up. The new guy signed off on everything, no questions asked."

Estelle pulled up another document. "Iffy credentials if I know anything about credentials."

I felt the pieces starting to click into place. "First Southeast brings in their own inspector who approves whatever they want. Edward and Carmela figure it out—"

"Or start to protest—"

"And suddenly they're both gone." Nia snapped her fingers. "With all the proof of shady dealings, not just on this project but probably every project they're running."

"So where would they keep documentation like that?" Estelle asked.

"I'm positive we'll find it when we find Edward and Carmela."

I went back to my office with the boxes spread across my floor. All this time, we'd been looking for evidence of why Edward left. We should have been looking for evidence of who he'd been before. Who he'd known, who he'd trusted enough to help him vanish.

"What did you two get mixed up in?" I muttered.

CHAPTER
TWELVE

WESLEY

SUNSET HAD PAINTED YOUNG INVESTIGATIONS' windows orange when I pulled into the parking lot. As I knew it would be, Yvette's El Camino was in its usual spot, the glossy black paint reflecting the security lights that had just flickered on. I gathered the aromatic bags from Surin of Thailand and headed to her office suite.

Yvette forgot to eat when she was deep in a case.

I used my key and stepped inside. All the lights burned bright despite the empty desks. Papers and photos littered every surface, a testament to a day spent chasing leads. Bell Biv Devoe's "Poison" pumped from the Bluetooth speakers on top of the file cabinet in Yvette's office.

She still played loud music after hours. She used to say it helped her drown out distractions, that it was a kind of mental white noise. These days, I was sure it drowned out a lot more.

Yvette sat cross-legged at her desk, her boots kicked off,

reading glasses perched on her nose. This was my favorite version of her—guard down, comfortable in her own space.

I knocked on the door frame, but she was already aware that I had arrived. The volume on the music lowered to a reasonable decibel. "I hope you remembered crispy spring rolls," she said without looking up.

"And extra soy sauce."

I dropped the bags in the kitchen and started pulling out containers. "Young, when's the last time you ate?"

She thought about it too long. "Define...*ate*."

"Consumed more than a donut and coffee." I eyed the pink box sitting on the counter in the kitchen. I flipped it open, shaking my head at the crumbs and tissue paper sitting at the bottom. I tossed the box into the garbage. "What's with all the paper? Is this all Miller Creek stuff?"

"Yup. Deep dive into public records..." She trailed off, obviously not intending to answer my question. Which was fine; attorneys never ask questions when they don't already know the answer. "What did you get?"

"Pad Thai, extra spicy, extra peanuts."

A smile flickered as she unfolded her legs and climbed out of the chair. She grabbed the nearest container and cracked the lid, huffing steam and the scent of well-prepared Asian cuisine.

"Reminds me of Thai Bowl...remember? At Fort Campbell?"

"Where you tried to convince the cook to make it spicier every time? Pretty sure he was worried about you."

"No one believes me when I say you build a tolerance." I watched her dig into the dish with a plastic fork and rake a mouthful of noodles into her mouth like she hadn't eaten in days.

"Lounge?" she suggested after she swallowed. "There's a *Bones* marathon on."

"You still watch that show?"

"Don't judge me," she said, laughing as she dropped to the couch.

"I just think you can do better than reruns."

"It's relatable. Woman with trauma, emotionally repressed, way too much brain for her own good." She tipped her head at me. "Grab a couple Cokes from the fridge."

The TV mounted on the wall played quietly. She curled into one corner of the couch, feet tucked under her. I parked myself on the other end of the sofa, not too close but not too far, and popped open both Cokes. She flipped through channels until Dr. Brennan appeared on screen, then dropped the remote on the table and picked up a spring roll, dipping it into chili sauce before taking a bite.

"You don't like *NCIS*," she said, chewing. "You don't like *Bones*. I'm starting to believe there's not a single procedural that meets your high standards."

"Procedurals are alright," I argued. "I like *Bones*. I complain about it for different reasons than I complain about *NCIS*."

"Such as?"

"Such as…" I flicked my eyes up to the screen, then blew on a forkful of noodles before putting them in my mouth. I chewed, then continued. "Them two fools dancing around feelings they won't acknowledge. Everybody knows from episode two that they want each other. Even *them*."

"That's the draw of the show. The B-story is the mutual denial, and the question of the week, every week is *will they or won't they?*" She licked chili sauce from her thumb. "The only reason procedurals make it past season one is delayed gratification."

"I know all about that, don't I?"

The words slipped out before I could stop them. And instead of correcting my intent, pretending I didn't mean something I fully meant, I let them hang.

On the TV, Booth and Brennan examined a skeleton, their

banter filling the silence I'd created. I watched her eat a few bites, then she said, "You're saying we're Booth and Brennan."

"Aren't we?" I asked her. "Isn't that why you love this show? It's the TV version of you and me. But Wesley and Yvette have had way more seasons of *will they or won't they?* than *Bones* ever had."

She set down her container and turned to face me. "Wesley—"

"I'm just saying what we both know." I set my container down as well, resting my elbows on my knees. "We've been circling this drain for years. Question is, how long are we gonna keep pretending there isn't this...thing between us? When are we gonna make the move those fictional people made so we can have what they have?"

"We're not characters on a TV show."

"No, we're not. We're real people who've been pretending for way longer than either of us will admit that we don't feel what we feel. At least one of us is. Eventually, Brennan stopped running."

"Brennan had good reasons for running. Abandonment issues. Trust problems."

"Haven't I already proven that I'm here and I'm not going anywhere? We already act like we're together half the time. I bring you dinner when you forget to eat. You call me when you can't sleep or need to talk over a case. Even when it's not mine. I have a key to your office. You painted my den."

"That's because—"

"Because we care about each other as more than friends," I broke in, taking over her sentence. I grabbed her hand and traced her knuckles with my thumb. "It is okay to admit that, Yvette."

She was quiet for a long moment, studying our joined hands. On the screen, Booth was making some joke that had

Brennan rolling her eyes, but neither of us was really watching anymore.

"What if we try and it ruins what we have?"

"We've already seen each other at our worst and still chose to stay in each other's lives. You think a relationship is scarier than investigating war crimes? We've both dealt with life-and-death situations. And what if we *don't* try and we spend the rest of our lives wondering what we could have had?"

I shifted closer, so close that I could feel the warmth radiating from her skin. "What if we try and it's everything we wanted it to be?"

She didn't pull away. Instead, her free hand came up to rest against my chest, right over my heart. "You make it sound so easy, Payne."

"And I know it's not. But maybe it doesn't have to be as complicated as we're making it." I brought our joined hands up between us. "I'm not proposing, Vette. I'm just asking you to stop running from me."

Her eyes flicked to my mouth, then back up. "And if I say…" She bobbed her head side to side. "I might take off my Nikes…what happens next?"

"You let me kiss you. We build from there."

She laughed, soft and breathless. "You got it all figured out."

"I've got exactly nothing figured out except that I want you, Yvette. And I want you to want me too."

She started to laugh at the Marvin Gaye lyric I honestly hadn't meant to drop in there. While she was off guard, I closed the distance between us and dropped my mouth onto hers.

Her lips were soft, warm, and she tasted faintly of chili and lime.

Jesus. *Finally.*

Years of wanting this, imagining this… Nothing had

prepared me for the reality of kissing Yvette Young. Every fantasy I'd had paled compared to the sensation of her mouth opening and her tongue slipping against mine. The moan she let out when I deepened the kiss imprinted on me so strongly that I knew I'd be replaying it for weeks.

Her body tilted into mine, the kiss spiraling higher. The half surprise, half gasp when I cupped her face in my hands and she fisted my shirt sent a live wire straight to my dick.

I shifted slightly, trying not to make it obvious. The last thing I needed was for her to be uncomfortably aware of how much I wanted to pull her across the couch and cover her body with mine.

Our lips parted, though reluctantly. A surge of exhilaration rushed through me when I realized our chests were rising and falling rapidly in tandem.

Yvette rested her forehead against mine while she caught her breath, a gesture that spoke volumes. "Damn," she whispered, the word rushing past my ear.

I ran my thumb along her jawline, marveling at how right this felt. "Damn...that was good? Or damn, I didn't mean for that to happen?"

She pulled back, absentmindedly brushing her fingers across her lips. "Damn, that was not...*weird* weird. Just... I..."

For the first time since I'd known her, Yvette seemed genuinely at a loss for words. She sat there, lips parted, two fingertips ghosting the path my mouth had taken.

"I promise I didn't come here to do all that." I shifted again, needing the space. "So it wasn't *'let's never do that again'* weird, was it? You liked that?"

"The rumors about you are still true, Payne," she said, bringing back the patented Yvette Young smirk. "I liked that."

She gave me a look that said I knew exactly what she was talking about. And I did. Military bases were worse than high schools when it came to gossip.

I was on a road that converged, and the way I wanted to

go was not the best route to take. I couldn't just sit there, though, hard as shit, pretending I hadn't just kissed the woman I'd wanted more than anything for as long as I could remember.

"Well, uh…" I stood, running a palm over my head. "I should probably head out. I have court in the—"

"You didn't even finish eating," she said, catching my wrist. "Don't leave. Not yet."

The plea in her voice stopped me cold. I looked down at her, hair slightly mussed from where my fingers had been, lips still swollen from the pressure of mine pressed against them.

"I promise I'm not leaving because I want to," I said. "I'm leaving because if I don't, parts of me are going to be very upset at not experiencing more of you."

I let my eyes drift down her body, past her breasts to her thighs and shapely calves and back up. "And sorry to be so direct, but…"

I sighed, contemplating the next few words, then going for it. "When I *finally* get to fuck you, it won't be on the couch in your office."

Her eyes widened slightly. "When you…finally get to…"

"Yeah," I said, leaning in to kiss her again. "Because we both know this isn't me scratching an itch or satisfying a curiosity."

I'd almost made it to the door when I heard her speak my name.

"Wesley."

I turned, bracing for her to run again. "Yeah, Vette?"

"Thank you." She looked down, then back up at me, eyes shining, wringing her hands. "For bringing me dinner. For always taking care of me, even when I push back against you taking care of me. For…not making me choose between holding onto Jason and…"

She gestured vaguely between us.

I gave her a cursory nod, encouraged. "Take all the time you need, Yvette. But please know that this is not casual for me. It could never be with you."

Driving home, I replayed the evening like a bad bootleg—the conversation I hadn't meant to have in the way I hadn't meant to have it. I'd gone to see her out of habit, a reflex to check in on the ones you love, and instead I'd fumbled us both into fresh territory. At every red light, I muttered a fervent prayer that we would keep moving in the same direction, because...*fuck*.

I could not take not having her anymore.

I had reason to celebrate, though. Yvette Young had let me taste those lips. Now all I could think about was when she'd let me have the rest.

CHAPTER
THIRTEEN

WESLEY

TEN HOURS at the courthouse had left me a dry husk in a navy blue suit. The only saving grace was that the last two hours of my day was in a court-ordered mediation between Marcel and Julia Simeon. I loosened my tie before it could choke me to death as I walked through the parking deck to my car, phone pressed to my ear.

I thumbed open the key fob with my other hand and the Range Rover chirped, the seats already moving to my preset position. The air conditioning kicked on automatically, a blessed relief from the Atlanta heat.

"Simeon looked pitiful. Like it wasn't his fault he had to give Julia twenty-five mil."

"He need to feel pitiful," said Yvette on the other line. "It's probably all for show anyway. Did you use any of my footage?"

"Played it like a highlight reel."

Yvette's laugh crackled through the speaker. "Good. I'm

sure he told some lie like he was working late. He was working something."

I dropped the phone into the holder on my dashboard and waited for the Bluetooth to connect, then pulled out of the parking space. I navigated through the concrete maze toward street level. "Julia's walking away clean with everything she wants, including the money."

"That's good. So glad I could help her out. Uhmmm..." Yvette paused, then asked in a lower register, "Are you coming by here?"

Young Investigations was clear across town from the courthouse, my office, and my house. I'd been driving out of my way to see her.

"Thought about it, but I'm beat. I'm heading home to try to forget about entitled attorneys who think a ninety-minute closing argument on a slip and fall case is necessary. But uh..."

I could hear her shifting around, maybe straightening papers on her desk. "But uhhhh what?"

"Come over. You haven't seen the latest updates to the house," I continued, coaxing her.

"You cooking? Or at least ordering? You know I eat."

"Nobody knows better than I do, Vette."

A moment's hesitation. Then, "You need me to bring anything?"

"Nah. When you get there, I'll have everything I need. See you in a while."

Then I hung up before she could click her tongue at me, like she always did when I openly flirted with her.

The driveways in Cabbagetown barely fit a car, but I'd paid extra to pour a new slab after the old one buckled in three places from the roots of a dying magnolia. I coasted into the garage and shut down the engine, just taking a second to breathe before I went inside.

The mill worker's house was almost a disaster when I

bought it. Rotting porch boards had been replaced, hundred-year-old paint had been scraped off, plumbing that probably belonged in a museum was replaced. It would have been less expensive to buy a brand-new home, but the character in my house couldn't be duplicated. The bones were solid, built to last when the Fulton Bag and Cotton Mill employed half the neighborhood.

Now the restored wraparound porch and original floors made it stand out among the shotgun houses lining the narrow street.

I grabbed my briefcase and the battered legal pad from the passenger side before locking up. Inside, I'd kept the high ceilings and wide-plank floors while adding modern touches. Yvette liked to tease me about finally breaking free of military minimalism, but she'd been here during every stage of renovation, offering opinions on paint colors and making fun of my attempts at decorating.

I'd barely changed into lounge pants and a t-shirt when I heard the El Camino pulling into the driveway. She appeared on my porch moments later, laptop bag over one shoulder, manila folders under her arm.

"Come on in. Make yourself at home." I took the files from her and set them on the kitchen island.

"This is so...*domestic*," she said, smirking in the doorway as she took in my casual attire. Gone was the sharp-suited attorney who wore a diamond stud in one ear. This was the Wesley few people got to see, relaxed, at home in the space I'd curated.

"Off-duty vibes," I said, moving to lower the volume on the lo-fi music piping into the room through overhead speakers.

Evening light caught the rich colors in the Turkish rug I'd added to the living room recently. The whole house felt different in this light. Warmer, more lived-in. More me.

"The place looks good," she said. "Remember when the

kitchen was all dark cabinets and tired linoleum and closed off?"

"I remember when you told me I was a fool to buy this house. You didn't see the vision."

"It looked like the civil rights era in here," she dead-panned, looking around at where I'd torn the walls down to create an open concept space. "I can admit I was wrong."

She wandered to the doors leading to the back deck. The wooded lot behind the house was one of the reasons I'd bought the place. It was a rare patch of green in a neighbor-hood where developers were cramming condos into every available space.

"The deck is finished." I loved the awe and appreciation embedded in her tone.

"Can't wait to break it in." I headed to the bar cart, opened a bottle and poured two fingers of scotch, then glanced at her. "Want something to drink? Water, Coke…"

I chuckled, then jokingly offered, "Scotch?"

"Hmm. What are you making?"

"Chicken and pasta arrabbiata. The real thing, with enough chilis to make you sweat."

I was practically seducing her. Yvette liked her food to clear her sinuses.

For a moment, she stayed at the window, her silhouette framed in the evening sun blazing through the kitchen. Then she turned from the window and walked over to the bar cart.

"Pour me one."

"Pour you one what?" I asked.

"Scotch," she answered. "Pour me one."

I paused, glass halfway to my lips. "Vette. You sure? You haven't drank much since—"

"I'm sure," she reassured me. "I need to turn my brain off for a minute."

I studied her for a few beats, then reached for another glass from the cart and poured a smaller measure than mine. I handed her the glass. She looked up at me as she took it.

No makeup. Loose khakis. Plain t-shirt. Hair pulled back with a wide headband. Still the most beautiful woman I'd ever seen, not because she was trying but because she wasn't.

I wanted to taste her again. That kiss was still with me, occupying every other thought. It must've shown on my face because she cleared her throat and stepped back.

She sipped the scotch and made her way to the other end of the kitchen. "Mmmmm. This is nice. Smooth."

"Nick's housewarming gift."

I went back to the stove and stirred the sauce, trying to focus on cooking instead of the way she'd looked at me just now. I hoped we weren't going backwards.

"What kind of man leaves his kids?" she asked suddenly. "I keep coming back to that. Even if Edward found proof of fraud. Even if he was in danger…"

"Maybe he thought he was protecting them." I stirred the sauce, adding diced chilis, then dropped pasta into boiling salted water. "If Barrett's as connected as Nick says he is…"

"Still." She downed another sip, larger this time. "Those boys needed their father."

I turned off the heat under the sauce and faced her. "You think he had a choice?"

"Maybe not a good one, but still a choice."

"I keep thinking about what I would do. If someone threatened my family…" She trailed off, then met my eyes. "I wouldn't run. I'd fight."

"That's because you're stubborn. And ex-military. And you can fight."

"I can only fight skinny, annoying men named Yancey," she said, giggling into her glass. "I'm going to see if there's a *Bones* marathon on."

"Leaving me in the kitchen to do all the work?"

"I'm a guest, Payne."

The familiar sounds of the TV clicking through channels drifted back to me as I cooked and drained the pasta and plated our dinner. We moved to the living room, settling into the oversized leather couch I'd splurged on.

Yvette balanced her plate on her knees and loaded up a fork. "This is so good," she said around a mouthful of pasta. "Your sauce has gotten better. Must be taking notes when Mama Payne cooks."

"I choose to take that as a compliment."

She gestured at the house with her fork. "Nice place, good job, can burn up a kitchen. Why aren't you married yet, Wesley Payne?"

The scotch was loosening her tongue. I recognized the faint slur riding her words. "I'm not the one holding up that show."

Her eyes dropped to her plate. "Shots fired. Center mass."

"You asked a question you already know the answer to, Yvette."

She didn't respond—unless swirling the scotch in her glass was supposed to say something.

"You doing alright over there? With the drink?" I asked gently, not just as a formality but because I remembered the way her face had crumpled the last time I saw her drunk.

She nodded. "Bringing back memories of the last time I drank and said too much."

Her lips flattened into a line as she nudged the glass back and forth. The ice cubes shifted. I felt the memory unfolding, enveloping her.

"I yelled at his mother about not talking him out of going to Afghanistan. Had a screaming, crying breakdown like I was the only person that ever lost someone. In front of the people that had known him his entire life. I was so...selfish and emotional."

Her voice was steadier than I expected, but her hands

betrayed her. The left one clenched, the right one fidgeting with the edge of the paper napkin I'd handed her.

"Got carried out of the repast," she recalled. "How embarrassing."

"I was the one who carried you out," I said, hoping the words were not a reprimand. "That's what made you cut back?"

"That and the three-day hangover." She held out her glass. "Another?"

"Vette." I stared her down, brows riding high. "You're grown and all, but you're not leaving here drunk."

She rolled her head so she faced me. "I know. I'm okay."

I poured her another scotch, smaller than the first.

"I still dream about him," she confessed quietly, taking the second glass. "I wake up feeling so guilty."

"About?"

She stared into the amber liquid. "That some days I don't think about him at all. That I kissed you and it felt…"

Yvette stopped herself, shaking her head. I watched her try to keep her emotions at bay but lose the battle.

"The other night…at my office."

My heart kicked against my ribs. "What about it?"

She set the glass down, swiveling her knees so we were face to face, inches apart. "I have been thinking about what it would feel like to kiss you since I met you. Since before Jason died," she said, letting that land before she went on. "I committed to loving him harder because he loved me so much. I felt so guilty about how much I really wanted it to happen after he died that I would literally run from you. And…"

She shifted, feeling more brave, moving closer. "All I have been able to think about is that I really want to kiss you again…but…"

"But…"

"I used to feel like I was betraying him," she said, the

words spilling over each other. "Especially when you and I were working together and he was off in some godforsaken location, stuck under a vehicle in the elements, covered in motor oil and I was at, like, the Heidelberg Marriott, having a glass of wine with a handsome, *sexy* superior officer who was rumored to be an amazing fuck. And who had made it clear he was attracted to me."

I had to force myself to breathe normally. In my peripheral vision, I noticed two peaks under her blouse. They weren't the only body parts rising to the occasion.

"Yvette… We—"

"I know," she said, cutting me off. "I had to get drunk to say this and now you have to wait for my ass to cut the check my mouth is writing." She squinted, shaking her head. "That made sense before I said it. Something to think about, though?"

Yvette stuck her tongue out to swipe it across her bottom lip, then scooted even closer to me. "I should feel guilty about how wet that kiss made me. About the things I did in my bed while thinking about you kissing me again. Doing…all kinds of things to me."

She shook her head. "I don't, Wesley."

I set my glass down before I dropped it. The confessions I hadn't expected to hear from her hit me like a physical blow, every nerve in my body firing at once. She was close enough that I could smell her perfume. And the scotch on her breath.

She pressed closer, her hand on my chest, fingers spread wide across the cotton t-shirt I wore. Her body was so heated, I felt her temperature through the fabric, and the slight tremor in her touch that had nothing to do with how much she had drunk.

I pulled her close to me, dropping a kiss on her cheek. She clung to me, her face buried against my neck.

Then I felt wetness on my skin. She was crying.

Not the loud, dramatic sobs I'd witnessed at Jason's

funeral, but the quiet shedding of something deeper. I held her tighter, one hand stroking her back in slow circles. "Hey. Talk to me, Vette."

She buried her face against my shoulder. "I'm sorry," she whispered.

"What you sorry for? Feeling something? Being human?"

"For being such a mess." She lifted her head, swiping her fingertips under her eyes. "For wanting you and missing Jason and hating myself for wanting you while I miss Jason."

"You're not a mess. You're human with a heart and mind and feelings and that's a lot going on. I get that."

I brushed a tear from her cheek. "Jason would want you to be happy. I'm not just saying that because you being happy means me getting something I want. If it wasn't me, it would be *somebody*. It should be *somebody*."

"He's probably up in heaven cussing both of us out."

I laughed at that. "Now, you know that ain't Jason because he loved you down, girl. And people who love you want you to live, not just exist. If Jason's up there cussing anybody out, it's not because you're moving on. It's because I took too damn long to make my move."

She pulled back to look at me, eyes still glassy. "You... think he knew?"

I smirked. "Baby, pretty sure everybody knew then. Just like everybody knows now. To his credit, he never said a word to me about backing off or staying away from his girl. You know why?"

She shook her head.

"Because he trusted you. He knew you loved him, and he knew I respected that."

I swiped another tear with my thumb. "But he also knew that if something happened to him, he'd want someone who actually gave a damn about you to be in your life. That's why I stuck around. That's why I landed here in Atlanta. I figured you'd come home after you got out."

She was silent for a long time. "Am I ever going to not feel like I'm cheating on him?"

"Yeah. And there's no timetable for that. I'm man enough to know two things can be true—you can love and miss Jason and..." I smiled. "You can wonder about the things I plan to do to you when you're not drunk."

She sniffled, flipping me off. "You are evil, Payne."

I grinned wide. "Payback is the biggest bitch, ain't she?"

She looked at me with something that might have been wonder. "Why, Wesley? You're always here, waiting for me to get my shit together."

"Because you're worth waiting for. Because what we could have together is worth waiting for, no matter how long I have to wait."

I meant that...but hoped I'd never have to prove it.

"Not trying to freak you out about it, but things between us are already different. You just need to take your time with it. And sober up because..."

I looked at her, narrowed my eyes, and issued a gut-level grunt at her. "I *been* ready."

"You are a fool." She pulled back and wiped her face with the heels of both hands. "God, I'm sorry. This is supposed to be dinner, not...whatever this is."

"This is us figuring it out." I stood and grabbed her plate. "Let's warm this up and eat some more. I'm cutting you off."

We moved back to the kitchen and I reheated our plates while she got us both water from the fridge. The conversation shifted to lighter things at first—cases we'd worked, people we knew.

After dinner, we went back on the couch in front of the TV. The mood grew more serious.

"What made you leave the Army?" she asked quietly. "You loved JAG, and you could have separated at a higher rank."

I inhaled deeply, bracing myself for this conversation. It

was an emotional decision that hadn't become easier to talk about since my release.

"Sofia Herrera," I answered. "Nineteen-year-old recruit from some dust-bowl town where going to school on the G.I. bill was the only way college was happening." I stared at my hands, willing them not to clench in reaction to telling this story. "First time I met her, she was sitting outside my office at 0700, uniform perfect, waiting to file a complaint against her CO."

"This sounds familiar," she said slowly, her brows knit together. "Delacroix, right?"

I nodded. "She wouldn't look at me when she talked. Kept her eyes on the floor. She was so quiet and shaking so bad I could barely hear her." My jaw worked back and forth, releasing pent-up tension. "She wanted to know if certain practices were a normal part of training. Private discussions, personal and sexual in nature. How he'd lock the door if she came to his office for these sessions. How he said her career depended on keeping him happy, in whatever way he deemed necessary."

Some nights, I still saw that scared woman in my office, the way her hands shook when she tried to drink the water I'd given her.

"She had bruises, Vette. And when I asked her about them, she just…broke apart."

Yvette gasped. "God, Wesley."

"I told her we'd get him. Promised her." The old anger flared, the same rage that had consumed me during those final months in uniform. "I spent weeks building a case. Had three other women come forward with comparable stories. Physical evidence. Witnesses."

Yvette shifted closer, her hand finding mine.

"Delacroix was appointed to a Pentagon job while Sofia was shipped to Fort Leonard Wood to complete her training in a more suitable environment, or so they said."

"Missouri? That was a punishment."

"She got swallowed up there. They disappeared her. And when I tried to fight it…" I ran my free hand over my face, resisting the urge to scream. "Colonel Hill told me some fights weren't worth risking my career and ordered me to stand down."

"That asshole," she muttered. "He must have some skeletons in his closet."

"For sure. I think Delacroix had something on him." I reached for my water. "But that's when I knew I had to get out. I wasn't going to spend the balance of my good, healthy years supporting a system that protects predators."

"Is that why you push hard on cases now? Even the small ones?"

I shrugged my shoulder, frowning. "I just know I won't be told to back down again."

She was quiet for a long while after that. We moved on to other topics—lighter memories, shared stories. But the weight of what I'd told her seemed to sit between us.

As the evening wore on, we both relaxed, sinking deeper into the couch. She curled up and tucked her feet under her. I stretched my legs out, and somehow we ended up with my arm wound around her body. It felt natural, easy. Like we'd been doing this for years instead of taking the tiniest of steps toward each other in recent days.

By the time her words started getting loose around the edges, she was leaning into me completely. Her head found the space between my shoulder and chest and her breathing evened out. I stayed still, not wanting to wake her, watching the rise and fall of her chest in the dim light from the TV.

When I was sure she was deep under, I eased out from beneath her and grabbed a blanket from the matching leather chair. I tucked it around her, brushing her hair back from her face and dropping a light, airy kiss on her temple.

She stirred but didn't wake, just burrowed deeper into the couch cushions.

I stood there for a moment, watching her sleep, then shuffled off to my bedroom, stripped out of my clothes, and headed for the shower, letting the hot water wash away the long day.

Yvette curled up on my couch was never far from my mind.

Yvette admitting her feelings and her desires amid the war that was raging inside her was playing nonstop on a loop in my head.

After brushing my teeth and rubbing body oil into my skin, I pulled on a pair of boxer briefs, slipped under the covers, and stared at the ceiling fan slowly rotating in the shadows of the vaulted ceiling.

The king-sized bed felt particularly huge tonight. Empty. I wished she was beside me, wishing I could pull her close, feel her warmth against me as we both drifted to sleep.

———

HOURS LATER, I awoke to a sensation I couldn't quite place. The mattress felt different. There was warmth where there shouldn't be, a subtle floral scent that hadn't been there when I'd fallen asleep.

I held perfectly still, barely breathing. Then I felt soft skin brushing against my arm as she shifted slightly.

Yvette.

CHAPTER
FOURTEEN

YVETTE

I WOKE UP TO SILENCE.

Not a morning that came too soon where I'd sit bolt upright straight out of sleep, with Jason's name stuck in my throat and tears already rolling down my face.

Not the sounds of Yancey stomping down the stairs and yelling at full volume, like people weren't trying to sleep in the house.

Not my parents lovingly bickering about Daddy's hard hat always hanging off the back of a chair, ruining Mama's Southern Living Magazine-inspired decor.

I was still on Wesley's couch, wrapped like a burrito in the soft plaid throw he'd tucked around me at some hour I couldn't remember.

My jaw wasn't clenched. My eyes weren't gritty. The suffocating, instant grief that came most mornings was absent. My mind rolled that fact around and found only the unfamiliar smoothness of having slept, *really* slept, for what felt like a century.

No dreams about Jason. No crying myself awake.

My hand was at my throat, fingers groping automatically for the thin chain that held Jason's ring.

Nothing. Bare skin.

I shot up in a panic, tapping around the couch. Then I remembered I'd taken it off to clean it and left it on my nightstand.

Well... I'd told myself I was taking it off to clean it, but that wasn't the truth, not really. And in the clarity of morning after a good night's sleep, I couldn't let myself off that easily.

I pressed my palms to my face as the memories of the past few days with Wesley played back in high definition.

Wesley and I in my office. Our mouths, our lips, his hands where they had never been before. I'd been a little weirded out by it but not enough to not almost beg him to stay. He was right to leave. If he'd stayed, I would have been unable to stop myself from giving in to him.

Then I showed up last night and made sure I got nice and tipsy because I knew Wesley wouldn't touch me unless I was sober.

You sneaky bitch.

Not my finest moment.

I'd worn that ring since Jason proposed with it. After he died, I couldn't look at it on my finger, so I strung it on a chain and wore it every single day. Until yesterday.

I sat for a minute, waiting for the guilt to assault me, to collapse in tears amid a crushing weight...but it didn't come. I'd worked all day and spent time with Wesley and slept through the night without that ring around my neck.

And I felt...fine about it?

Well, shit, as Leslie Jordan would say.

These days, I made an appointment with Paula when I needed an appointment with Paula. I...should probably call Paula. She'd want to know about this development, about how kissing Wesley had shaken something loose, something I'd been holding onto way too tight for far too long.

About how I was done fighting what I felt for Wesley. She would love to hear that.

I threw the blanket back and quietly took the stairs to Wesley's bedroom. The door was cracked, allowing the sounds of deep, slow breaths to seep through. Jason would want me to be happy. Wasn't that what Wesley said?

I pushed the door open and stepped inside, scurried to his bathroom, and found the spare toothbrush I knew he'd have in his linen closet. I brushed my teeth, then soaked a towel in hot water and washed my face.

When I came out of the bathroom, Wesley was spread out across his bed, one arm flung wide above his head, muscles relaxed and palm open. The other was folded against his chest. The sheets were twisted around his waist as if he'd had a fitful night of sleep.

I pulled off my clothes down to my bra and underwear, leaving them in a pile on the floor. My skin prickled, not just from the cooler air but from the knowledge of what the next few minutes might hold. I hesitated at the edge of the bed, propped up on one knee, not sure if I should wait for him to wake or just slide in and risk the awkwardness.

I pulled the sheet up and slid in beneath it. My thigh pressed against his as I wriggled closer.

He didn't wake right away, but I could tell the instant he became aware of me. The rhythm of his breath stuttered and his body went still as he processed what he was sensing.

"Vette?" he managed, his voice shredded by sleep. First came a flicker of panic in his eyes, then it stilled, replaced by the slow bloom of surprise.

"Hey," I whispered.

He took me in as I lay next to him—hair loose around my face, in nothing but my bra and underwear between his sheets. "What...what are you doing?"

I rolled onto my side to face him better, my elbow digging into the mattress. I felt absurdly calm lying in his bed. "I'm not really sure," I admitted. "But I am sober and I want to be doing it."

The distance between us closed as I scooted closer until our faces were inches apart. "I keep thinking about what you said last night. And the other night in my office. And everything you've been saying this whole time."

"What I say?"

"That you've been waiting for me." I reached out and traced the line of his jaw with my fingertip. "This morning I woke up and for the first time in three years, I felt…peaceful. Rested. Not guilty."

I sucked in a shaky breath. "And I remembered that Jason wanted to live a full life with me and he would hate that I wasn't living one without him. He would hate that I've been half-living since he died."

Wesley's hand covered mine where it rested against his face. "So…what are you saying?"

"I'm saying that I want to be done feeling guilty. I want to be done pretending I don't want you. I want to be done wasting time we could have had."

"You *want* to be?"

"Yes. Because you and I both know that I am stubborn and nothing comes easy to me, but as hard as I've fought against you, I can probably fight as hard to make"—I gestured between us—"this work."

"Are you sure?" His fingers tightened on mine. "Because I don't mind waiting if you're not—"

I kissed him. No hesitation this time. No tears. Just the solid warmth of him as he pulled me closer.

He felt like home.

When we broke apart, I rested my forehead against his. "I took off his ring, Wesley. Because I wanted this to happen without him between us."

I let my index finger map his chest: collarbone, sternum, the dip at the hollow of his throat where his pulse beat beneath the skin. He shivered, and I felt the current pass through my body too.

Wesley's eyes squeezed shut for a second, like he wanted to believe me and was afraid to. "Vette…are you *sure*? Because—"

"We already know you're not turning me down, Payne," I said, a smile starting in the corner of my mouth and refusing to be tamped down. "So relax and be the man I've always known you to be."

I pressed my lips to the pulse point in the dip in his neck, tasting salt and the faint remnants of his body wash. "Be the man you were last night when I told you what I've been dealing with, and you didn't make me feel like I need to be at the nearest hospital on a 72-hour hold. When you seemed so hurt telling me about Sofia's case. When I fell asleep in your arms and woke up on your couch all tucked in."

"Yvette," he rumbled, then let out a laugh. His hands were at my waist, pulling me closer, drawing the length of my thigh up against his body. His thumb traced the curve of my hip where underwear met skin. "You know what I mean when I ask if you're sure—"

I didn't let him finish. I reached for his face, one hand at each cheek, and pulled him in gently. My lips met his in the quietest, softest kiss I could manage, then pulled back to meet his eyes. "I know what you mean. I know exactly what you're asking me, and I want you to do everything you've been stopping yourself from doing. *Everything.*"

He searched my face in the early morning light filtering through the blinds. Whatever he saw there must have convinced him this was real because his demeanor shifted. The restraint I'd grown used to seeing in his eyes melted away. He rolled me onto my back, settling his weight over me. Every nerve ending in my body sizzled from the anticipation of experiencing something brand new with a man I knew like the back of my hand.

His mouth claimed mine with a force that made my toes curl. I responded in kind, my hands smoothing over the broad expanse of his shoulders, pulling him closer to me. I liked Wesley unleashed, welcoming every bit of want he'd been holding back.

When he broke away to trail kisses down my neck, his beard set fire to my skin. The sensation made me ache for him, made me need to press closer to him. A desperate sound escaped my lips. Wesley froze, his fingers splayed at my rib cage.

"You okay?"

"Mmmhmmm," I hummed, looping my arms around his neck. "Hope you don't mind, but I'm... I plan to make noise."

A slow grin spread across his face. "Good to know," he breathed against my lips. "Because I've been thinking about the sounds you'd make for a long time. I don't think you know how long I've been wanting this."

I curved into him, feeling a deliciously hard length between us. "Yes, I do."

Wesley's hands were everywhere at once—sliding up my ribs, cupping my breasts through the thin lace of my bra. His thumb brushed over my nipple, coaxing it to a taut point. I gasped, electricity shooting straight to my core. Deftly, he unhooked my bra, tossing it aside. For a moment, he just looked at me, his dark eyes taking in every inch of exposed skin from my deep brown nipples to the curve of my belly and the expanse of my hips.

"You're perfect, Vette," he whispered. He grazed a nipple with his lips, then—*fuck!*—drew it into his mouth. "Just like I thought...but better than I could have imagined."

I sighed, both in bliss and relief. Wesley sucked and teased, rasping across the bud with his tongue. I gripped him, holding him close while waves overtook me again and again.

"Wesley," I panted, moving restlessly beneath him. "I want it. I want you. Please."

He switched sides, giving the other breast the same attention while his hand slipped beneath the waistband of my panties. When his fingers found me wet and ready, he let out an animalistic grunt.

"God...*dammit*, Yvette!"

His fingers slid through my slickness, exploring me with a deliberate slowness that made me writhe and whimper as I tried to follow them, seeking out the friction that would send me over the edge.

"Don't tease me," I gasped, gripping his shoulders, nails digging into his skin as he circled my clit at a maddeningly slow speed.

Wesley's eyes locked with mine, dark and intense. "I've been waiting a long time for this," he said while he slipped a thick finger inside me, then another, coaxing a moan and stretching me. "This isn't going to go fast, baby. I'm years behind in learning every inch of you."

"I don't want slow," I whined, trembling. "We can do slow after you put me through this mattress."

Wesley's laugh was dark and rich. I was pleased that he was having a good time.

"That's not how this is going to work, Vette." He curled his fingers inside me, finding a spot that made stars explode behind my eyelids.

"Ah! Oh my...God!"

"That's it, baby," he encouraged, his thumb circling that sensitive spot while his fingers moved inside me. "I can't wait to hear you come for the first time."

I was already close, wound tight. When he increased the pressure on my clit, I nearly shattered. "Oh, God, please make me come," I gasped, grinding against his hand.

His eyes darkened. "Say that shit again."

"Make me come, Wesley!" I demanded, voice breaking.

He moved down my body, quickly kissing his way past my belly, and pressed his lips to the mound covered in thin cotton. He nipped at my clit through the fabric before hooking his thumbs under the waistband of my panties and pulling them down. I had kicked out of them in record time and splayed my legs, ready for whatever he was prepared to give me.

Warm breath teased my sensitive flesh. When his lips finally made contact, I came up off the bed with a loud screech of, "Fuck!" One hand flew to grip the top of his head and pull him into me. His nose was buried in the thin strip of hair I maintained and his tongue was bathing my clit like I was the most delicious ice cream cone.

I was coming undone beneath his skilled mouth, my thighs shaking as they bracketed his head. "Fuck, fuck, fuck, fuck!"

I whimpered and Wesley hummed with my clit in his mouth. His big hands had my thighs in a vice grip, holding me open to his assault as I writhed in his grasp; I couldn't pull away if I wanted to.

And I didn't. I rode his mouth, humped his face, shamelessly shed everything that had been holding me back since I'd met Wesley. All the grief I'd folded into myself since I left the Army and made sure I settled in Atlanta—not because my parents lived here but because Wesley settled here.

His tongue flicked mercilessly, building to a crescendo that made me want to scream. The pressure surged until I couldn't hold back anymore.

"Oh, shit! W-Wesley!" I stuttered as I screamed, my body seizing as the orgasm hit. I pulsed around his fingers, practically levitating as my hips undulated, eking out every pulse of climax.

Just as I began to ease down the other side, he made his way back up my body. I grabbed his face between my hands and pulled him in for a kiss. The intimacy of the gesture made my heart pound harder against my ribs.

"Please say it's your turn," I whispered, pushing against his chest. He was a bulky wall of a man, immovable unless he wanted to be.

"It's my turn, alright. But not like you think. Hang on a minute."

He rose to his knees and reached across me to pull open the nightstand drawer. While he rummaged through the drawer, I peeked between us. The bulge in his briefs made my mouth water.

I wrapped a hand around the rigid length through the fabric, then slid down the shaft until his balls were in my palm. I gave him a gentle squeeze; he twitched in my grasp.

"Ahhh...*Vette!*" He hissed, momentarily abandoning his search to close his eyes. His head dropped forward as I squeezed him again. "That shit feels good."

"Keep looking," I urged, massaging him while pulling his dick out and stroking him base to tip. He was warm, thick, and heavy. "If you take too long, this is going in my mouth."

"That's...not a threat," said Wesley, laughing. But he resumed his search of his drawer until he retrieved a box, removed the shrink wrap with his teeth, pulled a condom out, and tore it open.

I watched, transfixed, as he pulled his boxers down and kicked out of them. Now free and unencumbered, his dick bobbed freely. Wesley rolled the condom on, then checked to make sure it was secure.

He was longer, thicker than I'd heard. Not unmanageable, but I almost came just thinking about how good he was going to feel.

"You ready for me?" Wesley asked, noting my wide-eyed stare.

"Yes." I nodded, deliriously reaching for him. "Come here."

Wesley positioned himself between my thighs. "Look at me," he said softly. I had to tip my head up to find his eyes. When I did, his gaze held mine as he pushed forward slowly.

The stretch was *exquisite*.

My jaw dropped and I sucked in a sharp breath.

"Breathe, baby," he said, pausing. "You feel so fuckin' good."

"Don't stop," I begged. "Give me all of it."

We both let out a raw, lusty groan as he sank further into me. Then we went still, each of us overwhelmed by the sensation of finally being connected.

"*Fuuuuck*," he moaned, drawing out the word as he began moving. His strokes were long and tortuously slow until he had completely seated inside me. My eyes were closed, head tilted back, savoring the sensation. I gripped his biceps and paced my breaths to his.

"Relax, baby. I got you. Breathe."

I exhaled, letting my legs fall open. "You remember how long it's been, right?"

"Yeah. Tell me what you need. Slow? Light?"

"No." I laughed, shaking my head. "I need you to fuck the *shit* out of me, Wesley."

He laughed, his belly bouncing against mine. "You *sure* you want that?"

"I'm sure. I want it," I said, rolling my hips against his.

That was all the permission he needed. Wesley pulled back and thrust forward hard, setting a rhythm that was anything but gentle. Deep, powerful strokes that had everything on me bouncing.

It was exactly what I needed.

"This what you want?" he growled, panting with exertion.

"Fuck! Yes!" I gasped. "Give it to me."

The sound of our bodies coming together filled the room, along with my breathless moans and his low grunts of pleasure. His weight was a delicious pressure, like a security blanket. I met him thrust for thrust, our bodies moving together like we'd always been made for this.

"Harder," I gasped. "I can take it."

He obliged, ramping to a force that made the headboard knock against the wall and the air leave my lungs. I pulled my knees up to my chest, yearning for any way to take him deeper.

"You good, Vette?" he panted. "You like that?"

I moaned, arching my back to meet every pound of his body against mine. "Fuck, I like it! Don't stop."

"Shit! You feel so good." He began to chant, the words filtering out between his panting, ragged breaths. "God *damn*. It's so fucking good, Vette. Jesus Christ, you don't even know."

He raked a palm up my thigh, locking my leg high around his hip. His eyes kept flicking from where our bodies joined to my face to the bounce of my breasts, greedily cataloging the whimpers and moans he pulled from me. He ate it up like he had been starved and every noise or quiver was another meal.

Wesley slid a hand under my body and palmed my ass, kneading me while grinding down on every push. He bent low, sucked my earlobe into his mouth, then sent a harsh whisper in my ear.

"You are mine, Yvette Young."

There was something in the way he said it, fierce and hungry, but also profoundly needy, like claiming me out loud was the only way to believe it was real.

I could only nod since he was beating me up in the absolute best way.

"You...are mine," he rasped, thrusting harder. "You're mine, Vette. You're *mine*, Vette. You're *mine*, Vette!"

A moan that ended in a growl curled from his mouth as I felt something snap inside him.

"I'm about to come in this pussy. This pussy that is *mine*.

Come with me, Vette. Come all over this dick, baby. Come with me, Vette! Vette! *Vette!*"

The combination of his words and the force of his thrusts and the grit in his voice as he climaxed while claiming me sent me over the edge. A white-hot flash tore me apart; I released everything, everything, *everything* with wild abandon as we convulsed together.

We collapsed together, heaving air like we'd been choking, our skin slick with sweat. Wesley held me close, remaining inside me while pressing kisses to my hair.

"Can't go nowhere now. You're mine."

"I am," I whispered, burying my face in his damp neck. "I'm yours, Wesley."

For a few minutes, we just breathed, our bodies still tangled, his hand lazily stroking my thigh. I was weightless; I'd shed so much I hadn't even known I was carrying.

"Vette."

"Mmmmm," I croaked, still buried beneath him and not complaining about it. I knew what he was going to ask me when he paused. I almost smiled.

"You and Jason…y'all went hard like that?"

I giggled, dropping kisses along his chest. "I loved that man and we got the job done, but…no, not like that. This was about me and you. What I wanted with you. From you."

I traced patterns across his back and forearms, following the ripple of muscle. "You should have told me it was gonna be this good. I wouldn't have fought it so long."

"You're the one always talking about the rumors. Did they lie?"

I laughed loud and hard. "No, sir. They did not."

Wesley shifted, pulling out, then rolling away. He left the bed and headed to the bathroom. The toilet flushed. I heard his sonic toothbrush, then water running. When he returned, he brought a warm towel.

He tenderly wiped me clean, his touch gentle and possessive. I laid back, letting him perform an aftercare ritual, thinking about his quiet inquiry.

My relationship with Jason was a loving one, but it was fairly innocent. We were each other's firsts, fumbling through intimacy and still experimenting with what felt *really* good. Most of our relationship had been long distance, with quiet sessions in the barracks when we could manage to be alone.

We were excited to get married and really get down and dirty.

I would always cherish what I had with Jason, but Wesley's patient attention to my needs after a strenuous bout of fucking was very much my current speed.

Grown and sexy.

"Thank you," I whispered, watching his face as he worked. The sun was up, rays of light catching the angles of his handsome features, highlighting the slight furrow between his brows and the thickness of his lips as he frowned in concentration.

When he finished, he grabbed my hands to pull me up. "You need to hit the bathroom. I'm not missing any time with you because you have a UTI from not peeing after sex."

When I hesitated, he playfully scowled at me. "That is an order. Go."

I got up, shimmied naked to the bathroom, took care of my business, then slid back into bed. I felt the ghost of him inside me, a pleasant ache that reminded me this was real.

"So..." Wesley began, his fingers tracing the rise of my hip. "That happened."

"And I loved every minute of it."

"Loved it, did you?" He seemed proud of himself. "No regrets?"

I propped myself up on an elbow to look at him. "Only that I didn't give in sooner."

A smile spread across his face. "Same. But it's not like we wasted that time. We got to know each other. Became friends.

Developed a respect for each other. I didn't mind taking the time to build a foundation."

"Suck up. I know I've been a pain in your ass for a long time."

"I ain't admitting to that shit. I'm just glad we're here now."

"And we can move forward."

He cocked a brow at me. "Is that a promise?"

"It's...an intent," I admitted.

His chuckle rumbled through his chest. "Good enough for now. Do you *intend* to stay for breakfast? And lunch and dinner?"

I grinned, kicking my legs under the sheet at the mention of food. "Depends on what you have planned."

"The plans I have for you..." he said, rolling us over so he hovered above me. His eyes, dark with renewed passion, locked onto mine. "Do not involve food."

I was giddy at how easy this had become. My legs were already opening. "Care to share?"

Wesley lowered his head, pressing a trail of kisses from my lips to my shoulders, then down through the valley between my breasts. He pulled a nipple into his mouth, then the other before he came back up, pressing his lips to mine.

"I plan," he whispered between kisses, "to keep you in this bed and make you scream my name until you got no voice left." His hand slid down my body, his breath catching at finding me already wet again. "Then I'm gonna feed you, run you a bath, make sure you rest... And start all over again."

I leaned into his touch, amazed at how quickly my body responded to his fingers, his tongue, his voice. "That sounds like a full day."

"Baby, that's just Saturday." His fingers worked their magic, coaxing gasps and moans. "I got plans for the whole weekend."

I pressed my mouth to his, letting him swallow my words. This time, when he slipped his fingers inside me, I was already primed. My hips bucked against his hand as he built me up with steady strokes. I was so sensitive from before that it didn't take long for the pressure to mount again.

"Yeah, baby...get it," he mumbled against my lips. "Take what you need."

When the orgasm hit, it was no less intense than the two before it. "Wesley," I panted, coming down. "Shit, you're going to kill me."

"What a way to go," he said with a grin, then kissed me softly. "I would have waited a lot longer if that's what you needed," he said when he pulled back from the kiss.

"You would *not* have." I studied him. "The way you always found a way to bring up your feelings for me? You were not waiting much longer. You would have made a move or given up."

"Nah." Wesley shook his head.

"What do you mean, *nah*? You would have just hung out forever, waiting for me to come around?"

He was quiet for a moment. "I've waited since Germany, Yvette. You knew that. Paula knew that."

"Yeah, you should not be discussing me with my therapist, by the way."

Wesley laughed, the sound rumbling through his chest. "I was discussing a woman I was interested in with my *friend*. She helped me see you needed time and to not give up."

"Like I said. *Plotting*. You owe me a kiss for all that subterfuge."

His kiss was slow, thorough. I hummed with satisfaction.

"So, uhm..." I said against his lips. "You mentioned breakfast. And...lunch and dinner?"

"There's no sense in going to sit at the office where you don't have shit to eat but granola bars. I'm making schnitzel tonight."

My mouth dropped open. "Seriously? You know I haven't had that since—"

"Germany," he finished for me, his thumb tracing along my jaw. "Yeah. I found a recipe I think I can follow. Gonna give it a go."

"Oooh..." I grinned. "Somebody is trying to compete with my mama's cooking."

"Maybe I'll get an invite to Valerie Young's dinner table now."

CHAPTER
FIFTEEN

WESLEY

WAKING up with Yvette in my bed was surreal, like something I'd imagined too many times to believe it was real. Her leg was draped over mine, her hand rested on my chest. Sunlight filtered through the blinds, casting thin golden lines across her brown skin. Her breathing was deep, even.

The noise inside my head had gone silent. I did not immediately reach for my phone to scroll through unread emails or mentally cycle through the day's obligations. There were no nagging reminders about filings, no accusatory pings from an inner to-do list. The mental jury had finally gone home for the day.

There was just me and Yvette.

Her phone buzzed on the nightstand, bringing me out of a part asleep, mostly awake fugue. I stretched to pick it up. Estelle's name flashed on the screen.

Slipping out of bed, I padded into the hallway and answered quietly. "Hey, Stelle, it's Wesley. Is everything okay?"

"Wesley?" Estelle sounded surprised. "Is Yvette...okay?"

"Yeah, yeah. She's good. She's knocked out. We worked late last night and she stayed over."

It wasn't a complete lie. After she stopped home to grab a change of clothes, we had gone through Edward's files again and tried to piece the timeline of his disappearance together. We had a solid theory of how this case played out but needed the evidence to present the case to the official bureaus.

Then we made dinner, uncorked a bottle of wine, and had sex until well past midnight. Yvette was knocked out because I wore her ass out.

Estelle clucked her tongue but thankfully didn't press. "Well, I dug up something interesting. Back in the day, Carmela Verona's father used to work for First Southeast Partners."

"The investment firm behind Miller Creek?" The name Richard Barrett flashed through my mind.

"Bingo. More to come on that, I'm sure. Now the other thing is...there's a bit of an underground community among investigators. Word is Barrett's looking for Edward. He's got a man with a reputation for playing fast and loose with the law, if you hear what I'm saying to ya."

A knot twisted in my gut. Barrett was hunting. Men like that didn't leave witnesses.

"Stelle, can you dig into Carmela's father's connection to First Southeast? I want to see if there is a connection to Barrett. There's something in there that we need to know."

"On it. And Wesley?" Her voice softened. "Take care of our girl. Something tells me this case just got dangerous."

"I will." I glanced up as Yvette appeared in the kitchen doorway, wearing nothing but one of my shirts. Her hair was mussed, eyes still at half-mast. "Thanks, Estelle."

I hung up and set the phone down, crossing the kitchen to pull Yvette into my arms.

"Morning, beautiful." I kissed her forehead. She melted

against me, her arms circling my waist, her hands rubbing my back. She felt good in the morning.

"Mmmmm."

She tipped her head back, lips puckered for a kiss. I obliged, brushing my lips against hers and lingering for a moment before pulling back.

"I should start keeping clothes and a scarf here," she mumbled against my mouth. "And like...skincare. My face is crying without my moisturizer."

"Got plenty of room," I replied, chuckling. "Bring it on."

"Was that Stelle?" she asked, pulling back with a pat to my chest.

I moved to get a pot of coffee started, pulling the water reservoir out of the machine to fill it.

"Yeah. She got some intel. Turns out, Carmela Verona's father used to work for First Southeast Partners."

Her eyes widened. She had been looking through my cabinets but paused and turned to me. "Richard Barrett's company."

I nodded, then filled her in on the other bit of news—that we weren't the only people looking for Edward.

"Shit." She slumped against the counter, palms down. "That feels like confirmation that Carmela is wrapped up in this. We have to find them first."

"I know. But Vette, this might get dangerous. Barrett's folks don't play by the rules."

"All the more reason to get to Edward—and we assume Carmela—before he does."

"I agree, but we do this together, okay?" I reached for her, tucking a finger under her chin and lifting her head so her eyes met mine. "No going rogue, Young. You hear me?"

"Yes, sir. Same goes for you, Payne."

———

I'D SPENT most of the next day in court, but Yvette was already deep into the case when I arrived at her office. She was pacing, phone pressed to her ear.

"We need those records yesterday. It's time-sensitive..." She paused, giving a frustrated eye roll. "Alright, stay on it."

She ended the call with a sigh, tossing the phone onto her desk. "Nia is hitting roadblocks at the county clerk's office. Maybe Barrett has friends there too."

I shrugged out of my suit jacket, draping it over the back of a chair. "I told you—all kinds of friends. In all kinds of places."

"How was court today?" She glanced at her watch, then brought her eyes back to me. "You're getting out kind of late, aren't you?"

"Judge Humboldt loves the sound of his own voice." I sank into the chair, rolling my shoulders. "My day just got way better."

An eyebrow rose. She fought the smile tugging at the corner of her mouth. "Did it now?"

My eyes traced the curve of her hip, the way her jeans hugged her thighs, the roundness of her breasts under her t-shirt. She leaned against the edge of her desk, legs crossed at the ankle, arms folded, expression casual like she didn't know how good she looked to me.

Like she hadn't rocked my shit twelve hours ago and then got out of my bed to get dressed for work.

We'd agreed to keep our relationship under wraps for the time being. We wanted to explore this thing without opinions and other people's wishes holding their thumbs on the scale. But moments like this, alone in the office with no need to mask the sensual touches and lingering looks, made me hyperaware of how easy it would be to drag her over to the couch and pick up where we'd left off that morning.

As if reading my mind, she pushed off the desk, sauntered

over to me, then leaned over just enough to plant a kiss on my mouth. I smiled through the kiss, humming happily.

"You're a mess," she said, landing another softer kiss before stepping back.

"Nia is at the county clerk's office…where is Estelle?"

"She's been at the library for hours looking up incorporation histories."

"Mmmhmmm…" I hooked a finger through her belt loop, tugging her back over to me. "So whatever we're gonna do, we gotta do it now. Can't have her walking in on us."

"Not that we're not good and grown." Yvette smirked, bracing her hands on my shoulders. "We agreed to keep things quiet, though."

"I am very quiet when my lips are occupied." I slid my hands up her body, taking in the heat of her skin through the thin cotton shirt. "You're too tempting."

"How am I tempting? I'm just…at work." She dipped her head, full lips brushing against mine. I groaned, tightening my grip on her.

"At work," I replied. "At play. At home. Asleep. Just standing here. Don't matter, I'm never not going to want you."

Yvette ducked her head, forehead resting against mine, hands idly massaging the nape of my neck. I slid my hands up under her shirt and cupped her breasts in the plain t-shirt bra I knew she was wearing. She made a breathy, delighted sound when my thumbs went searching for the erect nipples I knew I'd find.

For a moment, there was no case, no secrets, no lurking danger. Just this woman who was finally willingly in my arms.

The door to the suite swung open so fast it banged against the wall behind it. Estelle rushed in wearing an aggressive floral print tunic and her standard jeggings.

"Uh-huh," she said, pausing in the doorway.

We didn't have time to move away and pretend we weren't doing what we were doing. So we didn't. I pulled my hands out from under her shirt. Yvette straightened her clothing and stepped back.

"Hey, Estelle. What did you find out at the library?"

"Hey nothin'! I knew there was a reason he answered your phone yesterday," she drawled. "Anyway...I come bearing gifts."

She brandished a thick manila envelope, crossing the room to spread its contents across Yvette's desk. "Incorporation records for every company associated with Miller Creek. They're not just connected to First Southeast. They're all interconnected—they all even have the same PO box address as First Southeast. It's a maze, but the architect is the same."

Yvette leaned over the pages as she studied the tangled web of LLCs and holding companies. "Barrett's really working overtime to cover his tracks. Would Nick have advised him to do this?"

"Nah. This ain't Nick's style." I moved to stand beside her. "What's he hiding?"

"Laundering?" Yvette mumbled. "Moving money around, making it impossible to trace?"

"Likely," said Estelle, nodding with great satisfaction. "And I'd bet that money's tied to whatever Edward and Carmela discovered."

"Estelle, you're a gift," I told her.

She waved a dismissive hand. "Tell me something I don't know." Then her expression grew more serious. "Actually, there's more on Marcus Verona. He was Project Finance Manager at First Southeast. Worked directly under Barrett for about three years before he took early retirement."

Yvette looked up from the documents. "How early?"

"Fifty-eight. Left a lot of money on the table." Estelle pulled out her reading glasses to check her notes. "But here's the interesting part—he retired right around the time some of

Barrett's other projects started having structural issues and cost overruns. Same patterns we're seeing with Miller Creek."

I felt the pieces clicking together. "He saw what Barrett was doing and got out."

"That's my thinking. And when Carmela started asking questions about Miller Creek's finances…" Estelle shrugged. "Daddy told her to run."

Then her expression turned sly. "Speaking of things I already know…it's about damn time. And that's all I'm gon' say."

She turned to head to her desk but stopped. "Break it to Nia gently, though. I'm happy for you both, but she's going to be surly. You know she's been crushing on you, Wesley."

I blushed beneath my dark skin. "Will do, Stelle. Thank you. We're…figuring it out."

"Well, figure it faster. I ain't getting no younger, and I want to see some pretty Payne babies 'fore I go."

The thought of that kind of future with Yvette made me heady and weak. Suddenly, it was the only thing I cared about.

I looked between them, these two women who'd become family over the years. "Be careful, both of you. Keep your trails clean, don't get caught. Tell Nia too. Barrett plays dirty."

Estelle scoffed, pulling out her chair and dropping into it. "Honey, I was playing dirty while Barrett was still in short pants. Let's get to work."

CHAPTER
SIXTEEN

YVETTE

PROPERTY RECORDS, bank statements, and incorporation papers for at least a half dozen LLCs, some so freshly minted the notary stamp ink still looked damp in the photocopies strewn across my desk. For nearly a week now, my mind had run circles like a dog chasing its tail, with every lead sending me to the same conclusion.

Edward's sudden vanishing act overlapped too neatly with Carmela's abrupt resignation for my liking...was that a coincidence? Or was there a more sinister reason for them both to leave at nearly the same time?

Hovering at the periphery was Marcus, Carmela's father, who worked for Barrett for years before a sudden, unexpected early retirement. Was he collateral caught in the fallout or an unlucky bystander?

The more pieces I shuffled across the puzzle board of conspiracy theories in my mind, the more murky it all became.

"I'm missing something," I muttered, tapping a pen

against my lip, then flipping through the printed documents again. Under the stack I'd been rifling through were a set Estelle must have dropped on my desk the night before. I glanced at them…then glanced again. "Wait…what is this?"

My phone vibrated. Wesley's name and serious professional head shot lit up the screen. It was a photo I had seen a thousand times before, but seeing it now made me smile so wide it was embarrassing. It gave away every thought I held about him since our relationship had taken a turn from possibility into a reality.

Since I'd acknowledged that we were entangled in something more profound than friendship, I ended up at his house more often than mine. We hadn't been apart long enough to miss each other, but I compulsively snatched up the phone like we hadn't spoken in days.

"What do you want, Payne?" I murmured into the phone, though my tone carried more affection than annoyance.

"For you to stop leaving the house without giving me my kiss," he promptly replied.

"I kissed you, fool," I shot back in kind, an eye roll accompanying my words despite him not being there to witness it. "You were dead asleep and I didn't want to wake you up. I, uh…I know I wore you out last night."

"Here you go with that all that noise," he grumbled. "Pretty sure you were the one who was delirious."

His teasing brought flashes of the evening to mind. "I'm sorry, I should have known you would be worried."

"I need to know if you're leaving the house, Yvette. Even if I'm asleep. Not on some checking in shit, but how I'm supposed to protect your ass and I don't know where your ass is?"

"I *said* I was sorry—"

"What am I supposed to tell Mr. Young if something happens to you while you're out in the city at God knows what time of the morning?"

"You had no complaints when I had a bush up my ass at midnight to catch Marcel Simeon cheating—"

"I knew where you were and I paid you to be there. You've been doing this shit all week, dipping out at dawn because you can't shut your brain off."

He wasn't wrong, which I both appreciated and slightly resented. His intuition about me was almost surgical, peeling back the layers I preferred to keep concealed. It was comfortable under his wing, but that left me with no place to hide except inside my restless mind, which was on a timed release. Even if I wasn't awake, my mind was, and it would harass me until my body joined the party.

"This case is important, Vette, but don't let it eat you alive. And don't let it make you make poor decisions."

"My ass and brain are fine. This case is driving me up a wall, though. I feel like I'm running out of time to find this man. I just keep going in circles. Same information leading to the same dead ends. Where the *fuck* are they? Is Edward alive? Is he with Carmela or did we just make that up and run with it because it sounds good?"

"Your gut is usually right about these things," he soothed. "Use your investigative instinct. There's no such thing as a coincidence, remember? If you didn't think there was something connecting them, you wouldn't be obsessing like this. But maybe you're looking too close. Pull back some."

"I have pulled back. And pulled forward and dug in and extrapolated from every damn angle," I said, but I closed my eyes and pinched the bridge of my nose.

Wesley was right, as usual. I tended to hit the same nail harder if it didn't budge the first time, mistaking being stubborn for being thorough.

"There's got to be a trail. If you don't do anything else well, you can pick up a scent."

I rubbed my temples where an ache was building. I was

hesitant to mention it to Wesley because he would grill me about eating food and drinking water.

"Maybe you're right and I'm overthinking it. Maybe there really is nothing there. Maybe he really is dead somewhere and we just haven't located his bones."

"Maybe. Or...maybe you're the first person to look hard enough at the details to see the connections you see."

I sighed, blowing out a hard breath that was supposed to regulate my nervous system but did nothing of the sort. Pausing, I phrased the next sentence in my mind—how to bring up the topic that had been weighing on me since the night before.

The *other* reason I didn't sleep well and crept out of bed before dawn.

"So...my mother called last night."

"Mmmhmmm," he replied, sounding distracted. In the background, the coffee grinder whirred. "What she need?"

"Mostly a listening ear, now that I'm not there to regulate Yancey, but...she wants to know when you're coming to dinner so they can properly meet you. And full disclosure, they intend to interrogate you."

"Dinner at Valerie Young's table?" he practically squealed. "Say less!"

"I knew you would say that."

Wesley had chatted with my parents several times in passing but had never spent time with them and had certainly not sat at our dinner table. This was the height of approval from Michael and Valerie Young and I heard the utter joy in his voice. I was touched that he wanted to take this step with my parents. Wesley and I had been through a lot together, but meeting the family was crossing into new territory.

"What did you tell her?"

"That I'd ask you. It's a trap, though. I'm never home anymore and Daddy keeps muttering that my apartment isn't a storage unit to keep things I'm not using while I sleep else-where. And I know Yancey is in their ear about moving up there."

"It's up to you, baby. I'm a world-class litigator. They don't scare me. It'll be a dress rehearsal for dinner with my folks."

I sighed. I did not sign up for all of this. "I know *you're* ready for that gauntlet—"

"And I know *you're* not," he finished. "And don't ask me how I know. I've known Yvette Young for—"

"A very long time." I smiled. For Wesley, it was as if the years we'd known each other were a training ground. I had probably spent more time with Wesley than Jason, to be honest. And I couldn't say Jason ever knew parts of me as well as Wesley did.

"Hey, are you coming this way, by chance?" I asked, changing the subject. I was not in the mood to go down the path of meet-the-parents logistics.

"I could be. Why?"

I scoffed. "To see me. Come get that kiss you won't shut up about and walk through this case with me."

"Mmmm…" I knew he was looking at his watch, scrolling his calendar. I also knew he had a light day at the office—it was the only reason he was still at home—and would end up at my office anyway at some point. "I can come through. I know you haven't eaten—I hear it in your voice. I'm gonna roll by Bomb Biscuits on the way."

I pretended to faint even though he couldn't see me. I hadn't had a hot, fresh biscuit sandwich from the popular breakfast and lunch cafe in over a year. "I might be falling for you, Wesley Payne."

He was silent for a time that stretched just over a heart-beat, long enough that I wasn't sure if the call dropped. I'd caught him off guard; I was afraid he might be scrambling for what to say. I was uneasy, like I had misstepped or overestimated where we were in our relationship.

"You think you *might be* falling?" He scoffed, petulant. "Woman, I'm counting the days until you admit you been in love with me. I'll see you in a bit."

———

AN HOUR LATER, Wesley pushed through the door carrying a bag from Bomb Biscuits that smelled so good, it made my stomach growl. My headache was definitely hunger-induced.

"I brought the leftovers from last night too," he said, greeting Estelle and Nia as he headed to the kitchen. He began unpacking containers, placing the dish of Fox Bros signature smoked brisket we'd had last night in the microwave. While the machine hummed and rotated, Wesley came to stand in the door to my office, leaning a hip against the frame.

He was as casual as a downtown Atlanta lawyer could get. His crisp white shirt was rolled up at the sleeves, revealing strong forearms. His black slacks fit him like a glove and hugged him in every good place. I tried not to stare, but it was hard when he looked so good.

"'Sup, gorgeous?" he said, giving me a flirty nod of his head.

I was sure I appeared as ragged as I felt in sweats, a Spelman t-shirt that I stole from my mother, and my hair pulled into a puff.

"You don't have to suck up to me anymore, Payne."

He crossed the threshold and in a few steps was bending over me. He pressed his lips to my hair, then my forehead, then found my mouth. "I was never sucking up, Young."

"That was more than one kiss," I said, but angled my head up for one last peck.

When he straightened, he said, "Reparations," and left again to attend to the beeping microwave. He returned with plates piled with sauced brisket and hot biscuits, dropping one in front of me. Wesley settled in a chair on the other side of my desk, watching me eat while he glanced over the scattered documents.

"Walk me through what you're trying to put together."

I swallowed before jumping into the three-ring circus I'd invented in my office.

"Okay, so—" I spread out what I had. "A thing that might be promising is that Estelle found some property records that shows one company *not* tied to First Southeast. It's tied to Marcus Verona and is also tied to several properties in different states. All managed through an LLC."

"Hmmm. Investment properties?"

"Maybe." I plucked the records and laid them out in front of him in a row. "A cabin in Montana on a few acres. A couple of properties in Oregon. Farm land in north Idaho."

"That's a lot of real estate for a retired banker."

"Right? An interesting collection in relatively remote areas. And the timing is curious." I pointed to the dates of purchase. "The Oregon properties? One of them closed almost a year and the other four months before Edward disappeared."

Wesley sighed, running his tongue over his teeth. "Looking at things from the time Carmela quit her job and got out of dodge, that last property was purchased three months before she took off. That's enough time to get utilities hooked up and outfit it to be a secure location. If you needed it to be."

"That's what I was thinking, too…" My eyes flicked up to Wesley's.

"You think that's where they are."

"At the very least, I think that's where Marcus stashed his daughter. Whether Edward is also there is a question, but like you said…coincidences are rare. I think Marcus knew something was coming down the pipeline and was preparing to disappear. Except Carmela needed to go first, and he couldn't just up and relocate. It would draw suspicion."

I pulled up satellite images on my laptop, turning the screen so Wesley could see. "That last property in Oregon is on three acres with private road access that butts up to a thicket of trees. The nearest neighbor is probably a mile down the road and they're likely thirty minutes from civilization."

"Remote enough to hide, close enough to be in the mix if they need to be," Wesley mused.

"I just sent that utilities report!" Estelle called from her desk.

I checked my email and clicked on the enclosed PDF. "So, I asked Estelle to ask a friend to do some digging on the utilities on these places." I scanned, feeling my eyes pop open wide. "And look—"

Wesley got up, moving around the desk to view the screen. "What are we looking at?"

"The property has active power, water, and broadband services. Internet was activated almost a year ago. And there hasn't been an interruption in service since it was turned on."

"Do any of the other properties have power, water, internet?"

I checked the other attachments. "Power and water at the Montana and Idaho locations. But I don't see a broadband connection. They could be using satellite but I doubt it. I don't see any surges on the other properties. This one Oregon property near Newport must be lit up like a Christmas tree."

"This kind of power usage isn't just keeping the lights on. Someone's living there." Wesley stood abruptly, energy radiating off him. "They're there. Gotta be."

I clicked to another report. "Property taxes are all current. They all still belong to him."

I felt the pieces clicking into place in my mind—the shell

companies, the fraudulent materials, the missing inspector. Marcus Verona's properties. It was all one big, mottled operation.

"What if..." I folded my arms across my chest and leaned my head back against the cushioned seat. "What if Barrett didn't know there was a connection between Carmela quitting and moving away and Edward disappearing? We didn't until you got that call from Anjelica's brother."

Wesley's bottom lip curled. "He can't find Edward because he's looking for one man in hiding—"

"Not two people being hidden by someone that knew he'd be looking for them."

Wesley pulled out his phone. "We need to get to Oregon. I hate to tip anyone off, but we need eyes on the ground and some backup."

He stepped outside with his phone, his voice dropping as he started talking. I watched him through Estelle's window, gesturing as he spoke, building his case with whoever was on the other end.

In just a few weeks, we'd gone from searching for a dead-beat dad to uncovering what could be a massive criminal conspiracy. Somewhere on the Oregon coast, Edward Foster and Carmela Verona could be hiding the truth that could blow everything wide open. If we could find them before Barrett did.

Wesley returned, tucking his phone away. "You up for a road trip?"

"Sure, but Oregon's too far for driving. I suggest we fly."

"Smart ass. Flight leaves at 7 a.m. Can you handle that?"

I was already mentally cataloging what I'd need to pack. I hadn't been on a real stakeout in years; I had missed the thrill, the adrenaline, the whirlwind of processes and information that wove complex patterns in my mind.

"You keeping up on target practice, Payne?"

He frowned, appearing offended. "Who you talking to?

Sig P226, same one I trained on. I'm not new to this, I'm true to this."

"Alright, Rambo." I started gathering the documents, sorting them into my bag. "Pack it. We might need more than your sunny disposition on this one."

Wesley's expression hardened. "I really don't like the sound of that."

"Neither do I. But let's be safe."

"I'll work on flights and hotel," Wesley said.

"No, I will work on hotel. You'll have us at the damn Four Seasons."

"Fine. Pack cold clothes. The Oregon coast is cold this time of year."

"Will you just worry about yourself, Payne? Remember when I had to handle that investigation—by myself, mind you—at Ft. Drum? I know how to dress for cold."

Ft. Drum, New York was practically Canada. I spent two weeks in February investigating a staff sergeant suspected of running drugs through the mailroom and using military postal privileges to distribute narcotics off-base. The heating system in the building kept failing and I spent long nights reviewing testimony in a freezing office. Biting winds, waist-high snow, and temperatures that made your face hurt every time I had to walk between buildings on post.

The Oregon coast in October didn't scare me.

"You were not alone, Young. I was there." Wesley handled the administrative separation proceedings after I gathered the evidence.

"For like...five minutes. I was there for *weeks*."

"Poor thing." He smiled, but concern lingered in his eyes. "I need to clear my calendar for the next few days. I'll see you at home."

I watched him head for the door, eyes tracing the way his shirt pulled across his broad back, how he moved for a man his size--built like a linebacker, and somehow still graceful.

I'll see you at home rushed over me like a tidal wave. We'd spent the night together, shared breakfast, made plans to leave the state and spend several days together—and I didn't want him to leave my office right now.

It was ridiculous is what it was.

This is what happens when you let yourself feel things.

We were getting the band back together. Travel, investigation, long days in unfamiliar towns. Just like old times... except now we didn't have to pretend we didn't want each other.

After he left, I looked again at the satellite images of the isolated Oregon property. For three years, Edward and Carmela had been protected by Marcus's foresight and Barrett's inability to connect the dots. And by the fact that no one had ever looked at them as anything but runaways.

We were looking now. And Barrett wasn't the only one closing in. The truth couldn't stay buried forever and one way or another, we were going to dig it up.

"Stelle!" I called, sweeping the pages across my desk into a stack. "The Oregon lead is looking promising. Payne and I are headed out there. I'm going to need all my camera batteries and cords packed up."

"Alright, honey," she answered. "I know your mama ain't raised no fool. Keep your head on a swivel out there. You're taking the Glock, right?"

CHAPTER
SEVENTEEN

WESLEY

"I STILL SAY we should have gone with the Four Seasons," I muttered, striding alongside Yvette into the lobby of The Nines Portland, rolling our suitcases along each side of me.

"This spot is nicer, believe it or not. There are better security cameras and staff that mind their business. Even if they saw us, they didn't see us."

She had a point. The staff certainly didn't question our story about a couple scouting investment properties. Once the clerk at check-in saw my Platinum card, he practically tripped over himself upgrading us to a suite with a view.

Once we were alone in the elevator, Yvette's facade dropped. "Estelle said two locations are clustered near Newport, one's further up the coast near Astoria. Both are small coastal towns. Astoria is way up north near the Washington border, more tourist traffic. Newport is farther south—quieter, easier to disappear."

"What's your gut say?"

Yvette pondered. "Astoria's exposed," she said. "Tourist

town, lots of traffic. They could blend in, though. Newport is isolated, especially out on the peninsula. I think I want to check Newport first."

"Makes sense." The elevator dinged and she led the way down the plush hallway. "Didn't Stelle's utility records show more consistent usage there?"

I followed Yvette into the suite, letting out a low whistle at the panoramic windows and upscale furnishings. "Nick's going to have a heart attack when he sees the expense report."

"Add it to the tab." Yvette dropped her bags and made a beeline for the desk, pulling out her laptop. "Usage logs show both Newport properties are drawing power, but one's using a shit ton of bandwidth."

I removed my jacket moving to look over her shoulder at the data. "Remote work, maybe?"

"That's my guess. Carmela has the kind of skills where she can work anywhere as a contractor. She probably does freelance accounting or something similar." She pulled up satellite imagery, tapping on a location. "This property has the best security setup. Restricted access road, clear sight lines."

"The kind of place you'd choose if you were hiding but could escape if necessary," I finished.

"Exactly." She zoomed in on the image. "We should do a drive-by, get the lay of the land. Then tomorrow—"

"*Tonight* we rest," I cut in firmly. "We've been up since four and flying all day. We need clear heads and fresh eyes. We won't even be able to see anything by the time we get there."

She'd started to protest but was cut off by a yawn. "Oh… man. Guess I'm beat."

I couldn't help smiling. Even Yvette Young had limits, though she'd never admit it.

"Fine," she conceded. "But first thing tomorrow—"

"First thing tomorrow, we'll check out both properties. Carefully." I caught her hand, tugging her away from the laptop. "First thing tonight, you need food and sleep."

She let me pull her close, melting against me in a way she never used to and I welcomed. "I only get room service when Courtney & Payne is paying the bill."

"I'll take care of it," I said, though the words came out as little more than a distracted mumble. I caught her lips in a kiss that would have been brief but lingered longer because it could. "Grab a shower, get comfortable."

"Or…" she began, letting the single syllable float between us, tilting her head up so I could see the devious gleam in her eye. "We could share the shower. Save water. Very environmentally conscious."

Heat pooled in my belly, the kind that made rational thought impossible. "Vette…" I warned before my body and mind could take over.

"You're not interested?" Her fingers toyed with the button on my jeans. The zipper coming down echoed in my ear. "You loved shower sex yesterday," she murmured, her lips brushing the stubble along my jaw.

The past few days flashed across my mind, the way things had shifted between us. I couldn't seem to get enough of her now that I'd had a taste. It didn't take much to tempt me as far as Yvette was concerned.

"You know damn well I'm interested," I managed, my throat tight as her hand slipped inside my jeans. "You need to pace yourself. You know how you get to begging and I don't like to rush."

She shivered slightly, pupils dilating. "Promise?"

"Clock it." I pulled her hand away from the already hard length she'd been stroking. Sighing, I stepped back before I lost my resolve. We had all night. "Go. I'll deal with room service."

She opened her suitcase, plucking a small case from it

before heading to the bathroom. Soon, the sound of running water filled the suite, along with her voice drifting out, unmelodiously offering backup to some GloRilla track.

Yvette should not quit her day job.

While she showered, I finished setting up our makeshift command center with both of our laptops, phones, tablets, files and notes. I texted Nick; he admonished me to be careful and stay vigilant. We had to assume Barrett had eyes everywhere and he could be following us to get close to Edward. One wrong move could blow this whole operation.

A knock announced room service. I tipped generously and was arranging the covered dishes when Yvette emerged wearing sleep shorts and one of my t-shirts, her hair wrapped carefully in a multicolored silk scarf. She sat cross-legged on the bed, pulling out tubes and containers of serums and elixirs from her toiletry kit.

"You're staring," she said, smoothing cream over her face.

"Can you blame me?" I asked, watching her like she wasn't killing me softly. "You took a long shower. Is there any hot water left?"

Yvette grinned. "Give it a few. You will appreciate the benefits of an everything shower later."

"An...*everything* shower?"

"Yes. Clean, exfoliate, shave, deep condition, moisturize..." Yvette ticked each step off on her fingers, voice trailing as she caught me staring, not even trying to hide the way I was thinking about her naked and glistening under a spray of water.

"Huh. I'm inspired."

And honestly, I was. The ritual of it, the discipline, the tease of knowing my partner would enjoy me that much more was worth the effort.

By the time I emerged from the bathroom in a t-shirt and boxer briefs, she had finished her routine and was ready to dive into the meal I had ordered from the hotel restaurant,

Urban Farmer. Herb roasted chicken and grilled vegetables with rice for Vette, Oregon grass-fed ribeye and fingerling potatoes for me, and a dark chocolate brownie with vanilla bean ice cream and salted caramel sauce to share.

"You're staring again," she said, after she had inhaled most of her dinner in minutes. The habit of eating quickly when you had the chance while on active duty was a difficult one to break.

"I'm *looking*," I said, somewhere between a confession and a cover. "And thinking."

"I want to think too," she shot back. "What about?"

"Germany, believe it or not." I stabbed a steak chunk and watched her eyes flicker, searching my face for the catch.

Her expression softened. "Have I mentioned that you were an ass?"

"A couple times. I think once with a PowerPoint presentation."

"*Special Agent Young, I expect you to interview every soldier on post about this case if need be!*" She mimicked my voice, making it deeper and more officious than it actually was.

"That case was a shit show from the get-go. But aye, all I hear is my name still holds weight."

Yvette rolled her eyes, but the corners of her mouth twitched upward. "Clearly your ego was not impacted."

"Never has been, never will be."

She speared a broccoli floret and pointed it at me. "You made me a better investigator, though. With your asshole self."

"You do the same for me."

Her smile turned genuine then, a flash of white teeth against deep brown skin. "I don't know about all that."

I popped the last of my steak into my mouth, sopping up the juices with the remaining fingerling potatoes. "You keep me honest. You don't let me get away with my usual bullshit."

"Holding you accountable is the fun part."

"We make a good team. We don't run from shit and we keep each other on the up and up. That's how I know we're going to crack this case."

She nodded, but worry lines showed up between her brows. She moved on to the dessert, scooping up a spoonful of brownie. "I mean... Technically, we just have to prove Edward is alive, right?" She spooned the brownie into her mouth and talked around it. "What if they don't want to be found? What if staying hidden is the only thing keeping them alive?"

"We figure out how to protect them. Get them into witness protection. Build a case against Barrett..." I set down my plate and scooted next to her. "But we have to find them."

"We have to consider that Barrett has people already watching the properties."

"That's why we brought hardware." I kissed her temple. "Let's worry about that tomorrow, though."

"Good idea." She set her plate aside and turned to face me, draping her legs over my lap. "What should we worry about tonight?"

I slid my hands up the inside of her bare, moisturized, tempting thighs and kept moving north until she twitched. "I can think of a few things to keep us occupied."

"Show me," she said, smoothing her palms across my chest, then lower until her fingertips hovered at my waistband.

If this was a test of patience and control, I lost.

I slid my hands under her thighs and lifted her onto my lap. Her mouth was insistent as it melded to mine, tongue probing, teasing, then pulling away, dragging out satisfaction for as long as she could manage. The flavor of chocolate and caramel lingered on her lips as she bit mine, tugging just hard enough to make me remember how easily pleasure and pain could become indistinguishable.

She pulled up the hem of my shirt with her eyes locked on mine like she was waiting to see if I'd stop her. "You love this, huh?" she whispered, lips brushing my ear, pushing the shirt up further until I took over, yanking it off completely. "Letting me feel like I can tear you apart."

"Affirmative. Give it your best shot."

Yvette laughed against my mouth, the sound vibrating through my chest. Her fingers traced the defined ridges of my six-pack. "You really would like that, Payne. You're not slick."

"I'm not trying to be, Vette. I really want you to wreck my shit tonight."

She traced my jawline with her fingertips, eyelids at half-mast. "Your wish is my command, Major."

The way my former title rolled off her tongue sent a lick of excitement up my back, almost like we had traveled back in time to the nights when I wished I could have her. My pulse quickened at the thought of Special Agent Yvette Young beneath me, breaking the chain of command and every regulation in the book.

She took my hands and guided them under her shirt—my shirt—letting me feel the softness of her skin, the firmness of her muscles underneath. No bra. Just Yvette, warm and real against my palms.

I pushed the fabric up, revealing her inch by creamy, delicious inch. The sight of her never failed to leave me hard, even after these past few days of discovery. Her body was a landscape I was still learning—the dip of her waist, the swell of her breasts, the lumps and scars and imperfections that made her so fucking perfect.

I lowered my head to taste her skin, savoring the gentle slope of her neck, the hollow of her collarbone. She sighed, her head falling back as I traced my tongue along her shoulder down to the swell of her breast. When I took her nipple into my mouth, she gasped, fingers clutching at my shoulders.

"Wesley," she breathed. My name on her lips was more than I could take.

I pulled back just enough to meet her eyes, seeing my own need reflected there. "Bed?"

She nodded, then laughed in surprise as I stood and scooped her up.

"Showoff," she teased. "This is why you're pushing four hundred pounds on the sled in the gym, huh?"

"I'm just saying... I have transferable skills."

I carried her to the bed and laid her down, trailing kisses along her neck and collarbone.

Yvette flipped us—I *let* Yvette flip us. Giddy, she laughed, straddling my hips and pinning my wrists.

"What you doin' up there, Vette?"

"You told me I could wreck your shit," she said.

"You got me," I whispered, relaxing beneath her body weight. "What you gonna do with me?"

She released my wrists to pull my boxers down. I kicked them off eagerly. Her eyes raked over me with appreciation that never failed to boost my ego.

"Damn, Payne." She trailed her fingers along my erect length. "Impressive."

"You say that every time."

"Just...appreciative. Every time."

When she took me into her mouth, I hissed, fingers digging into the sheets. She knew exactly how to work me, alternating between teasing licks and taking me deep, almost down her throat. Her hands followed the rhythm of her mouth and the way she was moaning, I had to fight myself to not fuck her face.

"Jesus, Vette..." I reached for her, trying to grip her, but my fingers slipped against the silk scarf covering her hair. "You're going to end this before it starts."

Yvette pulled off with a smirk. "Stick to the plan, Payne."

She shot me a wicked grin before returning to her task

with renewed enthusiasm. The sight of her—eyes closed in concentration, cheeks hollowed—sent fire racing through me. I settled on gripping the back of her neck, needing the connection as pressure built at the base of my spine.

"I'm close," I warned.

She hummed acknowledgment but didn't stop, working me with her hand and mouth until I couldn't hold back anymore.

"God*damn*...shit! Fuck, I'm comin'!"

I groaned her name as she worked me through it, only pulling away when I was spent and oversensitive.

She wiped her mouth with the back of her hand, looking pleased with herself.

I chuckled, wiping beads of sweat from my forehead. "Guess you think you wrecked something, huh?"

"Oh, you must think I'm done. At ease, Payne."

I watched as she stood and shimmied out of her sleep shorts, then moved up my body. She straddled me, this time hovering just above where I wanted her most. "Tell me what you want, Wesley."

"What I *want*? Or what I *need*?"

"Same thing at this point, right?"

I laughed. "I keep forgetting you can read me, Vette. Okay, then." I inhaled...then went for it. "Right now, I need you to sit on this dick and ride it while I suck your titties until you come all over it. Can you complete the mission?"

"Yes, sir."

She reached between us, guiding me to her entrance, slick and warm. When she sank down, taking me inch by inch, both our mouths dropped open in a groan. Her eyes fluttered closed, head tilting back as she adjusted to the feel of me inside her.

"*Fuuuuck*," she moaned, beginning to move, setting a maddeningly slow pace. "Damn, you feel good."

I gripped her hips to steady her as she rocked, rolling in a rhythm that made my toes curl. The sight of her above me—deep brown skin glistening, full breasts with big areolas bouncing—had been a fevered dream for so long I almost didn't believe we were really here in our relationship. I'd fantasized about Yvette riding me but the reality of it made me faint.

I let her control the pace, watching her face contort with pleasure, feeling her thighs tense around me.

"Yeah...ride it, baby," I encouraged, my voice rough. "Take this dick. Take what you need."

She leaned forward, bracing her hands on my chest. I seized the opportunity, capturing one of her nipples between my lips, swirling my tongue around the peak. She cried out, her inner walls clenching around me.

"Unnnhhhh...yeah," she grunted, grinding down harder, faster. "Just like that."

I switched to her other breast, showering attention on the neglected nipple while my hands gripped her ass. Her rhythm faltered as she chased her climax, eyes squeezed shut, bottom lip caught between her teeth. I slid one hand between us, my thumb finding her clit and circling it.

"Wesley!" Her eyes popped open wide and her pelvis jerked in response. "Shit! Shit! Shit! I'm gonna come!"

"I know, baby. I feel you. Your pussy is milking me good. Your thighs are shaking. Let it go. Come for me."

When she fell apart, it was glorious. She stiffened and yelped, her inner walls clamping down on me like a vise. I held her through it, whispering encouragement as she rode it out.

Before she could recover, I flipped us, careful not to slip out of her. Her eyes widened in surprise as I settled between her open thighs. I braced myself on my forearms, pleased at her flushed face.

"What happened...to letting me wreck your shit?" she asked, breathless.

"I'm a team player," I replied, rolling my hips slowly, teasing her with a slow withdrawal. "Got to get the job done, Young."

I started a deliberate rhythm, watching her expression shift with each thrust.

Her fingers dug into my ass, pulling me closer as I deepened my strokes. The slow, gentle rocking became faster, more urgent, the bed frame creaking beneath us as I drove into her.

"Fuck, yes...Wesley," she gasped, her legs wrapping tight around me. "Yes, baby! God, yes!"

Every inch of me was alive with sensation, hypersensitive and hungry for her. I pressed my forehead to hers, watching her face contort as she drew closer to her orgasm.

"You feel so *fucking* good, Yvette," I groaned, my voice ragged, barely recognizable as mine. "So good. So tight. So wet. So warm."

I lost all sense of composure, rutting into her with abandon, chasing the high of her body wrapped around me. I needed to fill her, to fulfill her, to mark her. I needed us to melt together until there was no longer me and her—it was just us. Forever.

She clung to me, her thighs locked tight at my hips. Her walls fluttered around me, the prelude to her release.

"Come with me," I demanded as my climax approached.

I was dimly aware of her chanting my name, her body arching and convulsing beneath mine. Watching her—eyes squeezed shut, mouth hanging open in ecstasy—took me out. I hunched forward, burying myself deep, and followed her into oblivion. We spiraled out together, clutching and clinging to one another as we rode to the edge.

Afterward, I collapsed beside her, completely spent, heart jackhammering an erratic beat. I wrapped my arms around her and pulled her across the bed, up against me.

"The way we just disrespected the fuck out of these sheets," I said.

Yvette snorted, her giggles vibrating against my chest. We lay there, a mess of sweat and limbs, neither of us making any move to fix the aftermath like drying off or straightening the sheets or covering up nakedness.

After a lifetime of order, the chaos felt good.

"Couldn't be helped," she mumbled, her lips brushing my skin. "I follow orders to the letter." She yawned, then kissed a spot just above my breastbone before nuzzling her cheek into me.

"You absolutely do." I ran the tips of my fingers down her back. Her skin was starting to cool and goosebumps were cascading across the expanse of her skin.

I shifted, pulling her more fully on top of me, tucking the top sheet around us as best I could. She let me, pretending to protest, but I already knew Yvette's secret: she liked being coddled. Taken care of.

I looked down at her, scarf just barely hanging on, her face bare, lips chapped from being ravaged by mine. She grinned, lazy and unguarded, then reached up to poke my cheek with her finger.

"You're staring *again*."

"I'm looking."

"Why you *looking* at me like that?"

I shrugged. "It's still weird to wake up with you in the bed after wanting that for so long. I'm always trying to figure out if I'm dreaming. And if I am dreaming, I don't want to wake up."

She made a scoffing sound, then traced her finger from the bridge of my nose down to my lips, pressing there as if to say hush.

"If you're dreaming, we are in the same dream, Payne."

We lay there for a while, saying nothing, trading little touches and half-baked jokes and commentary on the local evening news. The heat in the room settled, sweat cooling on our skin, but still, she didn't move away.

I pulled her tighter, palm splayed on her lower back. "You were well worth the wait," I said out of nowhere, but not really.

She smiled, shy, then curled into me. Her breathing deepened, soft and steady.

And I lay awake, holding her, already planning how to keep her safe tomorrow.

CHAPTER
EIGHTEEN

YVETTE

WESLEY HAD PARKED our rental SUV on a graveled turnout facing the target house. We had a dash-mounted camera recording everything through the telephoto lens and a mounted iPhone logging timestamped footage for review later.

"What's our story if someone stops to ask questions?" I asked, peering through the lens of my trusty Canon Rebel. It was more portable than my Nikon.

"We're just a friendly middle-class couple from California, exploring spots for our future retirement," Wesley said, fidgeting in the driver's seat. "We absolutely adore birds. Really, we just can't get enough of them."

I gestured to the Peterson's Guide conspicuously displayed on the dash. "That's the story you came up with? What kind of birds are we even looking for?"

"Tufted puffins, obviously. This is a known nesting spot." He grinned over at me, looking smug. "I may have done some research while you were in the shower this morning."

"Showoff." But I was impressed.

"How's your view of the house?"

"Perfect sight lines to both floors through those trees. But we'll need to move soon before someone notices we've been here too long."

I focused the camera on the cabin, the lens calibrated to cut through the early haze rolling in from the Pacific. The property was isolated but not suspiciously so—exactly the kind of place wealthy tech workers bought for weekend getaways. It backed up to public forest land, thick with pines and steep drop-offs that made it easier to vanish on foot. Access roads provided escape routes. Solar panels suggested they could live off-grid if needed. Professional-grade security cameras covered every approach.

"Motion sensors on all the walkways," I noted, zooming in. "Those cameras probably feed to an internal server, not cloud storage. Harder to hack."

"Someone's learned about security since they disappeared."

I was about to respond when movement caught my eye. A figure passed the large kitchen window—female, medium height, hair cropped in a stylish bob and colored a warm honey blonde. Different from the yearbook photos, but the bone structure was unmistakable.

"Got her," I said under my breath, firing off a rapid series of shots. "Kitchen window. That's definitely Carmela."

Wesley leaned closer to study my camera's display screen. "You're sure? Hair's totally different."

"Good dye job, but that's her." I zoomed in as she moved to the sink. "She's altered her appearance but not enough to hide basic features."

"What's she doing?"

"Talking to someone off-camera." I kept shooting as Carmela disappeared from view. "They're living a regular life here. Just…hidden."

Wesley was quiet for a moment. "Hard to imagine walking away from everything, starting over completely."

I lowered the camera, rolling my stiff shoulders. "Question is, do we really want to drag them back to the life they left?"

"We just need to prove Edward's alive. After that..." Wesley shrugged. "Maybe we can help protect them instead of exposing them."

A silver Tacoma drove past for the second time since we arrived earlier that morning. The driver kept his eyes straight ahead, too deliberately casual.

"Clock that truck again," I mumbled, lifting the camera and switching to burst mode to catch the plates if it passed again.

"Maybe Barrett has people watching the property already."

"Could be. We should move soon. Even with the birding cover, we've been here too long." I froze as motion caught my eye. "Movement. Kitchen window again."

But this time it wasn't Carmela. A tall figure—male, broad-shouldered. He paused, head turning toward our position.

"Edward?" Wesley asked.

"Has to be." I snapped a few photos. "He's lost weight, looks fit."

"So they're still together. Still hiding together after almost four years."

"They don't have any choice but to be together. If we're right, Carmela's father is financing this. Edward has nothing if he leaves."

This wasn't just a man who'd abandoned his family. This was something bigger, something that had forced both Edward and Carmela to rebuild their lives in secret.

"We need to move," I said after a long span of time with no movement in the house. "This spot is stale and that truck's making me nervous. We can come back later, try a different—"

A tap on my window made us both jump. I spun, hand instinctively reaching for my weapon. Then I realized I was face-to-face with Edward Foster.

He looked harder than his photos, leaner, weathered, staring right into my window. A Ruger Mini-14 hunting rifle rested in his hands. His eyes, cold and evaluating, studied us through the glass.

"Roll down the window," he said quietly. "Nice and slow."

I glanced at Wesley, who gave a slight nod. I pressed the button and the window lowered with a soft hum.

"Hands where I can see them. Both of you." Edward positioned himself just behind the hinge of my door—smart angle, hard to disarm and harder to predict. "The camera too. Pass it over. Slowly."

I did as he asked, watching him examine it one-handed while keeping the rifle trained in our general direction. His expression darkened as he scrolled through the photos.

"Did Barrett send you?" The question was casual but his finger had shifted closer to the trigger.

"No," Wesley said. "Your wife hired us to find you."

An emotion flickered across Edward's face—a tiny, involuntary flash.

"Your father's dying," Wesley added. "It's bad. Late-stage pancreatic cancer. He's not expected to make it through the year."

Edward's jaw clenched. "I know all about the will," he bit out. "I figured he'd just add the boys, but this is his way of bringing me out of hiding. I can't just pop up alive and well to make sure Anjelica gets her money."

"That works for Eileen. She wants you declared dead so she doesn't have to share."

Edward's laugh held no humor. "Of course. Eileen hates

Anjelica. Anjelica isn't too big of a fan of Eileen either, but she'd be willing to get along for the boys. Can't believe my sister would cut her nephews out."

"Anjelica just wants her sons taken care of," Wesley countered. "They're growing up without their father."

"They're *alive*," Edward snapped, voice pitched low and teeming with an anger he barely bothered to restrain. He was still pointing the rifle at us, but his attention had shifted, for a moment, to the woods behind our car. "Which is a hell of a lot better than the alternative."

He gave us each a look, assessing. "Who are you people?"

"This is Yvette Young," said Wesley. "She's a private investigator I use a lot. I'm Wesley Payne, an attorney."

"You got ID?"

"Sure. We can—"

"Slow!" he yelled, holding up his free hand as Wesley reached for his wallet.

I watched him examine our credentials, noting how his hands remained steady on both the rifle and the IDs. This was not the same man who'd walked away from his family four years ago. That Edward had been soft and impulsive.

This Edward was thin, lithe, wiry. He moved like someone used to looking over his shoulder.

"We've found a lot of evidence that suggests there's more to this story than a man walking out on his family," I said carefully. "Edward, let us help you."

He studied us for a long moment, then said, "The only thing that'll satisfy Barrett is a body. If I have to go, fine. But not without taking him with me."

I kept my eyes on the rifle, but my tone was calm. "Look, we're not bounty hunters. We don't have to give your exact location, just confirm you're alive. That's all your wife really wants out of this. If you want us out of your life, you'll never see us again. But if you're interested in not hiding out anymore and Barrett getting what he deserves, there's a better way to end this."

I tried to sound less like a cop, more like a confessor. "I know you've been running, and you have to be tired. I know you believe you have good reason to hide. At some point, don't you want to live a normal life again? Don't your sons deserve to know you, to hear why their father left, in his own words?"

Edward's gaze flicked from the woods to me, and for a second I saw the exhaustion in his posture. "You think you're going to solve this with a couple phone calls and some forms?"

"It'll take some work, but I know people, Edward," Wesley picked up. "I can get someone with a badge to listen, to take Barrett and all of his companies down. To get protection for you and your family. Carmela, too."

"Out of the car," Edward said after contemplating for a few moments. "Both of you. Keep your hands visible."

We complied, gravel crunching under our feet as we stepped away from the vehicle.

"Weapons?"

"On my hip," I admitted. "Wesley's wearing his, too. A few extra pieces in our bags in the trunk."

Edward nodded toward the car. "Grab your bags, pull the weapons out. Slowly. Eject the magazines and clear the chambers."

Once we'd disarmed, some of the tension left his shoulders, but the rifle didn't waver.

"You said Barrett's looking for us? How do you know?"

"Heard it underground," Wesley confirmed. "It's only a matter of time before he finds this place."

"Probably Tony," he mused. "And you probably led him straight to us."

"We figured we might, but we also hoped we'd find you

first," I countered. "Whatever you found at Miller Creek—whatever made you run—let us help you fight it."

"Fight?" Edward's laugh was bitter. "You don't fight people like Barrett. You survive them. Or you die trying."

His eyes found a focal point on something behind us.

We turned to find Carmela standing at the edge of the trees, a compact Glock 43X held steadily in a two-hand grip. Like Edward, she'd changed in four years—harder, slimmer.

"They need to go, Ed."

"Wait." Wesley stepped forward, freezing when both weapons tracked his movement. "You've stayed hidden this long and we're not here to blow your cover, but there's more happening here than meets the eye. There's a criminal conspiracy and you're holding a big key. We want to help you. On your terms."

Edward and Carmela exchanged a long look, years of unspoken communication passing between them.

"Trust gets people killed," Carmela said finally. "We'd rather not learn that lesson the hard way."

"You trusted your father to help you hide," I pointed out. "Trust us to get you in touch with people who can keep you safe. We might be your only chance at stopping Barrett for good."

Another silent exchange. Then Edward motioned with the rifle. "To the cabin. We need to talk."

———

THE MODERN CEDAR and glass cabin reflected everything we'd seen from a distance—intentional isolation, discreet surveillance, and a life built to be left at a moment's notice. Security cameras disguised as outdoor lighting covered every approach. Multiple satellite dishes sat behind the house, and a solar array stretched across one corner of the roof.

Inside, the great room was spare but efficient. Laptops and portable drives littered a workstation near the window. Go-bags sat by an exit.

Edward paced near the fireplace as he spoke. "I was site supervisor at Miller Creek. I started noticing irregularities in the material deliveries. Orders that didn't match what we needed for construction. Containers being diverted to warehouses that weren't on our approved list. The manifests showed shipments of high-end materials, but what arrived on site was garbage. The cost difference was being skimmed."

"Meanwhile, I was reconciling irregularities in the accounts," Carmela added. "Shell companies, fake vendors, inflated costs. Barrett was using Miller Creek as a front for something much bigger."

"What was he moving?" I asked.

Carmela shrugged. "I can only guess but probably guns, drugs, people. *Bribes.* Money washing through fake contracts and bogus suppliers."

Edward's jaw flexed before he spoke. "We were going to report it. We had the documentation ready. Then the site safety inspector disappeared."

"The one asking questions about substitutions and holding up the project?"

Edward nodded. "They found his weeks later. *Accident,* supposedly."

Carmela moved to a nearby desk and flipped open a laptop. "After the inspector disappeared, I started pulling threads. The same patterns showed up in other construction projects in multiple states. Always the same markers: same shell companies, same false manifests."

Wesley joined her at the desk, scanning the documents she'd pulled up. "So...this is why left Miller Creek?"

"I called my dad," Carmela said. "He told me to get out. Quiet, fast...but do it now. He said Barrett had done worse on earlier jobs. I quit, disappeared. Edward followed a few months later."

"I tried to act normal," Edward muttered. "But it's hard to live a normal life when I knew I was being watched. I couldn't risk staying."

"But...you left your kids," I said.

His eyes met mine. "Because if I didn't, Barrett's guy, Bianchi, would've come after all of us. A man walking out? Believable. A whole family vanishing? That sets off alarms."

"We had to make it look impulsive," Carmela agreed. "Like he cracked under pressure. Enough people bought it that the police didn't hardly look for Edward and no one was looking for me."

"You've sat on all of this?" I asked. "All this time?"

"We didn't know what to do with it," Carmela said. "Or who to trust with it. It's all encrypted. Distributed to multiple secure servers. If we disappear, it all goes public."

"It's the only thing keeping us alive, honestly," Edward said. "But it won't stop Barrett forever."

The same truck we'd seen earlier appeared again driving slowly down the access road.

"This location's compromised," Carmela said, already closing laptops.

Edward moved to the security monitor, his face grim. "Three vehicles. They're setting up a perimeter."

"How long before they move in?" Wesley asked.

"They're not rushing," Edward observed. "They're just setting up, looks like." He turned to Carmela. "Time to wake up the neighborhood?"

She nodded and pulled out a tablet, fingers flying across the screen. "Motion sensors are installed around the property. Once they're armed, the first person who steps wrong is going to set off every alarm we've got."

"That'll buy us time?" I asked.

"Maybe ten minutes of chaos while they figure out what's happening," Edward said. He shouldered a go-bag and handed another to Carmela. "There's a trail that leads through the forest to the service road. We can circle around to your vehicle if you're willing to move fast."

"What about your vehicle?" Wesley asked.

"Hidden in the forest, different trail," Edward said. "Carmela takes that route, we go with you. Harder to track two vehicles on separate roads."

A harsh electronic screech suddenly split the air—the motion sensors had triggered. Through the windows, we saw floodlights blazing to life, pulsing around the perimeter.

"Now," Edward said.

Carmela was already at the back door, weapon drawn. "Stay low, follow me close, don't stop for anything."

We slipped out into the forest, the alarm still wailing behind us. Shouts echoed from the front of the property as Barrett's men tried to coordinate over the noise. The flood-lights created a strobing effect through the trees, making it hard to track movement.

Edward led us along a narrow trail that wound through dense undergrowth. Branches caught at our clothes, and more than once I stumbled over roots in the dim light. Behind us, the alarm continued its relentless shrieking.

"How much further?" Wesley asked.

"Just ahead," Carmela replied. "The service road curves back toward your parking spot."

A new sound cut through the alarm—the roar of engines as vehicles moved to reposition around the property. They were trying to close off escape routes.

"They're mobile," Edward noted. "We need to move faster."

The trail began to slope downward, and through the trees I saw the gravel road where we'd left the SUV. But as we got closer, I spotted headlights sweeping the area.

Edward cursed under his breath. "They found your vehicle."

We took cover behind a stand of trees, watching as two men examined the vehicle. One of them spoke into a radio, then both moved toward the road to block any approach.

Edward checked his watch. "The system will shut down in three minutes. We need to be moving by then."

The men by our car were distracted, one of them shouting into his radio trying to be heard over the alarm. The other had moved closer to the tree line, scanning the undergrowth.

"When the alarm stops, they'll spread out looking for us," Edward said. "We go now, during the noise."

Carmela nodded. "Stay together. If anyone gets separated, the rendezvous point is the Lincoln City cabin." She gave us a hard look. "You found us here, so I assume you know where the other house is."

The three of us broke from cover, but only Edward followed Wesley and me toward our SUV. Carmela had already disappeared into the undergrowth, heading for their hidden vehicle.

The three of us moved in a low crouch. The alarm masked our footsteps as we circled wide around the guards. Wesley had the keys ready, and I watched him calculating the fastest route out.

Just as we reached the car, the alarm cut off.

The sudden silence felt deafening. For a moment, nobody moved. Then one of the guards shouted, "Movement by the vehicle!"

"Go!" Edward hissed.

The three of us dove into the SUV as the guards turned toward us. Wesley had the engine started before our doors were closed, gravel spraying as we accelerated away from the turnout.

In the rearview mirror, I watched the guards running back toward their own vehicles.

"They'll follow us," Edward said from the back seat.

"Let them try," Wesley replied grimly, taking the first turn at speed. "I know a few things about evasive driving."

CHAPTER
NINETEEN

WESLEY

"NEXT LEFT," Edward said from the back seat, eyes fixed on the side mirror. "Then we double back through those hills."

I took the turn, keeping my speed steady but not too slow. Three hours of swerving through Oregon backroads had taught me Edward's rhythm—random turns, doubling back, taking routes that would confuse anyone trying to follow. My hands stayed relaxed on the wheel, but every muscle in my body was coiled for whatever came next.

"Still clear?" I asked, checking the rearview mirror.

"No headlights." Edward shifted to get a better view. "Take the next right, then straight for about five miles."

Yvette kept watch out the passenger window, occasionally lifting compact binoculars to scan the road behind us. Her bag sat at her feet—nine years in the Army and three years as a PI had taught her to stay ready. I kept a similar bag in my office and car, a habit I'd developed after some of my more dangerous cases.

"Keep watching behind us," Edward said quietly.

Yvette lifted the binoculars, scanning the road we'd just traveled. "Clear. But we should assume Barrett's people are out there somewhere."

The narrow forest roads wound through dense stands of pine and fir, no streetlights, no houses visible through the trees. Perfect terrain for losing a tail—or for getting ambushed if you weren't careful.

"How much further?" I asked.

"Another hour. We'll hit the main road soon, then back into the forest near Lincoln City." Edward's phone chimed. He checked it, then relaxed slightly. "Carmela's clear. Took the coastal route, no problems."

Smart move, splitting up. Harder to track two vehicles moving independently, especially when one took Highway 101 while we wound through back country roads.

"You mentioned protection," Edward said after several minutes of tense silence. "What do you actually have in your pocket, Wesley? Who do you trust at this point?"

I kept my eyes on the dark snarl of road but measured my answer carefully. "FBI, U.S. Attorney's office. People who can put Barrett away and get you into witness protection if needed."

"Witness protection means giving up everything again. New identities, new lives."

"But your boys would know you're alive," Yvette said. "They'd understand why you left."

Edward was quiet for a long moment. "Barrett's reach goes far and wide. Federal judges, prosecutors, law enforcement. How do we know who to trust?"

"We document everything first," I replied. "Get your evidence to multiple sources simultaneously. Make it impossible for him to contain or refute."

"And if that doesn't work?"

"Then we disappear you again. But this time with federal resources behind us."

An hour and a half later, I turned off the main road onto an unmarked gravel drive that disappeared into dense forest. No signs, no mailbox numbers—nothing to indicate a cabin lay ahead.

"Just a little way to the gate," Edward said quietly.

A compact sedan poked through the trees, parked at an angle for quick departure. Carmela stepped from the shadows as I pulled up, weapon holstered but ready.

"You guys make it okay?" she asked Edward through his window.

"No trouble. You?"

"Doubled back twice. Nothing." She glanced toward the tree line. "But we should get inside. Being outside makes me nervous."

The cabin sat further back, larger than I'd expected. Like the Newport house, it had multiple security lights and cameras, but this place felt more defendable—clear sight lines in all directions, dense forest providing natural cover.

"Sensors are active," Carmela reported as we approached the door. "Perimeter's clear, but we should do a full check. Ed?"

He nodded. "I'll run the outside route. You take them in."

We followed her into a great room that was sparsely furnished but ready for occupation with emergency supplies stacked against one wall, bags by the exit. A basic security setup occupied one corner, two monitors showing camera feeds from the driveway and back trail.

"Nice setup," I noted. "You've gotten good at this."

"Had to." Carmela was already checking the camera feeds. "The first safe house, we barely had burner phones and dial-up internet. Now…" She gestured at the modest setup. "Basic early warning system, secure internet, backup generator. Nothing fancy, but it works."

"Multiple escape routes," I observed, noticing the back door and side windows positioned for quick exit. "Your father finances all this?"

Her expression went stone cold as she straightened. "I haven't seen my dad in four years. He said the only way to keep Barrett from using him to find us was to cut contact. He gave up everything to make sure I stay safe."

She turned away without saying anything more.

Edward came in from his perimeter check, securing the door behind him. "Motion sensors active, cameras clear. No signs anyone's been here since our last check."

"Good. For now. They found Newport, so it's only a matter of time before they find this place too."

Sunset began to color the sky outside the windows. We'd been going non-stop since morning, running on adrenaline.

"Take a few minutes to clean up and regroup," Edward said, noting our exhaustion. "Guest rooms are upstairs. We'll get something going for a meal, then we need to plan our next move."

As Yvette and I climbed the narrow stairs to the sparsely furnished loft, I heard Edward and Carmela's quiet voices in discussion below. I'd seen Edward's face when we talked about his sons—under all that control was a father desperate to protect his family. A man who'd walked away from everything to keep them alive.

Yvette did a quick sweep of the small room out of habit. There wasn't much to sweep—a bed, one window. Bathroom down the hall.

I set my bag near the door, within easy reach. "So…what's your assessment?" I asked quietly.

"They're definitely tired of running." She settled on the edge of the bed, lowering her voice to a whisper. "Do you think Edward and Carmela are…you know…"

"Together?" I whispered back, moving to sit beside her. "I was wondering the same thing."

"Did you see how they look at each other whenever we ask a question?"

I nodded, thinking back through the day. "But then again, four years of depending on each other for survival would create some intense bonds, whether there's romance or not."

"True."

"When she came out of the trees with that gun, she called him Ed."

Yvette grinned, clearly enjoying the speculation. "*Everyone* calls him Ed. Even his wife."

"Fair. He defers to her on the security protocols. He's used to letting her take the lead on certain things."

"Maybe she's just better with technology," Yvette countered. "I mean, her background is finance and accounting, his is…hammers and nails."

I considered this. "You think they were involved before they ran?"

"Possible. They definitely knew each other well enough that she jumped in to help him." Yvette shifted position, getting more comfortable with our gossip session. "But he was married with kids. Even if they had history, acting on it while he's married…"

"Happens every day, Vette. Nobody knows that like you know it. Some people compartmentalize differently when their life is falling apart."

"True. And his marriage was already struggling before he left." She paused, thinking. "If they *were* having an affair, it would make his decision to run easier. He wouldn't just be leaving his family, he'd be going *to* someone."

"That's dark, but probably realistic." I kept my voice low as footsteps moved around downstairs. "On the other hand, maybe the attraction developed after they were both hiding."

"Four years is a long time to be someone's only companion," Yvette agreed. "Even if it started platonic, feelings could have developed."

I thought about Edward's reaction when we mentioned his sons. "He seemed genuinely torn up about leaving his kids. That doesn't read like a man who ran off for love."

"No, but it also doesn't mean he didn't find love along the way." Yvette leaned back against the headboard. "What's your gut say?"

"Honestly? I think they care about each other, but I'm not sure it's romantic. More like…" I searched for the right words. "Like soldiers who've been through combat together. That bond goes deeper than friendship but isn't necessarily sexual."

"I could see that. They move like a team that's been together a long time. Like me and you."

She picked at a stray thread on the thin comforter, gaze distant. "When we'd be out on surveillance for days at a time, I could predict your next move and you could anticipate mine. It's not even conscious after a while. With them, I bet it started out as necessity, but then it just became habit. When you depend on someone and they don't let you get killed, that kinda sticks."

"That comes from time and close observation. You learn someone's triggers when you're with them all the time."

I watched her stand and move to the window, checking the view outside before pulling the blinds down.

"Speaking of triggers," I said carefully. "We need to talk about what happens next."

She turned, immediately wary. "What do you mean, what happens next?"

"I mean…we've done what we were hired to do. What I hired *you* to do—find Edward. He's alive and well. He'll inherit. Anjelica gets whatever the law says she gets as spouse to a disappeared person who pops up after four years. Technically, your job is finished."

"Technically." Her tone had gone flat. "But not *actually*."

"You could head back to Atlanta. I'll handle connecting them with the Feds if that's what they want."

"Excuse me?" The look she gave me let me know my proposal was not met with appreciation. One day, I was going to learn to think before I just blurted something out to Yvette.

"Vette, this is about to become a federal investigation. Barrett's people are dangerous—"

"And I can't handle danger?" She kept her voice low but the anger was unmistakable. "I've been *handling danger* since before you knew my name. It's been my entire job for more than ten years."

"That's not what I'm saying—"

"Then what the fuck *are* you saying?" She moved closer, invading my space. "Because it sounds like you're trying to bench me."

"I'm trying to keep you safe."

"By sending me home right when the case is really heating up?" Her eyes flashed. "I didn't sign up for safe. And I didn't turn into a fragile flower when we started fucking, Payne."

"I know that, *Young*," I shot back at her.

"Do you? Let me remind you of something." She poked my chest with her finger. "I'm the person you hired to track Edward and prove he's alive. I'm the person who figured out Barrett's operation and tracked these two here. And I'm the person who can put you on your ass if you keep patronizing me."

"Yvette. Come on, now." I had to fight back a smile. She was all fire and fury, making threats we both knew she couldn't physically carry out, but damn if I didn't love seeing her this fierce. "Let's not get carried away."

She huffed, obviously not in on the joke. "All I'm saying is I didn't turn into a cupcake in the last couple of weeks. You hired me to do a job and I'm staying involved until it's done. The part of me I only let you see doesn't cancel out the badass you and I both know I am. Don't make me regret showing you that side of me."

The heat between us was electric, part anger, part attraction. I tracked her pulse jumping in her throat.

"I'm not trying to patronize you," I said quietly. "I'm trying not to lose you."

That stopped her cold. For a moment, we just stared at each other.

"You think I can't take care of myself?" she asked.

"I think the stakes are high." I reached for her hand. "I think I'm not going to walk you into something if I don't know I can walk you out of it. I think I love you enough that it scares the shit out of me to think about something happening to you."

She didn't pull away, but her jaw was still set. "This was never a problem when we served together, so you need to figure out how to handle that without treating me like I'm made of glass."

"You're right." I squeezed her hand. "I'm sorry. It's just... we're good together. The thought of being responsible for you getting hurt—"

"Makes you want to put me in a safe little box while you play hero?" Her voice was still laced with malice but she was losing her edge. "That's not how this works, Wesley. We're a team or we're not."

"Of course, we're a team. We work better together than apart—"

"Then act like it! These people need advocates who understand what Barrett has done. Neither of us can walk away right now."

"You're right," I conceded, sighing. "Edward needs to see his sons. Carmela wants to stop running. That doesn't happen unless Barrett goes down."

"Right," she agreed, pushing out a hard breath. "Besides...you think I'm missing out on watching you take down a criminal conspiracy? I want front-row seats to that show."

She seemed satisfied, at least for now. We sat together in the hush, letting the adrenaline ebb. I wondered if any version of this could ever end simply—no betrayals, no final firefight, no lingering guilt for the innocent people who got caught in the crossfire.

Downstairs, Edward's voice carried through the floorboards, too low to hear him, but with an obvious terse choppiness to his speaking cadence that suggested difficult decisions were being made.

"Listen…" I leaned over so I could whisper right in her ear. "I trust you with my life. I'm just trying to manage my personal feelings about you and I want you to be safe. And let me tell *you* something, Yvette Young…."

"What, Wesley Payne?"

I grabbed her chin and pulled her face close to mine, then kissed her. There was nothing delicate about the move. Her lips stiffened in surprise, then she relented, kissing me back.

When we parted, one of her hands had fisted in my shirt.

"If you *ever* doubt how capable I think you are, remember who I call when I need the job done right."

———

"THE FBI WON'T MOVE without proof Edward is alive and evidence of credible threat," I said, pocketing my phone. "But my contact at the Portland field office says once they have both, they can mobilize quickly."

We sat around the cabin's kitchen table as night settled over the forest outside. The smell of instant coffee lingered in the air—Carmela had made a pot while Edward and she spent the evening hours pulling their documentation together and I worked my contacts. Empty sandwich plates sat pushed to one side, crusts and crumbs the only evidence of the hurried meal we'd grabbed.

"What exactly do they need?" Carmela asked, hands clasped tight on the tabletop.

"Proof Edward's alive is only the beginning. To get them to act, we need to tell a story. They need evidence that not only are you threatened, but the threat is coming from people with resources. The more organized, the more real it looks to the Feds."

My thumb tapped a nervous rhythm against the mug of black coffee in my hands. "We need more than smoke. We need fire."

"We can give them fire," Edward said. "What do you need from us?"

"Recorded testimony laying out what you found and any supporting evidence you can provide."

I glanced at Yvette, who nodded at me. "We do it like a formal deposition with our camera. Upload it to a secure address. Once they have that, they'll take it straight to DC."

"Does that get my family protection?" Edward asked.

"It gets the ball rolling. The Bureau can get you and your family out of reach before any kind of public announcement or leak puts you at risk," said Wesley, explaining further. "They specialize in quietly extracting high-value witnesses. You'd be on a plane before Barrett even gets wind of it."

Carmela's fingers trembled, her fingernails leaving marks in her pale skin. "I have years of records showing the shell companies, faked shipping manifests, the locations of warehouses. We'll keep the most damaging files in reserve until we're safe and face to face with them."

"Insurance," Edward said quietly. "In case Barrett's reach extends further than we think."

Lots of friends in lots of places, I recalled.

Edward and Carmela's eyes met across the table in a wordless conversation born from four years of survival.

"Barrett knows you're both out here," I said. The thought of him somewhere out there, mobilizing his people and swarming a north Oregon cabin sent a cold jolt through my veins. "You're not likely to escape again. Please let us help you."

Finally, Edward nodded. "Let's do this."

I pushed aside my coffee and stood, straightening into the expert, the professional, a man ready to take it from here.

We moved to the great room where the light was better. A table lamp cast a halo of brightness around Edward's chair as he faced the camera. I positioned myself beside it, legal pad in hand.

Carmela stayed by the window, dividing her attention between the darkening tree line and the interview about to begin.

"State your name for the record," I said, once Yvette gave me the sign.

"My name is Edward Patrick Foster. I worked as site supervisor at Miller Creek Development until the project collapsed."

"Please describe, in your own words, the nature of the corruption you uncovered," Wesley said.

CHAPTER
TWENTY

YVETTE

EDWARD PUSHED the chipped mug away from him and seemed to relax as he began to lay out the story.

"The official story behind the collapse of Miller Creek was structural issues and cost overruns. But I was boots on the ground. Site construction, material orders, inventory. If something went wrong, it came back on me."

He stood and wandered to the window, hands shoved deep in his jeans pockets. "About four months into the project, I started spotting inconsistencies—materials showing up that didn't match what was on the books. I thought it was clerical at first. Mix-ups happen when a company has multiple sites going. But my inventory was useless and my counts were off and nobody could explain why everyone kept saying it was fine, just use it."

Wesley looked up from his notebook. "What happened when you asked questions?"

Edward returned to his seat but didn't sit down, instead gripping the back of the chair. "Stonewalled. Nobody wanted to touch it. That job was my livelihood, so I kept my mouth shut and worked around it. Then the project went belly up."

Wesley nodded, pen still moving across the page. "How did that impact your family?"

"We were barely scraping by. Anjelica took double shifts. We stood in food bank lines and hit up different churches every Sunday."

Wesley shifted his attention to Carmela, who had been sitting quietly in the corner chair. "Ms. Verona? Tell us about your role?"

"I worked in finance," she began. "Miller Creek was a mess from day one, so I was watching it closely. Edward and I reconnected when he came to my office to ask about the stuff he was seeing at the job site. It was...it was like a mini-high school reunion." She glanced at Edward, then back to the camera. "We hadn't seen each other since graduation."

Carmela stood and began pacing behind her chair, one hand trailing along the back of it. "After what Edward shared with me, I started digging. The financials were a maze. There were overlapping shell companies, invoice trails that looped back into each other, vendors that didn't seem to exist." She stopped pacing. "It looked like they were ordering high-end materials on paper, billing full price, then swapping in cheap knockoffs and pocketing the difference through fake vendors."

She walked back to her chair but remained standing behind it. "Other Barrett projects showed the same pattern. Same vendors appearing across multiple sites. Same invoice amounts. Same material substitutions. We're talking about *dozens* of projects over years. That amounts to millions in fraudulent billing."

Wesley's pen stopped moving. "Edward, what was happening? In detail."

"Yeah, here's how it worked. You bid out the job, get funding based on premium specs—say, grade-A steel, high-end concrete, top-tier electrical systems. Then you swap out the good stuff for bottom-barrel materials and sell the original shipments off the books."

He was animated, hands gesturing as he walked us through the process. "They were profiting twice—once from the inflated bid to the client, then again by reselling what they never delivered to the actual job sites."

He rubbed the back of his neck, his face growing red.

"I wasn't gonna take the fall for that. The building codes we were violating could've killed people. So I asked Carmela for help. She started cross-referencing every invoice with the actual financials, and the deeper we dug, the more we realized this wasn't just corner-cutting. This was fraud."

Carmela stepped around her chair and sat down, pulling one leg up under her. "The paper trail led back to at least three shell companies, all with Barrett's signature on the incorporation documents."

Wesley closed his notebook and set it on the small table beside him. "You mentioned Carmela's father?"

She finally sat, gripping the arms of her chair. "I called my dad when I started piecing things together. I knew he had worked with Barrett, who was the principal partner at First Southeast Holdings, the investment firm basically controlling the project. He would be able to tell me if it was something to worry about. Sometimes a project is a bloody mess until the structure is up and then they get their act together to close it out and get paid."

Carmela shook her head. "Well…Dad kind of…went quiet when I went into where I was working and what I was seeing."

Wesley hummed, nodding as if he didn't know any of this information. "What did he say?"

"He said it looked shitty. He said there was no way that project was getting to completion, that Barrett was basically wasting time and money using this project to move substandard equipment and God knows what else. He said he always suspected there was dirty money flowing through that company and he couldn't, in good conscience, keep working there. He took early retirement as soon as he was eligible. He started pushing for me to leave. I finally put in my notice in June...but that left Edward there."

She leaned forward. "My father said Barrett would bid legitimate jobs, then use those projects to wash dirty money through fake vendors and inflated invoices. The construction work was just cover for moving cash."

Wesley picked up his notebook again, flipping back a few pages. "But you didn't leave." His eyes moved to Edward.

Edward stopped pacing and crossed his arms. "I had mouths to feed. Carmela had her father looking out for her and she could find other work. I didn't have those options."

"So what made you finally act?"

"Joey Martinez," he answered, his tone flat. "Safety inspector for this site. Martinez was a good guy who actually cared about his job. He started flagging things we couldn't explain—missing inspection reports, unauthorized electrical work, concrete pours that didn't match the engineering specs. He kept asking questions. Kept documenting violations. One morning he didn't show up to the site. Joey never missed a day of work as long as I knew him."

He pressed his lips together before he went on. "Two weeks after Miller Creek shut down, his car was found half in, half out of a flooded ravine. He was in the car."

Carmela wrapped her arms around herself. "I read that the police ruled it suicide. Said he was depressed about losing his job when the project folded."

Wesley looked up from his notes. "But you knew better."

Edward shook his head slowly. "Joey Martinez wasn't suicidal. And he disappeared before the project folded. He was about to blow the whistle, though. That scared the shit out of me."

Nobody spoke for a moment.

"Tell us what happened the night you left," Wesley said, his voice softer now.

"I got a call about a job. Off the books, good money. I was desperate, so yeah...it worked on me. When I got to the address, it was an empty job site, all chained off. This guy was waiting, introduced himself as Tony Bianchi." Edward's knuckles went white as he gripped the coffee mug. "Tall, menacing-looking guy in an Italian suit, long hair, ugly face. Mob energy. He drove this...I don't know, old body Caddy. Across the trunk, he had laid out a series of photos. My boys, Anjelica, our house. He even knew their teachers' names."

Edward let out a breath and dragged a hand down his face. "He said the Feds were sniffing around and I needed to clam up about Miller Creek. Then he looked at the pics and... I got his point."

He looked over at Carmela. "We'd been in touch through burners. I called her, she told me what I needed to do and do it quickly. So the next night, I picked a fight with Angelica and left the house. Made it look like I cracked and took off."

Edward slumped forward, seeming exhausted. "And for the record," he added, looking between me and Wesley. "We're not a couple. Carmela and I have been through hell together, but we're just friends. Can't say I am still in love with my wife, but...she's a good mom. I want her and my boys to be safe. That's all that matters."

The next hour was spent cataloging what they knew—names, accounts, shipping records, flagged inspections. I stayed behind the camera, adjusting angles as people moved around the room. Wesley filled his notebook, only speaking when he needed clarification. Edward paced between the window and his chair. Carmela sat cross-legged, organizing documents into neat piles.

Wesley finally set down his pen and stretched his neck. "Anything else for the record?"

Edward stepped closer to the lens, his voice steady. "If anything happens to me or Carmela after this goes public, Richard Barrett and his people are responsible. Everything we've said is true. The evidence is real."

At Wesley's signal, I stopped the recording.

Edward dropped into his chair and heaved a sigh, running both hands through his hair. "What about my family? When will I know they're safe?"

Wesley stood up and walked to the window, looking out at the scenery. "The Georgia Bureau has a heads-up. They'll move on your house before we go public."

I began backing up the footage to a secure link while Wesley explained our process from across the room: upload to the Portland field office, then copies routed to the U.S. Attorney's Office, DOJ, and media if necessary.

Edward came over and hovered behind me, watching the progress bar crawl forward.

"How long before anything actually happens?"

Wesley turned back from the window. "Best case? Marshals move tonight. Realistically? Tomorrow morning."

"That's a long time to stay exposed."

I looked up at him from the laptop. "You've got backup now."

Carmela gathered the last of the documents and stood. "Feels good knowing Barrett can't stop this train. He can't hide now."

Wesley's phone chimed from his pocket. He pulled it out and read the screen. "Portland field office confirms receipt. They're passing it to the task force. No timetable yet."

Edward walked back to the small table and pulled out a burner phone, then hesitated, the phone halfway to his ear.

"I should—someone should know…"

Wesley crossed the room quickly, snatching the phone from Edward's hand. "Are you out of your mind? Four years in hiding and now you think you can just ring people up?"

His tone was firm; I recognized the near-snarl in his order. "Barrett's people are watching *everything*. Have a seat. Let the feds handle it before you get someone killed."

Carmela's hand froze over her own phone, which she'd been reaching for in her back pocket. "My dad knows all this stuff. I can't—"

"Same rules apply to you," Wesley said. "It's too risky."

Edward's shoulders sagged. "So close. And I still can't talk to my boys."

"You will," Wesley said, walking back toward the me, double-checking the progress of the emails going out. "Soon. But not yet."

CHAPTER
TWENTY-ONE

WESLEY

"HOME SWEET HOME. At least until the bureau says we can leave."

I dropped our bags inside the hotel room door.

Yvette kicked off her boots and fell back onto the bed, arms spread wide. The past few days had worn her down, though she'd never admit it. "Did you see how many cars they brought to transport Edward and Carmela? I thought I was watching a Presidential motorcade. Barrett's going to have a hard time touching them now."

"Let's hope he never finds out where they went. I can't believe they sat on all that information this whole time."

I loosened my tie and sat on the bed's edge. Yvette had worn her usual P.I. uniform—an oversized t-shirt, jeans, and boots. Smart choice. My dress shirt felt like a straitjacket after the long day of federal meetings, with more scheduled tomorrow.

"When your enemy has friends in high places, you don't

know who you can trust. They seemed to be waiting for someone to prove they could do more to help than harm."

"Well, between witness protection and the federal task force, I'd say our clients are well taken care of."

"*Our* clients?" She rolled onto her side, eyebrow raised. "Since when do you share credit?"

"Since I hired the investigator who was right about everything. You knew from the start there was more to Edward's disappearance."

Yvette's mouth dropped open in a gasp of mock shock. "Is that a compliment from Wesley Payne? Should I record this moment for posterity?"

"Keep it down. Our shadows will think I'm not as badass as I've made myself out to be."

She hooked her finger through my tie, tugging me closer. "Sounds like you need to find a way to keep me quiet."

I kissed her softly at first, a brush of lips with a tentative uncertainty that vanished the moment Yvette's arms snaked up and around my neck. Her mouth parted and her tongue found mine, sweet and hot.

Her fingers worked at the buttons of my shirt, cold fingertips sliding underneath the fabric.

"Your hands are freezing," I murmured against her mouth.

"More problems for you to solve, Payne."

She pulled my shirt free and off my shoulders. The hotel room's dim lighting caught the angles of her face as she moved closer.

"Right now, I want to celebrate closing our first big case together in…years. We're not counting how many."

I studied her face, the way her eyes held actual light for once instead of their usual guarded wariness. This kind of work, the thrill of victory, brought out a side of her I hadn't seen in a long time. I'd missed it.

"Might hurt yourself trying to count." I cupped her face in

my hands, kissing her again. She pushed me back against the pillows, then swung a leg over to straddle me. Her hands went to work on my belt buckle.

"I'm hearing you say...you trust my instincts."

"Not just your instincts." The words landed as heavy and deliberate as I intended them to. "I trust everything about you, Vette."

The old Yvette—sharp, skeptical, tempted to reply with sarcasm—held court for a second before yielding to a softer version I'd only glimpsed recently.

"Even when I'm pushing you away?" she asked. "Even when I'm horning in on your case and refusing to leave when it's resolved?"

"Especially then," I said, and the way she bit her lip told me I'd scored a direct hit. "You being right is half the fun. The other half is you gloating about it."

I let my hands graze the hem of her t-shirt, moving slowly, giving her every chance to shoo me off. She didn't. My palms settled on her hips while my thumbs teased the fabric higher, feeling her sharp inhale as the cool air of the room hit her skin.

She wore a navy lace bra; it looked expensive and well-constructed.

Yvette was a simple woman with odd, specific likes and luxuries, none of them the kind that could be purchased at a lingerie shop. The idea that she had picked up a few things she knew I'd like looking at made my heartbeat stutter.

"Back in the day, you used to tell me I was too direct with my personnel," I said. "Too honest. That I need a sparring partner who won't fold under my scrutiny. That's why I like being with you."

She lifted her arms so I could pull her shirt off. "Professionally? Or personally?"

"Both. Though right now, I'm more interested in the

personal side." I leaned in and kissed the soft skin just under her collarbone, drawing a shiver.

"For real, are there people outside our door?"

"Maybe. I hope they've heard two people enjoying the fuck out of each other before." I rolled us over, settling my weight against her. "Anyone who knocks on this door better come with a battering ram. I'm not stopping unless you make me."

"How about I dare them to try?" Her arms slid up around my neck again, legs locking at my hips to pull me in closer, turning the question of passersby and nosy Feds into background noise.

I mapped my way across her skin, memorizing every response, every sound. Her hands never stopped moving—down my shoulder blades, over the lean muscle of my back, dragging little scratch marks that would sting later.

Maybe that was the point. To make the memory of tonight last longer than tonight.

Her lips grazed my ear as she whispered a string of words that startled even me, and we'd been soldiers. Then she kissed the spot behind my ear she knew would unravel the last of my self-control.

Her rhythm was nothing like mine, but we found a pattern together. Yvette's breath came in sharp gasps, her body arching beneath mine.

"Wesley... Oh God...yes!"

Yvette's breath hitched on the last syllable, her shuddering cry echoing off the bland, beige walls of the hotel room. For a moment I lost any notion of who was leading, who wanted who more, who chased who, and who fought against it until there was no more will to fight what the heart wants.

There was only Yvette, open for me, desperate in my arms, nails digging half-moons into my skin gasping, "Yes, yes, yes, yes." I buried my face in her shoulder, grinding out her name as I followed her over the edge.

Seconds...or minutes, or an hour later, I collapsed onto the mattress beside her, lungs gulping air. The world was reduced to the can light on the ceiling, the sheen of sweat on her skin, the solid, staccato gallop of my heart.

After a few moments, I gathered her close, pressing my lips to her temple.

"Damn, we are good together," she mumbled against my chest.

I laughed, letting my hand glide down her back until it rested on the swell of her ass. "We should celebrate closed cases more often."

———

"DID you know you think real loud, Vette?"

She stretched beside me, her grin slow and Cheshire Cat-like. We got up, took turns in the tiny hotel bathroom, pulled two expensive bottles of water from the refrigerator, and came back to bed. Now we sat watching the preliminary details of the Barrett case play out on the evening news.

"I do?"

"Mmmhmmm." I hummed, dipping my head in a deep nod. "Your internal chatter sounds like it's coming through a bullhorn. I know exactly what you're thinking right now."

"You do not."

"I bet you lunch at Chops that I do."

She rolled her eyes, lurching up and bracing herself on one elbow. "No. Not because you're probably right but because I'm never buying you lunch at Chops."

"See how you are?"

Yvette snorted, then flopped back down, the covers twisting between us. Her head found a home on my chest. I let my hand drift up and down her shoulder, drawing lazy figure-eights that made her muscles flex and soften in turn.

"Fine, I'll bite. What am I thinking about right now?"

"You're thinking about what comes next for Edward and Carmela, of course. But mostly you're thinking about what happens with us when we get back to Atlanta."

Yvette hummed. "Two for two, but those were easy guesses. Coincidentally...what *does* happen when we go back to Atlanta?"

"Well, I think that's pretty much up to you, babe. What do you want to happen?"

She pulled her bottom lip between her teeth in that cute faux thinking pose. It was a nervous tell that I'd clocked the year we first met.

Yvette didn't need to think about the answer to the question. She needed to think about how to say what was on her mind and her heart. She needed to know she could trust me with her wildest dreams and I would turn the world upside down to make it happen.

Finally, she exhaled. "I don't think I can go backwards," she said. "I want what we felt for each other when we met. What might we have become if I wasn't young and in love. I've been through...the worst heartache anyone could ever imagine going through. I feel like I deserve some happiness. I deserve to take a chance at getting everything that was taken from me."

Her brows rose and a timid smile crossed her lips. "I sound *so* fucking corny—"

"You don't...that's not corny, Vette. If that's what you want, I want that too. I'm in. No fallback position."

She laughed. Actually laughed, the sound rolling out of her like it flooded the room with color. "Captain Payne! Do you hear yourself? *No fallback position,*" she mocked. "Is that your idea of pillow talk?"

"You knew this was me when you met me, Young," I shot back, but through laughter. "However I gotta say it so you know I'm here. I'm down. I'm with you. Do you read me?"

Yvette snorted. "I read you."

"And it's Major, if you're gonna keep using my rank."

"Fine, then. I expect to be addressed as Special Agent Young."

"Only if you're a good girl. Follow all my orders and don't give me attitude."

"Oh, see, that's never happening."

"That's what I figured."

The aftermath of our conversation buoyed my mood—and I was already feeling good. "I know you're concerned about what happens when we don't have a case as an excuse to spend time together, but I've always wanted to build something real with you. I got you. I'll give you all the time you need to be comfortable. Even the stuff you feel that you don't want to say yet."

"I'm scared," she admitted quietly. "I'm about to risk loving someone again...and the work we do means I could lose you too."

"I get that. I want to make it so you don't have to be scared, but I can't. I *can* promise that I want to come home to you every day. I want to spend a random, meaningless night with you where we don't even think about work."

She smiled, staring into space. "You, me, a cute restaurant on the Beltline on a Thursday night. And no reason to bring the Glock or the Sig out."

"If you can dream it..."

"Just understand that if something happened to you, I think I'd have to move in with Paula."

I burst out laughing, the sound probably carrying through the hotel walls. "You're a trip, Yvette Young. Just saying—I wouldn't mind working a lot more cases with you."

"I like pissing Nick Courtney off. I know he hates me."

"He doesn't hate you—"

"You don't have to lie, Payne!" She giggled. "Though maybe the next case can be something less dangerous than an international crime syndicate."

"I brought you a missing persons case. *You* turned it into an international crime syndicate."

"Potayto, potahto." She waved a dismissive hand. "A few boring slip and falls, some cheaters would be nice."

"So...no thoughts on joining the Georgia Bureau, then?"

Her eyes narrowed as she turned to study my face. "You been talking to my mama?"

"No. But if that's her line of thinking, I'm not against it."

"I have no intention of wearing business casual suits I bought at...wherever the young women are buying suits, and reporting to an office every day for eight hours of boring computer work. Tell that to Mrs. Valerie Young when you meet her."

"So I am meeting her?"

Yvette let out a long theatrical sigh, letting her head thunk softly back against the headboard.

"Does that tantrum mean yes?"

"Yeah," she answered. "I just haven't arranged it because she'll start calling you her son-in-law. I just didn't want her to get attached before I got attached."

"So you're attached now?"

"And I need to prep you for Yancey. He's used to being the center of attention."

"I'm not worried. I keep up on my PT and security training. You won't be the only person to put him on the kitchen floor."

"I would pay to see that, actually."

"Something I want you to start thinking about, Vette... I'm not pushing, but think about it."

She sat up suddenly, eyes wide. "You are not asking me to think about what I think you're asking me to think about. Are you?"

"No, I am not, coward."

I laughed, pulling her back down against me. "I bought a house and renovated the house and made sure you came over at every step. There's nothing in the house that you turned your nose up at. You know that, right? I knew eventually I'd share it with someone I wanted to be around all the time. You can have your own space if you need it. Then you don't have to hide out in your office to avoid wrestling your little brother to the kitchen floor."

She watched me, her gaze lingering on my face longer than usual. For a moment, something flickered in her eyes. Then she let out a single contented exhale, and the corners of her lips curved up into her standard smirk.

"I was just about to tell you that you're going to have to let me pick a room since I plan to be at House of Payne more nights than not."

"I thought you'd never demand it," I said, grinning like a fool. "We can christen every room if you want."

She threw her head back and laughed. My phone vibrated on the nightstand. Agent Billings' name flashed on the screen.

"You're too late to ask to join in, Sam," I said, keeping my voice as dry and unbothered as possible.

There was a snort at the other end, like he actually had a sense of humor hidden somewhere under that dark, unflattering suit. "You wound me. Just checking in. The new shift came on at 6 p.m.; the next shift cycles around 6 a.m. tomorrow. Nobody's getting in unless they want to become breakfast for a federal team with a lot of aggression to work out. You guys doing okay?"

"Yeah, we're great. About to get some rest. What time is our first meeting tomorrow?"

"Ten, but be ready at eight. The drive to Salem is an hour with no traffic, and we never have a day without traffic."

"We'll be ready," I said, then hung up. "Speaking of work…"

"Nobody was speaking of work." She groaned, swinging her legs off the bed. "Two days of debriefings and paperwork."

"Yes. But also...two more nights of our West Coast adventure. We're almost on vacation."

"With federal agents outside our door."

"They're probably looking forward to the next show." I reached for her, but she was already moving toward her suitcase. "Where you going?"

"Getting in the shower while you order dinner."

"Hell, no. I'm not missing another shower with you. First we shower, then we get some dinner."

"Fine." She paused to smile. "Can I pick the food tonight?"

"Why do I feel like we're having Thai?"

CHAPTER
TWENTY-TWO

YVETTE

"PASS THOSE GREENS BACK THIS WAY," Estelle called down the length of the dining table, her voice carrying that smoky tone she was known for. "Yours are better than my grandmama's, and I never thought I'd say that about anybody's cooking."

"Well, thank you, Stelle. That's quite the compliment."

Mama's face lit up as Wesley dutifully passed the bowl of collards back toward Estelle. The formal dining room glowed under the crystal chandelier, light catching the feast spread across the antique table. She'd outdone herself tonight—oven-fried chicken, tender greens seasoned with smoked turkey, creamy macaroni and cheese, candied yams dripping with butter and brown sugar, and cornbread still radiating heat from the oven.

The moment I'd told Mama that Wesley wanted to come to dinner, she'd been beside herself. She'd changed the menu three times. She made Daddy bring down the good china and she ironed every linen napkin with starch.

Even now, in the thick of the meal, her eyes kept darting between me and Wesley with an interest she tried to hide behind sips of sweet tea. Wesley, for his part, played the perfect guest, complimenting every dish, laughing at my dad's groan-worthy jokes, making sure to take a little bit of everything on offer.

Mama ate it *up*.

"Y'all see the news about Barrett today?" Nia plucked another wedge of cornbread from the basket, unconsciously slathering it with butter as she talked. "The federal grand jury dropped the hammer on him. Twenty-seven indictments! Money laundering, weapons trafficking, conspiracy to commit murder. Nearly every charge you could dream up, they're throwing at him."

"That's conservative for a RICO case," said Wesley. "The Racketeer Influenced and Corrupt Organizations Act is what they use to take down organized crime families, drug cartels, corrupt politicians with extensive networks. The murder charges will probably be added after they've completed the investigation into Joey Martinez's death."

Estelle whistled softly and shook her head. "I knew that man was bad news, but twenty-seven and more comin'?" She nudged her husband, who'd been quietly slicing yams into perfect half-moons. "You ever heard of anything like it?"

"They say he's going down for thirty years, minimum," Nia said around a bite of cornbread. "Even before they add on the murder charges."

"Good," Daddy said firmly. "Him and his whole crew deserve multiple life sentences. Making a father leave his children like that."

"And his crew will go down with him," Wesley said, adding more macaroni and cheese to his plate. "The feds are still unraveling his networks. Barrett had people in construction offices, building inspectors, even some folks in the DA's office—"

"The county clerk's office," I reminded him.

"It'll take years to sort through all the shit he had his hands in."

"Are Edward and his family alright?" Mama asked.

The Fosters and Veronas had declined federal witness protection for the moment. Edward and Carmela had been hiding for nearly four years. They'd lived under fake names and in enough secret homes to last a lifetime.

"As settled as they can be, but they're together," Wesley said. "The boys wouldn't let go of Edward for the first hour after they saw him. Just kept hugging him, crying, asking if he was really staying this time."

"Poor babies," Mama murmured.

"And Anjelica?" Estelle asked.

Wesley grimaced. "I heard she threw a coffee mug at his head during their first debrief. She's got some anger to work through."

"Can't blame her," I said. "Man disappears without a word, leaves her to raise twins alone, struggling to keep food on the table. I'd throw more than a coffee mug."

"They've got therapists working with them, but it's going to be a long road. Edward's guilt is eating him alive and Anjelica's rage is justified. Those boys are confused as hell."

"And Grandpa is dying," Estelle added. "At least they got to see him, spend some time with him as a family, no matter how broken the family might be."

"That's another reason they decided not to go in under protection. They needed to see and spend time with George while he's still here."

"The right choice is sometimes the hardest one to make," Mama said softly.

I felt Wesley's hand find mine under the table. He knew what Mama meant—how hard it had been for me to move forward, to trust again, to let someone new into my life.

"Young Investigations' reputation is growing," Daddy

commented, clearly trying to lighten the moment. "That Barrett case is going to bring in some interesting work."

"As long as it's not *too* interesting," Mama interjected. "I worry enough about Yvette running around out there doing heaven knows what. The GBI told her a long time ago all she got to do is apply and they can put her to work. It's time to settle down, do more than run around half the night after folks up to no good."

I glanced at Wesley, knowing only he saw me roll my eyes.

"She's in good hands, Mrs. Young," Wesley assured her. "I support whatever Yvette wants to do with her life."

"Thank you," I mouthed before shoving a piece of chicken in my mouth.

"I still can't believe y'all cracked that case," Yancey said around a mouthful of food. "I been telling' everybody at work that my sister did that! You might be kinda smart, Vette."

"Might be, Yance? I know that's the closest I'm getting to a compliment from you, so thanks."

"Well, Wesley, I hope you have room in your truck for Yvette's boxes," Mama said with a smile. "I don't remember the last time she slept at home. Might as well pack her up and cart all of her things over there."

"Mama!" I protested.

"Yeah, go ahead and get that handled so I can move up there," Yancey said. "Y'all doing that today? I'll help."

"You will not be touching any of my shit, Yancey."

"Yvette Young!" Mama scolded, giving me a glare over her bifocals. "Watch your mouth at my table."

"Sorry, Mama. Tell your son to keep his grubby paws to himself."

"The apartment served its purpose," Daddy said. "Gave you a soft place to land after separating from the Army and dealing with the loss of Jason. Let's be real, though. You been living at Wesley's for a minute. Seems like you're ready to move on and that's okay."

The table went quiet, just long enough for all of us to sit with the memory of Jason at this table instead of Wesley. Not long ago, this conversation would have sent me into an emotional spiral. Today, though, I caught myself smiling at the warm memory of him but also feeling excited about a future with a man I had fallen for completely and without reservation. I felt the heat on my cheeks and was sure my skin was red and inflamed. I didn't mind.

Wesley laid an arm over the back of my chair—a show of solidarity, I supposed. "Whatever Vette is ready to do, I'm in. I'm not in a rush to make any moves without her say-so."

I smirked, poking at a piece of candied yam. "Y'all are really just gonna plan my life while I'm sitting here?"

"Somebody has to," Estelle chimed in. "Lord knows you'd overthink it for another six months otherwise."

Nia snorted, almost spitting her tea. "Estelle got you dead to rights, cousin. You do be draggin' shit out. Know what I'm saying?" She used her fork to gesture between Wesley and me.

We moved to the back deck for peach cobbler and after-dinner drinks. The evening was balmy, slightly humid but not uncomfortably so. The sun had just set, a sliver of dusty rose on the horizon sending pinkish hues across the sky. A string of lights twinkled above the deep cushioned seats around a fire pit as conversation and laughter flowed.

I leaned against Wesley's shoulder, pushing out a long, contented sigh. He turned his head just far enough to drop a kiss on my forehead.

"Babe," I whispered. He leaned in to hear me over the din of conversation between my mother, Nia, and Estelle about some celebrity's very public affair. "How do you feel about running upstairs to fill up a couple boxes?"

"Mission ready, if that's what you want to do. I've been training for this."

I bumped his elbow with mine, grinning as I stood. "On your six, Major."

———

"NEXT SUNDAY, SAME TIME?" Mama asked a few hours later, handing me a paper bag filled with containers of leftovers. We'd already packed and loaded several boxes into Wesley's SUV. I also stripped the bed, leaving the place almost as good as I found it.

Yancey was already planning to move his things upstairs the next day.

"Wouldn't miss it," Wesley replied. "And we'll host once we get Yvette properly settled. Can't wait to impress you with my skills, Mrs. Young."

Daddy, behind Mama, let out a short, approving grunt. "I like a man who's proud of his food. Now you take care of my baby girl, Wesley."

He gave Wesley a firm handshake, the kind meant to size a man up and, if he passed muster, welcome him in. The two of them stood there for an extra beat, hands locked, nodding in something like mutual appreciation. It was a funny thing to see: my big, gruff father and my mountain of a man in tacit alliance.

"It's my honor, Mr. Young. Mrs. Young, thank you for the leftovers. They might not make it past the midnight snack checkpoint."

"Call me Valerie, honey," she said, leaning in and presenting her cheek for a kiss from Wesley, then from me. "And I'll be waiting for an invite to meet the Paynes—sooner rather than later. I know you both hear me."

"Yes, ma'am," Wesley replied, then led the way into the twilight.

The evening felt like the end of something...but also the beginning of something. I threaded my free arm through

Wesley's and tucked my hand into his elbow. He let me in on the passenger side of his Range Rover, waiting until I climbed in to lean closer.

"Tonight was good, Yvette. Wasn't it?"

"Yes, Wesley. It was very good."

He hovered, making sure he caught my eye and held my gaze. "You don't feel like we pushed you to—"

I reached over, wound a finger in his shirt collar, and tugged him close until our lips met. When I pulled back, his eyes were still closed.

"I love you, Wesley Payne. Take me home so I can show you how much."

"Ma'am. Yes, Ma'am."

EPILOGUE

YVETTE'S INVESTIGATION board sprawled across the wall like a crime scene: photographs, financial records, and surveillance shots pinned to the corkboard. I leaned closer, studying the patterns she'd mapped out in the case we'd been working on.

"Okay, here's where we are so far," she said, pointing to a series of bank records tacked to a bulletin board. "What do these look like to you?"

"Cash transfers?" I surmised.

"Exactly. Large sums of money being transferred from different accounts into one central account." She pointed to a series of bank records. "Every third Thursday."

I followed her finger and saw that the amount transferred was always the same range, between nine and ten thousand dollars. "Curious that it's always about the same amount of money."

"I'm still working on it, but interesting things are coming to light. Some of this stuff I've never seen before. It's kind of exciting." She glanced at me, beaming a wide smile before tamping down her giddy exclamation.

"How's your whistleblower?"

"Nova's legal team is brutal," I said. "They're doing everything short of hiring a team of snipers to keep her mouth shut. They can't fire her or it'll look like retaliation. Best they can do is a hostile work environment."

"Sounds about right. It's tough in these cases, but we'll try to get the info you need quickly. And you'll make sure justice is served."

Nia stopped in holding a box from The Salty Donut, opening the lid to offer us some. "My exploration of every donut shop within a five-mile radius of this office continues. I figured Wesley would be here, so I got maple bars."

"You don't know my life," I whispered, snatching one. "My mother is already grumbling about me fitting into a tux."

"Speaking of," Yvette said, reaching for a fritter, "she left me a voicemail about the engagement party."

My mind flashed back to an evening a few months prior, about a year after Barrett had pled guilty to the charges against him in exchange for a paltry number of years in a cushy corrections facility—which pissed me off, but at least he was in prison. The backyard gathering had been my mother's idea. *"Nothing fancy, just family,"* she'd said, which in Payne family speak meant forty people, catered barbecue, and enough string lights to illuminate a small town. Yvette had been talking to my cousin about the latest season of some police procedural when I pulled her aside to the garden gate. Jason had proposed in a backyard setting too, and I wasn't trying to beat him or copy him, but the setting was just... perfect for us, at the house I tricked her into helping me renovate to be a place she wanted to live.

"I've been carrying this around for three weeks," I'd told her, pulling the ring box from my jacket pocket. "Not because I was waiting for the right moment, but because every moment with you feels right and I had to decide which would be the best one. Since our families are here and we're both not working, seems like now is the best time to ask a very important question."

Her hands had flown to her mouth, eyes going wide. No tears, just the biggest smile.

"Yvette Young, I want to build a life with you. I want to argue about investigative techniques and whose turn it is to take out the trash. I want to solve cases together and fight about the thermostat. I want all of it, every ordinary, beautiful day of life... I want to spend it with you. Please say you'll spend your life with me."

She was nodding before I'd even finished talking, then laughed when I fumbled with the ring because my hands were shaking. "Yes, Wesley. God, yes." The party had erupted in cheers from our families, who'd been watching from the deck.

"You too?" I asked now, chewing my donut and trying to appear innocent.

"It's absolutely not happening, Wesley. I'm not even wearing a dress to our wedding." She paused, then, with a deadpan delivery perfected by years of investigative work, clarified, "You know that, right?"

I shrugged. "Vette, you could wear assless chaps, a thong, and red bottoms so long as you come down that aisle."

"Now that would be somethin' to see!" Estelle, who had been eavesdropping, called from her desk.

Yvette cocked her head, aiming a withering side-eye at me. "You'd like that, wouldn't you, Payne?"

"I don't hate it. Look, babe... Gloria Payne moves to the beat of her own drum. I told her I'm not your boss and you'll be wearing what you want to wear. I'ma marry you regardless. I'm not in the business of making my fiancée miserable. Anymore."

"Well, thanks for that. My suit will be stunning. It's a very feminine cut."

Estelle called from her desk, "You can't let the man's mama dress you up just once?"

"Stelle, stay out of this!" Yvette yelled back.

I finished my maple bar, balling up the napkin and tossing it into the wastebasket, then turned my focus back to the investigation board. "These transfers and the timing…they're obviously trying to stay under the IRS threshold."

She hummed in agreement. "Got to be a reason for that."

Yvette's proximity was distracting. Her hair fell in shoulder-length curls and whatever she'd showered with—something musky and vanilla—hit my nostrils every time she moved. I was so damn in love with her. Nose wide open, heart surrendered, all that hokey shit I used to roll my eyes at. I had been gone over Yvette Young for a long, long time. I spent most of our time together staring at her, trying to believe she was actually in my life on a permanent basis.

I leaned in, dropping a kiss on her neck, just below her ear. It was one of her favorite spots and it never failed to get a response from her. She let out a small, involuntary gasp and tilted her head slightly.

"I thought you came over here to get an update on the case, Payne."

I couldn't help my smile at her playful scolding. I loved bringing out the side of her that didn't pull away when I got personal at work. "I did. Can't help it if focusing is a problem when I'm this close to you."

"Try harder," she whispered but, unable to resist the pull of my lips, leaned into me anyway.

Nia cleared her throat loudly, leaning against the door jamb with her arms crossed. "Is our workday interrupting your bout of office sex? Y'all don't be fuckin' in here, do you?"

"Don't act jealous, Nia," Yvette shot back, laughing but also not pulling out of my arms.

She scowled, sucking her teeth, brows knit together. "Nobody jealous of y'all. I got my own man that can't keep his hands off me. I'm just trying to get shit done so I can meet him for dinner without having to hear Wesley mumbling in that Quiet Storm voice and Yvette giggling in response to it."

"I do not giggle," Yvette protested.

"Yeah. She does not giggle."

To make up for only ever having eyes for Yvette, I had agreed to set Nia up with a Courtney & Payne litigation attorney. Things seemed to be going well between them.

Young Investigations had grown. With the attention the Barrett case brought her, more work poured in, so she'd hired two more investigators and moved into a larger, nicer office space in Virginia-Highland. Yvette's work centered on investigating Courtney & Payne cases, while Nia and the others managed their own caseloads and jumped in to help us when needed. Estelle was busier than ever managing the office and making good use of her connections with the police department and the federal bureaus.

"Stelle has a contact running the encryption," Yvette said, her tone returning to professional. "Maybe there's a clue in the code."

"Let's see what they come up with." I reviewed the documents, already spinning strategy. "We need to prove a pattern of fraud."

"So we can break the entire network," she finished.

Our professional synchronicity was still seamless. Years of partnership had created an understanding that went beyond words. We knew how the other's mind worked and could finish sentences without missing a beat.

I pulled out my phone, checking my text messages. "Vette—"

"I am not wearing a dress to that damn party," she repeated firmly.

"Child, make the man's mama happy!" Estelle called.

I chuckled and leaned in for a long, warm kiss. "I will talk to my mama. I promise. But I was going to ask if you want to go to lunch. I have an appointment over by Surin this afternoon."

"Ooh! Red curry and drunken noodles on your dime?" She clapped her hands together and sprang up, reaching for the crossbody bag she still went nowhere without. "We can talk about the case over lunch."

"We can talk about our wedding over lunch."

She huffed, rolling her eyes. "Wesley—"

"Babe." I caught her hand, making her pause mid bag-swing. "We've got to make some decisions before our parents make them for us."

"You would think they're the ones getting married," she grumbled. "Why didn't we just elope?"

"Aht!" Estelle screeched. "I will be watching my Vette walk down the aisle. Think I'm playin'? Try Jesus, don't try me."

Yvette laughed. "Eloping is a fever dream. My mother would never, ever forgive us."

I reached behind me for the hand that I knew would slide into mine. The connection between us was an invisible tether —touches, glances, a shared language that had only deepened in the months since Yvette took off her running shoes.

She cast one last glance at the investigation board.

"Come on, babe. The case will be waiting for you when you get back."

We left the office suite and walked down the hall to the elevator. Vette suddenly stopped in her tracks and turned around.

"What did you forget?" I asked. "I'll run and get it."

"Nothing. I didn't forget anything. I just…" Her voice trailed off.

"You just…" I prodded, laying a hand on her shoulder. "We can elope if you really want to. They'll get over it."

"No," she said. She shook her head, then looked up at me, her eyes shiny with unshed tears. "I just sometimes get these huge waves of…happy. I'm still not really used to that. When Jason died, I never believed I'd ever feel this way about someone again. But I do. I love you so much and I can't believe how lucky I am," she said softly. "That you basically planted yourself in my way and didn't move and waited for me to be ready for this. That you love me like you do."

"Yvette Young…"

I pulled her into a long, tight hug, feeling overwhelmed with emotion. It had been a long road for us to get here. Jason's memory was honored, not replaced. A part of our story, but no longer a barrier to a better life for the both of us.

"This is not luck. You worked hard for what you wanted. I just stood here, where I wanted to be. Where I needed to be." I leaned in, kissing her temple. "I love your stubborn ass."

"I love your stubborn ass too," she replied, squeezing me tightly before pulling away.

I grabbed her hand, tugging her toward the elevator. "Let's go eat and try to plan our wedding. If we're not careful, we're going to end up with one of those grass walls, a tacky hashtag, and a gospel choir."

"Honestly," Yvette said with a content, satisfied smile, "as long as I get to wear what I want and you slide that ring on my finger, I might let our mamas turn our wedding into a big, fat, Black wedding."

"For real," I said, "I'm only concerned about you wrecking my shit in the honeymoon suite in Belize."

Yvette hummed a low, almost keening sound as we stepped into the elevator. "Those are orders I will be happy to obey. Sir, yes, sir!"

ACKNOWLEDGMENTS

As always thank you to my "seasoned" readers, my ride-or-dies, the first to buy my books whenever they pop up. I would not be here were it not for your interest in my work, so I am eternally grateful for your loyalty.

WELCOME to any new readers! Thanks for taking a chance on this writer and this book. I truly hope you enjoyed meeting Yvette and Wesley that you'll be on the lookout for more books and novellas in the near future. Right behind this section you'll find the "Also by" section. DIG. IN.

I owe so much to people who've held me up when I wanted to quit. Thank you all from the bottom of my heart for keeping me afloat.

No acknowledgement would be complete without thanking the Beta Readers, the ARC readers, the authors I ask for advice and feedback, my writing pals and my ever supportive ring of friends and family.

Special thanks to **AdotKEdits** for a professional touch.

I like to say that writing is a solitary art, performed in concert. Thanks for joining my band.

ALSO BY DL WHITE

RUBY'S

Brunch at Ruby's

Dinner at Sam's

Drinks at Minks, a Ruby's Companion Novella

BLACK DIAMOND BAY

Beach Thing, a Black Diamond Vacation Romance

Elysium, a Black Diamond Vacation Romance

The Pearl at Black Diamond, a Black Diamond Workplace Romance

POTTER LAKE SMALL TOWN ROMANCE

Leslie's Curl & Dye

Second Time Around (Potter Lake Holiday Novella)

The Guy Next Door

Home for the Holidays (A Potter Lake Holiday Novella)

STAND-ALONE NOVELS/NOVELLAS/SHORTS

A Thin Line

The Never List

Hey, Lover, a Second Chance Romance

Olympia's on King Street (newsletter exclusive)

Baking Bad, a Sweet Crumbs Mystery

Calculated Risk *(only available in print until Sept 2025)*

Missing Persons, a Young Investigations novel

HOLIDAY NOVELLAS

The Kwanzaa Brunch

Unexpected

The Festival at Evergreen Falls

Grumpy Valentine

Clover (website exclusive)

Anonymous (permafree!)